Flight

For Anthony Glavin, an inspiring writer, friend and mentor

Flight

Oona Frawley

TRAMPPRESS

This edition published in 2014
First published 2014 by
Tramp Press
Dublin
www.tramppress.com

A CIP record for this title
is available from The British Library.

5 7 9 10 8 6 4

ISBN 978-0-9928170-0-8

Thank you for supporting independent publishing.

Set in 11pt on 15pt Quixote by Marsha Swan
Printed by GraphyCems in Spain

Flight

the action or manner of flying or moving through
the air with or as with wings; a mounting or soaring
out of the regular course or beyond ordinary
bounds; an excursion or sally; a state of flutter or
agitation; a trembling fright; the series of stairs
between any two landings; a collection or flock of
beings or things flying in or passing through the air
together; the action of fleeing or running away from,
or as from, danger; hasty departure or retreat, also,
an absconding; a journey through air; the duning
drift of imagination; the abandonment of place.

|

The man of the house was mad when Sandrine came.

It had happened rather all at once. One Wednesday morning he rang his daughter to demand an explanation for the goings on: the postman had intercepted the ten-ton delivery of pepper and confiscated it, claiming that duty had not been paid; the postal service would destroy it tomorrow, all of his beautiful Vietnamese pepper that he'd worked so hard for. Did they have any idea of the trouble it had taken to set up a pepper exporting business in Vietnam? The red tape? The taxes? The interminable negotiations? The vagaries of weather that could consume a crop? The mould that could ruin it? The loss of the pepper seemed inevitable, and he could not see a way out of it. Why was the postal service interfering, for God's sake? Elizabeth reassured her father with as much calm in her voice as she could muster behind a computer screen at the office, and asked to talk to her mother.

At the next Sunday's lunch, Elizabeth watched her father as he sat to the side of her mother at the head of the table, one fist stuffed into the pocket of a hooded fleece sweatshirt. It was his concession to modernity, this fleece, he had once joked, but only because he was back in Ireland and it was too cold for anything else; until then he had maintained a disdain for such invented fabrics. The other hand was fastened around a cigarette that explained the yellowing, claw-like nails of an otherwise elegant hand whose fingers had smoothed through barrels of ground spice, selected peppercorn and ajowan and star anise by delicate touch. As was becoming more usual, he did not hear everything that was said, sitting behind the only cloud of smoke in the room with an impassive face that seemed, with age and against character, determined to slouch into a frown. When Elizabeth shouted to him, inquiring whether he had seen a tennis match televised the night before, Tom leaned forward with an attempt at a smile, shaking his head and saying loudly, I can't hear you. The tennis match, Clare bellowed. Elizabeth is asking if you saw the tennis match, the Agassi one we watched. They waited for a few seconds, and then Tom sat back, stabbed his cigarette into the ashtray on the left-hand corner of the table, and pushed it away. He smiled. Yes, he said, waste of time. I hear the fellow he was playing is going to retire, and the sooner the better, the way he played last night. The fool couldn't ace anything.

There was no talk of pepper. Elizabeth looked at her mother and relaxed.

But the next week the postman was at it again, and Elizabeth's mother rang her morning, noon and night. He's driving me mad with his pepper talk, she said, I'll crown him if he talks to me about the need for Vietnam to join the International Pepper Community and duties and postmen one more time!

The cracks one begins to see in families.

⌣ ⌣ ⌣

Sandrine had watched the flights of others from this airport. She had seen the diminishing windows through which one hoped to spy a face, a head, a desperately waving arm. And then it was Sandrine in the plane of diminishing windows, about to wave desperately towards where her husband and son might stand in the parking lot, or the sun-cracked fields encircling the airport, or in the lush ones further beyond, before the creep of the city began to turn the green to dust. But she realised from within the confines of that space that, just as they could not catch any glimpse of her, neither could she recognise those beyond. The departure had already taken place. And so her arm, poised to flutter like a bird's wing, fell back into her lap and rested on the not-yet-child which she sensed in her belly as one senses the pause of a bee on the arm before it stings.

As the sounds of the engines were lost in the clouds and in the static silence, Sandrine closed her eyes, unable to bear the blindness of her own mind. And in that moment none of it seemed worthwhile, despite all of the plans they had made for the future. On the ground, it had made a kind of sense to her, that, because they were certain George would be denied a visa, she should apply to go to Ireland – ostensibly to improve her English, but really to earn badly needed money and furnish their household with even more badly needed hope. In their conversations, there had even been the small, worrying possibility of remaining there, and of husband and son both joining her. And if they – if she – did not remain in Ireland, it would not be lost, that experience of hope, even beyond the useful-ness of any money she might make and send home.

George had said: Think of your return some day, think of a different president, think of our son, think of the experiences you will be able to tell him of in your letters. This country of ours, you will have seen all of it in an instant, from the perspective of the sky, and you'll be able to tell him that. And so she opened her eyes and peered out of the window, half afraid to heed his advice, fearing illogically that her movement would affect the plane's, and saw, to her amazement, her country spread out below as her husband had imagined. Plains and rivers and violence – all of that was there below, away from her, a miniaturised reality of which she was no longer a part. Farther and farther below her were the queues for petrol and for bread, the hungering bodies full of disease once banished by vaccination, the houses roofed with zinc that crackled when it rained, the wilting maize in tiny patches of garden. The far-away feeling and the not-yet-child in her belly made her ill, and for a long time she buried her head in her arms, bending towards her knees in what the laminated card in her seat pocket described as the brace position. What could be worth this, she thought, leaving my country, my home?

Sandrine spoke to no one on the flight except a young woman she met in a queue for the toilet. She stayed sitting for as long as she could bear, and then ventured, embarrassed, to the mid-section of the plane. The younger woman's body lolled against the outer wall of the toilet. She watched Sandrine approach and, after glancing over her clothes, which were no longer unwrinkled, had relaxed into informality, spoke in English.

You're going to London too? she asked hopefully, her posture improving.

Sandrine shook her head. No, she said, I'm going to Ireland. It was the first time she had spoken the words in an active present tense, and not in some mad futurity her mind never grasped.

Why? the woman asked bluntly, her body contracting itself back into a hunch of a question mark. Why Ireland?

The question brought her back to all of the discussions with George after Tobias was asleep. After they had been in to see the agency that arranged student visas and had heard of the possibilities from friends and relatives, they had debated. Don't go to England,

George had urged. I know that it would be better than here, but they did take over ours and many other countries. The Irish priests are so nice, gentle. Go to Ireland. They too have been conquered; they will be kinder. And everyone says the economy is doing so well. There is work.

I don't know, Sandrine replied. It was too much to explain in a queue for an airplane toilet.

The young woman watched her for a moment. Sandrine's hands unconsciously remained over the space of the not-yet-child, over the wrinkles that had developed in the lap of her plain skirt, recently rehemmed. Then, as one of the door latches broke the illusionary silence of the airplane, the girl turned to her. Don't go there, she said, because they kick you out for being pregnant. Or you have to marry Irish man.

She slipped into the toilet, leaving Sandrine to wait, full of a new terror. Despite her horror of leaving home, it would be far worse to be returned in disgrace. It could put her family in more danger if she were sent back. She cried in the toilet, wondering how she would survive the flight.

c c c

The second plane was smaller, and, as she made her way to her seat, Sandrine realised that there were no familiar faces; all of those on her flight from home had arced out in separate lines from London. She hadn't thought either, before boarding, that she might be the only black woman on the plane. Until that moment, Sandrine had never been in such an overwhelming minority. Here she was, alone in her skin, feeling – for the first time – the gaze of those around her as it rested not on her but on an idea of her. This gaze was not unkind, but neither was it friendly. It was a look of greed, as she came to think of it, full of desire to know her, to know what her skin meant. And it was a look bound to be disappointed, for Sandrine had never discovered what her skin meant – if anything. She no longer listened when Mugabe and Hunzvi talked about ridding the land of white scum. She no longer listened to them about anything, because there was no food, and no money, and nothing was improving with their words. The children came less and less to school; there was no money to send them. One of the worst things about her departure was the knowledge that she would not be replaced and that the school would lack a teacher.

What did she care if James Cloete, whose family had run the farm her husband now worked on for generations, was white? He paid the wages, and the community ate. Perhaps he shouldn't be there any longer, but time enough to do things peacefully. She knew well that all of them, James Cloete especially, were afraid of the black-skinned men wielding sticks and guns who might arrive unannounced. So to be gazed upon because of her colour now, in the exhaustion of travel, was puzzling. Gradually the eyes averted themselves, and she settled into her seat, pulled a toddler-sized green plaid wool blanket over her belly, and stared out at what was, for her, all of England.

Somewhere beyond the hundreds of planes parked, taxying, landing, taking off, spouting grey and black smoke like awful, voracious furnaces, beyond the complexes of hangars and sleek glass-walled buildings, England lay. Big Ben was not far off, the Tower of London close by. And something in those buildings contained something of the history of her own country. Of missionaries and railroads and the desire for gold and diamonds, space and victory. Sandrine could not connect these things to the people in the airport who stamped her passport and poured her the cup of tea she had allowed herself to buy, people who looked tired or troubled or stalwart, and whose accents were so starkly different from the neat BBC version she had heard. This England was beyond them, too, and belonged only to a handful of men, most long dead, whose legacies survived in place names and tales of flag planting.

England from the perspective of the sky was pale green and gold in an early morning sunshine as thin as glass, the landscape veined with blue-black rivers. When the captain announced that to the left might be spied the Thames and all of historical London, Sandrine's stomach tingled. She watched that central vein and pretended to make out the buildings she had recreated in poor pencil sketches for a history project as a child in the missionary school. She imagined the queen having her breakfast at that moment, with a tiara on in the palace and perhaps looking up through the window at the patch of sky where Sandrine was. Perhaps the queen was looking up, daydreaming, drinking tea from some other country, alone except for her circle of red guards and their gold braid and puffs of black fur that sat still and dead on their heads. Sandrine watched the river that down there was flowing in some direction but to her seemed stock still, a line only, and knew quietly that it was the river that was England. The waterway meant something that she intuited but couldn't name: empire? And yet other lands had rivers and did not conquer. Her eyes blurred on the ribbon of river that faintly glowed in the sun. The plane tipped then, and she watched amazedly as the sky reared into view and England disappeared: the sky was larger than England. When the plane righted itself, there was water, flat and blue and far away, and then there was Ireland.

 ᴄ ᴄ ᴄ

Despite the small trauma of the airport, Sandrine's first real memory of Ireland was the patterning of the fields as she saw them from the air, and then, when she was outside, rain.

From where she sat in the sky, Ireland was a green puzzle of shapes. Narrow runnels of fields that were scarred a deep, earthy brown, awkward triangles of gnarled pale-topped trees, squares of august green grass, rectangles of golden and green-apple crops. At the edges of cliffs and shores and townlands the shapes grew stranger, more curving, and also more abrupt as Ireland plunged into the sea and the field was forced to stop and yield, or a road interrupted the vegetation with no apologies for its mean grey streak. The sun fastened itself on favourite fields, aiming beams into clouds that the plane now skimmed through, so that here and there below were glowing golden nuggets of land whose greens were shot through with a wealth of spangling light.

As the plane lowered itself to the fields, Sandrine began to see the rain, tiny droplets hurtling past and dashing the windows of the plane like bombs. She felt a fondness for it, immediately, simply because it was the first thing of Ireland that leapt to her, and once she had managed to come through the difficulties with the airport officials, she found that the rain was still there. It was the softness of the first rain that she remembered. Soft rain that gemmed and misted on her hair and coat and sweater in colourless water jewels as she walked along the grey pavement outside the airport terminal, rain that clung to her and so seemed determined to be familiar, to tickle her earlobe or her neck or instep when she least expected it. The rain was a weeping that she could not herself submit to. Her photographs of Tobias were out of order, her bags didn't close properly.

Sandrine stood uneasily in the rain along with five other men and women from all over the African continent, awaiting the opening of the doors to a bus that would take them to their residence. A security man of some kind stood by, thumbing a small newspaper distractedly. The driver of the bus was talking into a phone and smoking a cigarette with the window rolled down slightly, aiming his smoke at the crack and sending it sinking into the rain and the heavy air. He took no notice of the passengers standing patiently with hastily re-packed bags, and dark skin and eyelids that twitched as drops of rain slid down their foreheads; it did not matter to him what the weather was.

Nor had it seemed to matter to the Irish officials in the airport that Sandrine held a valid passport (this was taken from her) and a student visa that would allow her to attend classes and work part-time: she was African, and so must be arriving illegally. Her papers would be returned to her, Sandrine was told, if they proved valid.

Remembering the mild British interrogation now, Sandrine protested quietly, asking why they didn't simply confer with her country's embassy in London, since there was not one here, or check with the Irish Embassy in South Africa that had issued the student visa. There was a bit of sniggering at this and one of the men said, right, love, we'll see about that then and ushered her out of the room. On the long bus ride, she tried to forget the snigger.

ᴄ ᴄ ᴄ

Later, when she had moved in with Tom and Clare and the new chaos had begun, Sandrine looked back at the ten days she spent in the small Wicklow town as a strange sort of holiday. The two-storey stone house was on a quiet road, surrounded by plum-leaved maple trees, run by a woman whose husband had died and whose children had grown up and long since absconded from the town. Deirdre had been a nurse and, later, a teacher at a nursing college, and when she discovered that Sandrine too had been a teacher in Zimbabwe, she began nodding vigorously. They were at the table in the kitchen, late in the evening on the second night. The others with whom Sandrine had arrived were in their rooms, as were a family of Romanian sisters who had been there for several weeks. Sandrine had crept downstairs, feeling the beginnings of nausea, to make herself a cup of tea, and found Deirdre sitting there reading a slab of newspaper, her fingers and a spot on her temple smudged with ink.

You're not like the others, she said after putting on the kettle and telling Sandrine to sit down. You're quiet, reserved. You speak good English. Married, she gestured at the ring.

I was a teacher at home, Sandrine said, faintly.

Her nods began. A teacher. And good English. And legal, from what your papers say, she added. Sandrine looked surprised.

Have my papers been returned?

Deirdre raised the newspaper from the table and indicated an envelope. Sandrine took it carefully.

I was going to tell you in the morning, Deirdre said with no embarrassment. They told me you could go, to tell you that. And to remind you that you're allowed only twenty hours' work a week on a student visa. But you can stay here for a few days, if you like, until you get an idea of what to do and where to go. They haven't anyone else coming down to me for another bit. It's nice to have someone who speaks English for a change. So, she said, dunking the tea bag with a spoon and watching as Sandrine fingered the envelope, what are your plans?

I'm not certain, Sandrine shrugged, suddenly open, the relief of the papers in her hands allowing her a respite. I have the phone number for an English school, and the name of a woman from two towns over who is somewhere here.

I have a friend, now, Deirdre sat down and leaned in conspiratorially, a retired nurse like myself, who runs a home care agency. They send people to live with the elderly, to cook and clean and chat to them. You could do that. No rent. It's not many of you that are married and speak English. And you're Christian, and amn't I a Christian myself?

Sandrine said that she would like that very much.

Right, Deirdre said, I'll ring her in the morning. Lots of blacks like yourself already work for her, the ones of you like yourself.

ɛ ɛ ɛ

There is a strangeness in arriving at a house as Sandrine did: suddenly, with two bags, to stay. The strangeness is that the house is already lived in, already functioning. There are schedules: the times people eat, sleep, wake, retreat to the television, bathe, run errands, listen for the post, stare at themselves with no recognition in a bathroom mirror after washing their hands. And into that schedule of life Sandrine arrived with her student visa and the silent pregnancy. It was hard to remember later what exactly she had expected. To find them not as mad as they'd been described to her in interviews? To find that these people, even if mad, might somehow help her? Tell her what she could do to remain in Ireland with her child? Or to find that she would be happy there, amongst madness?

When she arrived, Tom was well past the pepper preoccupation, and Clare beyond the wearing of watches. By that point the daughter was close to admitting that the madness had begun not so suddenly after all. Only a few years earlier – was it four already? Or three? – Tom had retired and returned to Ireland after thirty years in Vietnam and America broken by the odd visit home.

The boxes preceded them for weeks. Souvenirs and gifts – decades old – came back in crates that had been packed years earlier and shipped to the new quarters to remain unopened there. Now they all returned to Ireland like forgotten presents, a once-in-a-lifetime Christmas morning.

These were followed by small pieces of furniture picked up at markets and craft and antique shops over the decades that they had decorated their hotel suite with. Other, larger pieces had been in storage: carved teakwood tables from Laos, a 1960s American refrigerator with a rusty chrome door handle but a perfect icebox, a hardwood Shaker dining table with twelve chairs, embroidered silk duvet covers from Thailand, rolls of oriental rugs, carpets, throws and tapestries from Vietnam, Hong Kong, Laos, India, and Persia. These, Clare's extravagance, the items of which she remained hopelessly enamoured, came rolled in layer after layer of brown paper that concealed their weft, their imperceptibly perfect patterns woven by hand in an eye-aching array of coloured thread.

The other things – photographs of Tom and Clare with various businessmen and personages now forgotten, bolts of Thai silk, statues of Buddha in cold jade, sanded ebony, weathered brass, monstrous masks of papier mâché painted with the leaching dyes of spices, beaded necklaces whose beads were in fact miniscule seeds, hard and imperfectly oval – all of these came at the last, following the most significant items: the drums, barrels, jars and small plastic sacks of spices that Tom insisted they bring home.

It was very strange, Tom's love of herbs and spices. Men of his generation in Ireland didn't cook for one thing, and for another there were only a few herbs and spices to be found in the typical Irish pantry. Pepper, yes, and salt – although this, Tom corrected hundreds of people during his lifetime, was a mineral – and vanilla, but an artificial kind made into a brown alcoholic liquid, not the shrunken pods with their sticky dots of beans. Sometimes sage, a bit of parsley, cinnamon, clove, nutmeg. Beyond these, there would have been few staples. Even garlic, which grew wild in the forests and scented the steps of walkers and galloping horses and fat wild hares with strong legs, was shunned. It was too strong, too pungent, too likely to make one sweat the odour indefinitely or, worse yet, be overtaken by a temper or a passion better suited to an Italian or a Spaniard, or so his brother and his wife argued, in any case, when Tom suggested on a visit home they try some garlic bread with their Sunday lunch.

How, his daughter Elizabeth often wondered, had he come to care for spices? Just, she supposed, the chance of having gotten a job in a spice as opposed to a shoe factory. She imagined him in that factory with his nostrils flaring over vats of paprika, while his mind soared to Spain, into the Balkans, imagining goulash on an autumn night, the orange of the grind a glow that his mind would return to, earmarked as the very colour orange: warm, insensible to yellow, edging towards a fine passionate brown.

In his Arbour Hill bedsit, already bereft of parents at the age of twenty-four, had he tried to cook himself meals seasoned with pinches from the vats that filled his pockets: cumin left-hand trouser, fenugreek breast, brown bark of cinnamon interior jacket, close to the heart? Had the landlord wondered at the perplexingly sweet aroma that carried up the stairs, something like coffee but also vanilla and, mystifyingly, pepper as he tried to make the Moroccan coffee he'd been reading about? Had the other boarder watched Tom pat chicken with the pocket pinches, crinkled his nose in curiosity? Was he asked to taste, to describe for Tom the result of a chilli rub?

Elizabeth didn't know. Her father spoke nothing of those days when he shared a house with a family of nine and another male boarder. He spoke nothing of his morning walks along the Liffey, regardless of weather, before he caught an O'Connell Street bus to the factory, and the heat of the scents that warmed him in winter as soon as he spied the building. He never mentioned the occasional visits he paid to his parents' old home in Wexford, the small plot of land farmed by his brother now and his wife, the cooking seasoned only with the salt of endurance. He never told Elizabeth of the morose mood of the Sunday afternoon train back to Dublin, the sublimity of such early darkness for half the year, the parading noise of the wheels and tracks, rain sliding across the windows and the way he could see nothing except his youthful but aging face in the glass. This part of Tom's life, the several years of solitary time in a room he lined with books for insulation as well as company, he dropped from the registry of what he described to his child.

It was to Clare he had described it, but only briefly, because when he met her it was just as things were changing. His devotion to the spices had become obvious to every worker in the factory, and his knowledge of their uses and origins was beginning to be relied upon by his superiors. Realising this, Tom had swiftly and painfully hacked at his smoking habit so that his senses of smell and taste would heighten. Only after he left the place on a dry day and had taken his reverse journey back to the Liffey did he allow himself one cigarette, which he took leaning over the solid stone while the smoke swirled like rococo dreams into his nostrils, lips and lungs.

When the boss's son, the one who'd take over, began to drop down to the floor and call him outside on exceptionally sunny days for a smoke and a chat, Tom could not refuse: here was his chance. And so it was over reluctant cigarettes in the doorway that Tom's plans hatched themselves into the boss's son's ears, and the boss learned about the possibilities in Jamaican ginger and Caribbean allspice and Mexican chilli. The results of that early labour saw he and Clare leave Ireland.

Returning home from Vietnam after decades away, Tom could not bear to see the last of his sample stock thrown away or left behind. And so sealed jars of star anise, tubs of green peppercorns and lidded jars of different grades of cinnamon and cassia came with them. All of it, including the spices and their mingling scents, was piled up in a massive, specially built garden shed roofed with opaque perspex that paralleled the house and ran the length of the garden wall. It was undoubtedly the only house on the street that had a real photograph of the pope, taken at a short distance in Vatican Square one Sunday when Tom had closed a handshake deal to ship chillies and small amounts of lemongrass from Hanoi to Rome for an Italian businessman whose brother was a bishop. The photograph was in a cardboard box, beneath corrugated plastic in the shed, which leaked and drummed its own rain when it had collected enough moisture.

The garage, necessary on a sea road where salt would corrode car paint and the underbelly of the vehicle itself in a season or two, was quickly converted into a storage closet for trunks of ao dais and slippers encrusted with pale amber beads. The converted attic took on the appearance of a carpet showroom, with carpets for every imaginable space – for stairs, hallways, dining rooms, bedrooms, living rooms – enough for the rest of the suburb, laid out in a layered, ungraspable pattern all over the attic floor.

Following their return, the man of the house had increased his commitment to his smoking habit – it had been simply too hot to smoke in earnest in Vietnam, he remarked to Clare, and, anyway, excessive smoking would have interfered too much with his all-important sense of smell. He began another of reading every newspaper that was sold locally on a daily basis that had a business section. (Weeklies he thought hardly worthwhile since, if one read daily, there was little need for a summary chapter on a Saturday or Sunday.) It was because, he told his wife, he had gone without any reliable English-language newspaper for so long in Vietnam, where in the early days he had read what had happened at least several days after the fact, and sometimes, if he was waiting on the arrival of an Irish newspaper, weeks. Publications of the International Pepper Commission took even longer, and he struggled to keep up with the events of the trade. And it all arrived, eventually, but his knowledge had often been useless then, too tardy to make sense of the world, too late to take advantage of a jump in pepper prices, a Chinese need for star anise, or too late to know that the dockers in Rotterdam were planning strike action and a shipment already on the way.

Only when a colleague arrived on business and carried trade newsletters was Tom up to date. Only when a visitor arrived from somewhere like London or Paris or New York did he get a chance to enjoy an only day-old paper. Like scavengers, many of the permanent hotel residents crowded the front desk each afternoon to see if new arrivals had discarded their newspapers in the woven waste baskets scattered about the compound – and if they had, it called for a glass of lime juice at the bar with a cigarette whose smoke sank around the sheets of the used newspaper like lead.

Now Tom had the opportunity to consume the world as fast as the newspapers could print it out and transmit it to him. He subscribed to every publication of the IPC, of the European Standards for Spices, even the American Standards. But these were not daily publications, so there was a need for other material: *The Irish Times, The Guardian, The Times, The Wall Street Journal,* and the *International Herald Tribune.* Each day, he devoured broadsheets from the time he sat down at the table for breakfast, guarded by his wife's gaze and the ten empty chairs, ate a soft boiled egg sprinkled generously with freshly milled Vietnamese Chu Se pepper that made her sick to look at (it was he who cooked it), one croissant purchased from the local Londis that did a fair imitation of the Metropole croissant, and one piece of toast with jam from Bonne Maman, a French company that Clare found she particularly liked. Even though I could never live in France, she told Tom. They just eat the strangest parts of animals and they left such a mess in Vietnam, but they do make nice confiture.

Aside from offering an occasional answer to his wife's comments on confiture or the weather or her small plans for the day – the rehooking of a rug's corner, the tending to her orchids and her struggling lime tree that lived at the conservatory end of the kitchen – while at the table, he did not speak. He ate his peppered egg as he had his pho back in Vietnam, spooning it hurriedly into his mouth, slurping, then the crispy, flaky, strangely oily croissant with which he mopped any egg on the plate, then the toast and its oozing red mountain of jam. When his plate was stained with yellow and red and stuck with crumbs, Tom settled properly into the newspapers, which he had until then attempted to flip through with one hand over his food. When he sensed that his wife was finished with her toast and jam and her occasional indulgence of a rasher done to a crisped turn, he pushed his chair backwards, gathered the unread sheets of paper into his hands, and walked the ten yards to another chair in the corner by an enormous window that cast the shimmering light of the sea onto his sheaf. There he would remain uninterrupted until it was time for tiny cups of strong, thick coffee that, along with marzipan sweets as close to green bean candy as he could find in Dublin, leant his mouth the memory of Vietnam.

When friends from abroad directed visitors to his door, the newspaper information shaped conversation before it began. If a foreign visitor arrived, he was treated to an expedient run-down of all that had happened in his country in recent weeks, if not months, and was then expected to answer a barrage of questions about the issues at stake, particularly in terms of business, and, if it was at all possible, in terms of the spice business. Was there one? Was employment needed in the country? What was the export market like? What kind of export taxes were in place? Had the vanilla crop recovered in Madagascar yet, after last year's storms? Was Laos still trying to charge a fortune for second-rate lemongrass? Was the saffron reliable? Were the green cardamom pods able to dry properly in that climate? Was Israeli sea salt coming down in price this year? What kind of cleaning process were they using for Malabar pepper now? Cycloning? Destining? Or still winnowing, sieving? The Sarawak – what particle size was it ground to? What had the prices been like at Kuching after the last harvest? What was the volatile oil content of the Malabar berry like now? How was Nagpur doing as a site for trading? Did the EU really expect that banning irradiation in its own territory would mean that it didn't occur in the country of origin?

If no spice trade was to be hit upon, and if the guest showed bewilderment beyond an awareness of table salt and pepper of no distinct or known kind, Tom might try the carpet business – you know my Clare loves carpets. What kinds of thread did they use? Silk or wool? Or a combination? Was Sardinia still importing Moroccan carpets and selling them on at outrageous prices? Was

Assif still running his own showroom on 57th Street, or had he retired and let his son-in-law – who wasn't Pakistani-born and didn't know a good carpet from a bad – take over? (Clare might, on occasion, interject, if the visitor was from New York.) Had Tintawn corrected the flaw in the cleaning machine that ruined Henry Kissinger's order? Had they not heard the rumour?

God, it was funny alright, Tom would say. Kissinger had placed a huge order with the Tintawn company, and it had all arrived as it was meant to, it had been installed perfectly, and good old Kiss was happy as Larry. But then over the next coupla weeks his staff started noticing strange marks appearing on the carpet. At first faint carnation pinks, then plum, then crimson. As if someone was going around in the middle of the night, spilling dribbles of wine in the same places and then coming back the next night to make the stains more pronounced.

Kissenger's assistant called Tintawn, who were puzzled by the story of the marks. After trying to get off the hook by saying that the carpet had been in perfect order when they'd installed it, the company sent a representative out to take a look at it. And the rep is looking and looking, and in the other parts of the house he can hear someone he presumes is Henry Kissinger himself shouting and carrying on, and he's getting nervous, and it suddenly dawns on him, as he's thinking of how much he'd like to pack in this job and just go back home to his father's farm in Ireland. By God if the stains don't look like the spraypaint his father uses to mark his initials on his sheep. He looks closer, gets right down on his hands and knees on the creamy, knobbled carpet and looks the ink in the eye. It has to be. And sure enough, when he gets back to the office and rings the warehouse in Ireland and tells them what he thinks has happened, a fella eventually comes on and tells him, yep, you must be right. The machine that washes the wool is broken and ink rises again like invisible ink. So there's Henry Kissinger with the remains of the initials of Irish farmers coming up all over his carpet, and the whole thing has to be taken back. And that, Tom always finished the story, is why I never went into the carpet business – or any business – in Ireland. Bloody fools, thinking they can close down for a day and not answer their phones because Tipp are playing Kilkenny.

Elizabeth and her mother often had a good laugh at his dissections of world business, even if he did tell the Henry Kissenger story a few times in the space of a month. He could seem at times more like his old self. The former self that he sometimes resembled seemed to have been a much more jovial fellow, if just as obsessed with spices, and an uxorious man who once wouldn't have dreamt of slurping his egg behind the rustle of inky newspaper while Clare sat near him on the other side of the bedsheets.

But the madness, once it set in, made the former self only a shadow, only a memory, and the new man, the one that Sandrine knew, sat with his trade newsletters and his head full of international spice pricing and carpet designs and postal disputes that he undoubtedly read of on a particular page of one of the day's papers, or clung to in the vestiges of his slowly changing mind.

c c c

The interview at the agency had been nothing like Sandrine thought it might be. Anxious about being late, she had pored over the train and bus timetables like prayers, calculating how long it would take her to walk down Rathdrum's paint-peeling main street, whose shopfronts and buildings declined as the street did – rapidly. She would calculate on the train being early or late, but certainly not on time. This much she had learned about Ireland from Deirdre so far.

Deirdre watched Sandrine during breakfast. The youngest Romanian girl had realised that she didn't touch anything but toast and eagerly sat beside her to eat the extra sausages and eggs, and Sandrine sipped black tea and nibbled the toast, holding the Dublin bus timetable in her free hand. Deirdre said nothing and then suddenly stood up. Well, Sandrine, she said, we'd better make a move. I'm going into town to do a bit of shopping and I'll drop you off.

The relief – knowing that she didn't have to negotiate the train and buses and directions and the worry about missing her stop and rude stares – made her tremble. She could have wept. Deirdre was kind, but Sandrine thought too, as she gathered her bag and the coat that was already proving far too thin for Irish weather, that Deirdre liked the stares of the neighbours when she set off with a black in her car and waved daringly at their suspicious faces.

Stuck running a bed and breakfast for foreigners sent to her by an overstretched government, Deirdre herself felt she belonged elsewhere. She told Sandrine as much as she drove towards Dublin, describing the dullness of life in a small Irish town, the constant demands to stop and chat even if one were in a hurry, to prune the roses and clip the hedges so that passersby could stare in at your front window, to turn out for another quiz fundraiser at the parish hall, to pretend to give a damn about another GAA match that would mean only that wives would be given a terrible time afterwards with all the drink that was taken.

Now I know I have nothing to complain about compared with the likes of you, I know that much, she said, wagging her chin at the road ahead, but a woman wants a bit of a life, now. I told my husband, I told him I wasn't a country girl, but we ended up there near his people instead of mine, and I've been called a blow-in from the dawn of the first day until this day here. Our own children hightailed it out as soon as they were able, and who can blame them, not wanting to end up celebrating the end of another week at Pineto's with a hot bag of chips?

Sandrine listened and didn't listen, absorbing the constant stream of Deirdre's voice mingled with the road works and the ebbing flow of cars streaking after one another, trying not to worry about the interview. Deirdre didn't mind Sandrine's silence, in fact she was grateful for it. I'm just going across the way to do my bit of shopping and I'll come back for you in an hour, she told Sandrine as she idled the car outside of the agency. Sure we can head back together then, and you can tell me how it all went. I'm sure you'll be grand, now.

Deirdre's friend was an enormous woman with dyed hair the colour of ripe bananas who had not so many years ago escaped the very town they'd driven up from, so Deirdre had told Sandrine. Not to worry, now, Moira's a decent sort, was the way she'd put it. But Moira was hurried and curt, and seemed entirely uninterested in Sandrine's experience as a teacher or in her education, or in the status of her visa. Never once did she ask how many hours a week Sandrine was entitled to work. Can you work here legally? she asked immediately. Applying for a work permit is an awful hassle, now.

Sandrine told her that she had a visa and that it allowed her to work. She didn't volunteer that it was a student visa that officially limited her to twenty hours' work a week. She sat stiffly, a slight muscle in her lower back twitching while the woman scanned a listing of clients, and was relieved when the fattening finger rested at one line of print.

Here's one for you, she said, and if you can stick it out, you'll be the first. So don't worry if you can't, is what I'm saying. Give it a few weeks and see how you get on. Couple around seventyish, both losing the plot, need an all-purpose, live-in carer. That means you cook their breakfasts and dinners or make sure they don't burn the place down if they want to cook themselves, do the laundry, dust the grandchildren's pictures if there are any, that kind of thing. Clare and Tom Hughes. It's a gorgeous house, she added, putting down the list and giving a toss of her banana-yellow hair, right on the seafront. And if I remember, their daughter said they lived abroad for a long time, in Asia or Africa, I can't remember which, so they won't mind you being a black from the get-go. I know I shouldn't say so, but Deirdre likes you, so you won't mind my saying it. Some of the clients are just an absolute nightmare that way.

∪ ∪ ∪

When she came, the daughter told Clare and Tom that Sandrine was going to tidy up and sort through the boxes that had remained unpacked since Vietnam. Maybe even since before that, Elizabeth added ruefully a moment later. They might have packed these here when they went to the States. Whatever country the boxes had been packed in originally, they sat stacked in piles that made the house look as if it was in a constant state of being moved out of or into, but for Tom and Clare they had merely become part of the furniture, so long had they rested in the places that truck drivers had set them. I don't mean for you to actually unpack them, Elizabeth said to Sandrine, it's just a way of explaining why you're in the house without having to explain really. Sometimes my father can be a bit odd, Elizabeth apologised. Not to mention my mother. After the way she reacted to the first three people we tried, I realised I had to come up with a reason for someone coming to stay in the house, or it would never work.

∪ ∪ ∪

Sandrine was driven to the house that first morning by a curious Deirdre, who even hugged her at the gate after writing out both her mobile and landline numbers on a card and telling Sandrine to let her know how she got on. Sandrine was touched. She watched

Deirdre climb back into her car and hoped that she would see her again. Deirdre would be delighted to have an excuse to get up to town, as she put it, and perhaps when Sandrine had saved some money she might buy Deirdre a cup of tea somewhere. She waved as the car pulled out and traced its way along the coast towards Dun Laoghaire's spires, and then turned to the house.

The gate was heavy wrought iron, curled and curlicued in wave patterns that mirrored the sea that unsettled itself over and over again across the road. At the door the wife greeted her, shook her hand and smiled, and the daughter looked relieved. Sandrine followed softly down the hallway whose wooden floor gleamed dully in the autumn light.

She was gradually overcome by a faint but distinct scent of ginger as she was brought into the sitting room to greet the man of the house. Oh hello, Tom said. Something of the former self wakened. He rose and offered Sandrine a drink, though it was mid-morning, and then, when she declined, asked in conspiratorial tones if she too had flown in to attend the convention. Did she have any special shipping prices for large orders? And what was the coriander like at this time of year?

*   *   *

Sandrine had never seen people quite so old. For days, it was an astonishment to her, the whole experience, and she didn't know which had shocked her more, the age of these people or the extraordinary array of colour and objects in their home. She stared and stared at the couple whose skin fell into beautiful, concentrated lines on their faces and hands, the tone so uneven that it could be pale as milk in tender places like the inside of a wrist, rivered by blue veins, and then as brown as autumn leaves where spots had spread and joined, as on an arm. Then there were the yellows that seemed to dawn across Tom's face at the end of the day, when he was exhausted, and the pinks and reds that fought to determine Clare's countenance. Their hair she was fascinated by, the wispy softness of it. How fine it seemed, thread-like, and how odd that what had evidently been blond hair on Clare's head had become like glowing platinum, while Tom's had drifted towards a sullen, stern grey.

There was no one so old as this at home. There was her grandmother, it was true, who was alive at 70, but she had lived most of her life, unusually, with good food and in relative happiness, managing to skirt around the major troubles of her country, and her smooth brown skin had found only a few large creases as she aged, not these hundreds of thin lines and tracks. Sandrine's own parents were not as healthy, and that had contributed to her own anxiety to get away and earn better wages. Such people as these she had never observed up close before. It amazed her that they were still alive, and she had realised quickly to keep this amazement to herself. The daughter explained to her that, as her parents weren't yet very old, she wanted to try to keep them in their own home for as long as possible.

And then there was the house. The colour in it: the layers of carpets, the softest carpets she had ever seen, everywhere, strewn over those gleaming dark wooden floors, and full of the intensities of reds and oranges and browns and golds in the sitting room. It did not feel at all how she had imagined Ireland, all of this texture and colour on the floor, on the walls, which were covered with tapestries and vivid sketches in bold blacks and reds. The bookshelves were laden down with fat volumes and interspersed with so many ornaments and curiosities that Sandrine still, after a few weeks, felt she had not examined them all. She loved the squat Buddhas, the bellies of them in their different materials. How, Sandrine wondered, did one come to acquire so many things?

The bedroom she had shared in Deirdre's house in Wicklow had been plain, white-walled, flat-yellow curtained, duvets covered with a simple floral pattern in pale colours. There was no carpet, only a small shag rug between the beds. The kitchen had been orderly and clean and, to Sandrine's gaze, marked by every convenience. This house, with its chaos of colour and strange objects, with its excess of light from the sky and noise from the sea and its enormous kitchen that ended in a wall and ceiling of glass that sheltered orchids and lilies, was for her like entering a museum, like sleeping in a gigantic shop that sold everything.

꜡ ꜡ ꜡

November in Dalkey: the light low, fighting to descend through pillows of clouds stacked relentlessly in the sky. She is on her way. He knows this somewhere in the straining depths of memory. Sitting in the chair they moved him to after he'd woken, he gazes around the room, smoking the ghost of a cigarette. He raises his empty hand to his lips, pursing them into a stream of clear air, waiting for a few civilised seconds before taking another puff, even though what he wants this morning is to smoke like a train, one cigarette and then another and another.

At least there are things he can look at as he waits for she who comes bearing grapes. Elderly women, who are to him gnarled trees, sit in similar chairs, slightly atilt, contemplating their river-veined hands, their lips occasionally pursing, as if having reached some decision or heard something that has tried their patience. One man whose face is purpled frustration rocks incessantly to the quieting music that plays softly from hidden wall speakers: his cheeks are shot through with paprika and cayenne. Tom watches the colours merge like a sunset. The other men do not interest him: they mumble things he cannot hear, shuffle about the room like wayward atoms, bounce back in different directions, their trouser legs skating beyond their heels. He ignores them, looking instead to the relative still life of the rest of the space.

She is on her way. The memory of breakfast – salt, a cheap, sandy one – is in his mouth, but not in his mind; he licks his lips. For a fleet few seconds he wonders if he is at a salt factory to sample their wares. The thought vanishes as he blinks, thin eyelids sinking and rising. He fastens his eyes on figures he does not recognise as nurses, as they enter and begin to touch the gnarled tree women on the shoulder, their bright smiling teeth glittering. The mood in the room changes. The zigzag men gravitate towards them and they too are touched, patted, led to vacant chairs, wheeled into window patches of frail, struggling sunlight by a gentle hand on their elbow. One comes to him, touches his shoulders.

How are you today Tom? Are you ready to go for a walk?

She is cheerful and pretty in a fluffy way, high-coloured with flyaway straight blond hair. He stares at her, the static-raised strands recalling a small blond child who then vanishes from his mind. He then nods and says, thank you, thinks: Tom.

He does not experience the movements across the clean smooth floor. On either side he is supported by arms that talk to him. A deep voice. That's terrific Tom. There's life in these legs yet. You've just been joking with us, have you, trying to stay in your chair all day? I hear you used to play tennis. You must have done a lot of walking then.

In America, wasn't it, Tom, adds the other arms, a higher voice.

America. Tom. He stops without knowing it.

America, he says loudly. America. A few of the old women look up from their chairs, startled out of the trance of their knuckles. Tom stares at them.

She is on her way. Perhaps when she who comes bearing grapes arrives, he will remember to say this word again – America.

‹ ‹ ‹

It is morning now. Clare knows this because she can hear the garbage men on the streets outside. She climbs out of the sagging bed draped with fading hand-embroidered sheets and stuffs her feet into her shoes, wriggling her toes into them. There is no need to dress since she kept her clothes on. It had been too cold the night before to take them off – always too cold to undress in this hopeless country – and she had argued to that effect with Sandrine as they climbed the stairs. Fat chance, she'd shouted when Sandrine had suggested getting ready for bed. She remembers this now, the fact of Sandrine, and that she was cross with her. Remembering makes her more cross: that Sandrine was there at all, in her house, was aggravating. She would ring her daughter now and tell her that she was sending Sandrine packing.

Down the stairs then, stopping to pick up a painted porcelain knickknack in the shape of a tiny Buddha, his bellybutton a clean perfect circle of a black paint dot. She closes her eyes with the Buddha in her palm.

Vietnam, she says aloud. Hué. Puts it back on the shelf and goes down the stairs, which audibly ache in places. Footsteps start upstairs.

Clare? A voice comes falling down behind her. Are you up, Clare?

She doesn't reply at once. She ambles into the kitchen first, turning on the lights, opening the refrigerator and walking away from the slow-swinging door, eying the beautiful curtains before the conservatory glass made from a yellow and green silk tapestry of birds on branches she'd chosen where? Yes, she calls, I am up. I'm on my way to Tom, and you can just go home because I'm finished with you. *Where?*

Vietnam, she says softly again to herself, her hand remembering the cold little Buddha. And the tapestry curtains with their singing birds and sunshine-made fabric colour?

She leaves this question in the kitchen, goes to the front door then, automatically opening it (as she had done the fridge) and peering out. It is dark for morning, but she does not notice this. She watches her breath, small steaming clouds hovering over her, looks at the still-lit lamps of the quiet street that is full of the creeping, cold, sea air. The sea echoes over the road, sound falling into her ears. November in Ireland is miserable, she tells the street. It is dark all the time. The words in the dark are white smoke.

Clare? A voice behind her. You'll get a chill in that air. Sandrine is in a pair of thick flannel pyjamas with a kerchief tied over her hair, her eyes full of disturbed sleep, a slight, almost imperceptible ripple and bulge in the top speaking of something she does not.

I missed the garbage men again, Clare tells her. I wish you'd remind me to put out the rubbish. At this rate, the whole house will fill up! Clare walks past her in irritation but is not sure where she wants to go. She hesitates in the kitchen.

I wouldn't worry, Sandrine tells her, her voice gentle, her hand pushing closed the front door, shutting out the cold and the dark. They don't begin their collections for another few hours. It's only three a.m. She watches Clare to see how she takes this piece of news, but Clare is standing still with limp arms, gazing at a row of cupboards that are walnut like the floors. Something must have woken you. Will I make up a hot water bottle for you and you can get back into bed until the rubbish men come? It's still cold down here, the heating is not yet on. Sandrine watches her back, sees a slight droop of the shoulders that means that it will be okay, that Clare will go up without a fight this time, that there will not be a need to bolt the doors or call Elizabeth because Clare has run off across the dark street towards the sea with no coat on.

It is cold down here, Clare says, her voice slumped as her shoulders are. November in Ireland is always miserable. Sandrine is startled out of her half-consciousness by this. Clare knows what month it is. Clare turns to the stairs and pauses after climbing only a few. But I wish you'd reminded me! What will Tom think when he comes home to find we've a house full of rubbish? He has a sensitive nose, you know, he'll smell it out. Even if it's gone a day, he'll know it wasn't put out on time.

Back in her bed, twitching a bit of coverlet between thumb and finger, Clare watches the space that is Tom's and talks to it. I don't know what to do Tom. My house is full of strangers from all over the world and I don't recognise any of them. What's-her-name is always jabbering to her relatives on my phone, eating my food, and my daughter does nothing. Your daughter, Tom. I think the pair of us should run off back to Vietnam. We should just go and never come back. And I could grow lilies again. And it would be warm. And sunny. And you could sell your spices and we could go to Hong Kong for the weekend and the markets in Shenzhen, eat dim sum in one of the giant houses. And it would be bright and warm and sunny and never so cold as this, even when it's January and that mist blows in from the Red River. And we wouldn't have to talk to anyone but ourselves.

Sandrine comes with the hot water bottle wrapped in a button-down shirt of Tom's – this is a trick she has invented, knowing that Clare will recognise the smell, somewhere, or the shirt itself that once held her husband – and leaves quickly. She pretends to close the door and then half opens it again and stands outside to ensure that Clare is staying in bed. Clare holds the hot water bottle against her breasts, her arms folded around it.

When you were still here, Tom, I never needed one of these. The heat makes her close her eyes. It is like holding her life in Vietnam against her heart. Vietnam, Tom, she says quietly. But the fatigue of climbing the stairs makes her mind porous, and, without realising it, she is losing the memories that are those two words, losing the sense that they are memories at all, and she sleeps again, her still-blond hair spreading on the pillow like a faded peacock fan.

It seemed to Clare that Tom had gone before she knew it. One minute he was there in the bed beside her when she woke in the morning and there was no need for hot water bottles or electric blankets, and the next her days were filled with the arduous maze of trying to reach him in whatever home or hospital he happened to be. And no one seemed able to tell her exactly where he was, either. She couldn't remember exactly when all of this had happened. Initially he had been brought for tests to a hospital nearby. This, Clare remembered, had something to do with an adventure he'd had on Sandrine's first afternoon off, only two weeks after Sandrine had arrived, and so she vaguely linked Tom's disappearance to Sandrine's arrival.

On that particular afternoon, after Sandrine had left for her three hours of freedom and quiet, walking around the newness of Ireland thinking what to do about the not-yet-child and the fact that she had not yet attended an English class, Tom had gone into the last of the October garden. Drawn to its beech hedges the colour of the palest cinnamon bark, he'd decided to hack down an old apple tree that he violently proclaimed to Clare never to have liked. Not having wielded any tools beyond a hammer since he was a child on the farm in Wexford, Tom very quickly hurt himself with the shears he was hacking the tree with, and then, heading back into the house with bleeding arms, had slipped. Clare had bandaged up his arms in warmed tea towels without much real alarm, and hadn't called Elizabeth. When Elizabeth, knowing that it was Sandrine's afternoon out, appeared for a visit, she got a land. It was only several days later, after two trips to his GP, that Tom was taken to hospital by his daughter for some tests.

What kind of tests they were didn't concern Clare because Elizabeth had told her there was nothing to worry over, and she accepted this. She did not experience the weight of a new silence in the house. In fact, there was more conversation now that Tom was absent, for this absence provided an infinite stretch of enquiry about how Tom was, where he was, and when he might be coming home. For the first few days Clare had been startled to wake to an empty space in the bed, and immediately set about trying to find him, asking Sandrine where he'd gone and where she'd hidden him. Clare developed an acute sense of purpose. She single-mindedly sought her husband.

This sense of purpose took her over as these things do, suddenly, so that within a week she would have been hard-pressed to remember what she had done with her days before. When her daughter called in to drive her to the hospital to visit him, she often found Sandrine alone, helplessly explaining that Clare had insisted on going already, just ten minutes ago. She would have spent the morning gathering together bills and bits of mail, bags of soft sweets, bundles of backdated spice trade newsletters, and a small bunch of grapes, all to be thrown into one green Superquinn cloth shopping bag, and then snuck out when Sandrine had gone to the loo. Sandrine had been torn between looking for Clare and staying at home; she had run around the corner a few times and rushed back to see if Clare had returned, then had run across the road to peer over the railings that marked the start of the sea, to make sure that Clare was not in the water. It was time, Elizabeth told Sandrine exhaustedly, that she bought Sandrine a mobile, and time, too, for a new, more complicated lock on the front door.

While her daughter set off by car to search for her, Clare obliviously roamed away from the seafront through housing estates, taking short cuts across greens littered with leaves and seasonless cigarette butts, through gaps in walls that led to bicycle paths, collecting on her way bundles of sticks, for one never knew if Tom would need a fire lit. The weather often allowed her to forget that October – or November? – in Ireland was always miserable. The sun shone lower, but with a clarity that cast Clare into happiness. It had the appearance of heat, this sunlight, shot through with an orange glow, and the sky often a soaring, cloudless blue. Sometimes she would hum to herself as she walked blindly into the sun, or talk to Tom, and even if it was raining the time passed while she looked down at her feet in the puddles and pools that grew in spots on the paths. And, eventually, she arrived at the hospital, wet or dry, with her bag of things for Tom and a great deal of kindling tucked under her arm.

ⸯ ⸯ ⸯ

As a child Clare had occasionally collected kindling from the back garden of the house. It became a sort of competition, brothers and sisters frantically moving over the grass to peer beneath trees, into hedges, for sticks. Their mother laughed; she found the sight of the four of them dashing to the far corners of the garden amusing, their enthusiasm for the task charming. The smallest ones merely toddled, returning to her with handfuls of grass or, at a certain time of year, a few pinecones. Clare, since she was one of the two older children, took it more seriously. She wanted very much to win the unofficial game, to announce herself as the winner when her father came in the door in his train conductor's uniform, to loll against the counter near the sink where he wrapped himself in an apron and washed dishes and told her stories about the trains that day (how they had had to stop when a cow had gotten onto the tracks near Bray, a big old brown cow with a mouthful of cud and a bursting udder), and to have her own story to tell, about finding the sticks. Sometimes, only once or twice, Clare snatched at a green branch from a tree, and carried it shamefacedly into the firebox.

More than the others, she liked to see the firebox full. It had never been empty, and she had no reason to worry herself that the kindling would run out. Her mother, when she found the green branches, told her that her father had taken the pledge, and as a result they would never have to worry the way other Irish families did. The green sticks could be left alone to grow and flower in the spring. But despite her mother's assurances, still Clare liked the firebox best full, when the sticks were wedged in so tightly that to remove a handful was to spill out most of the box onto the bare stone floor.

It was the same with the pantry. If they were running low on something, milk, or sugar, or bread, and her mother decided she'd wait until the next morning to do a bit of shopping or baking that would fill the downstairs part of the house with smell and comfort, Clare worried privately. Her older sister Fidelma teased her that she was only afraid that she wouldn't get any of the milk, or sugar, or bread. But in fact it was more serious and less immediately selfish than that.

When she had been only a few years younger, the war had been on, and Clare had been much impressed by the rationing of butter. Before that time she had not liked butter more than any of the others, but she certainly felt its yellow absence on the table more than them. It was like the sun had gone in and never came back, except in minutely angled portions, and for a limited time. Unconsciously, in response, she had built the ideal of abundance into her mind, taking to an advance stockpiling for a time when the butter might become only a memory again. And while you couldn't keep butter forever (she'd asked about this at school and had been told by her Mayo-born daughter-of-a-farmer teacher that the only way to keep butter was to dig it down into a bog, the thought of which repulsed her. She'd been in the bog with her father in the winter, and it was soft, squelching and frightening), you could always use sticks. Clare reckoned that if it came to a choice, really it was better to be always warm than to have butter.

It was not hard for Sandrine to picture Clare as a child. Casually, unthinkingly, she told Sandrine these stories, the small details that make up a life, and Sandrine could see her: fair-haired with round cheeks, in a garden bordered with currant bushes that wept with fruit in the summer months and provided small children with hiding places that were filled with the scent of tangy, sun-warmed sugar. Clare gazed at her, after all, with the same watery brown eyes that had sought kindling in the bushes, and had admired the rubies of red currants as the sunlight filtered through their delicate, taut skins.

What was more difficult was for Sandrine to imagine Clare as an adult, not yet an old woman, during the years when she first met Tom outside a carpet warehouse. Week after week, Clare and her sister, selecting rugs before Fidelma's marriage, returned to the warehouse to check colour samples of fabric for curtains and uphol-stery against the rugs. And week after week, Clare noticed the gentleman who frequently appeared from the opposite warehouse whose business seemed to be something to do with cooking ingre-dients, and who occasionally smoked a cigarette, pretending not to look at her while she waited outside. After three weeks of watching each other across the road, Tom waved, called 'Hello again!' and bowed, the boldness of which made her laugh. Sandrine tried to picture this meeting, the casualness, the chance of it, and achieved an image of laughter crossing a street.

When he'd said hello his accent was stuck somewhere between Dublin and Wexford, a half-a-bog accent, Clare's sister joked for years. But Clare liked his accent, the strange awayness of it, the way it spoke of experiences beyond the port of Dublin. She listened attentively to his descriptions of his work as they strolled through Stephen's Green one afternoon. He had twenty minutes only, he apologised, for he had run down to meet her on his lunch hour and still had to get back again. Clare didn't mind, and for twenty minutes they wove their way between railings and flower-beds that were edging towards autumn. As they parted at a side gate, Clare was already rather enchanted with the world that his ambition offered her imagination. They arranged to meet again for 'lunch' the following day, and, in the only love-struck daze of her life, Clare returned to her own job as a secretary to an importer of fabrics, up the road.

Clare was remarkably quick as a typist and astute when it came to her own failings. The fabric importer was married to a Frenchwoman, and Clare thought her charming, witty and beautiful. She paled in comparison, she knew, even if the fabric of her clothes was exactly the same – which it often was, seeing that Clare received a discount on the cloth that made up a large part of the wife's wardrobe.

She took to wearing scarves and studying French at night at a local community college, and as she cycled home from work or the college, she would carry on conversations with herself in the language, causing those she passed to smile at what they took for her oblivion. But what they took for the unselfconsciousness of a girl only out of school was something else entirely: a determination to shape herself, to make sure that if the chance arose, she would be ready to go, to step into some role that demanded the poise and grace of that Frenchwoman. She would be ready for the stares that would come her way once she was the foreigner, once she was the beauty walking down new streets.

Most difficult of all to imagine were the years that followed when Clare and Tom left Ireland so that Tom could buy and sell spices, while Clare along the way collected carpets and rugs and tapestries in palates far more complicated than anything her sister had dreamt of back in Dublin. He always said he knew we'd marry when I told him which carpets I liked, and which spices. He said I knew my carpets and I knew my cinnamon and I was the girl for him, the one he could take around the world.

She told Sandrine about these years more than anything else, and of course there were many photographs, but to picture her happy, slightly pink-brown from the long-time exposure to the sun, strolling through a balmy stone courtyard with other expatriate guests, dressed in a tailored ao dai glittering with gold thread, or standing atop an exquisitely fine silken carpet tufted with dark blue in the house that had been hers in America – this was difficult. It was almost impossible if she returned Clare's gaze. When Clare spoke of such times, her eyes glistening and remote, Sandrine couldn't help but stare past her at the paintings on the wall, at the small carvings and statues, to avoid seeing only an old woman in unwashed clothes whose husband had disappeared into his own breaking-up mind.

⁘

When Tom was allowed to return home after a week, it had been on the understanding that permanent live-in help was already in place, and that he must not be left to his own devices. All sharp objects should be locked away, including knives, and the door was to be locked from the inside at all times. The doctor had recommended a nursing home, but Elizabeth could not yet face moving him out of his home permanently. It was one thing to tell Clare that Tom would be home soon, quite another to simply pretend it, or tell the truth. And Clare was delighted to have him at home again. Instead of trailing around town in search of him on foot, her eyes followed him round the room. Her lips turned into easy smiles, she celebrated with rashers for herself every day at breakfast, and urged her daughter to come for dinner each day, even if Elizabeth continually turned down the invitation.

Tom didn't notice this attention one way or the other. He still shuffled down the stairs in the morning, but began to go straight into the sitting room and to forgo his usual breakfast – prepared by Sandrine now – for palmfuls of sweets, biscuits and grapes that

Sandrine learned to pull into small sprigs and branches that he toted round with him. When she managed mid-day to sneak into Clare and Tom's room to change the sheets, Sandrine found the bloodied stains of grape juice on the pillowcases, smears of jam clutched into the edges of blankets. Like a child, he hid things in his pockets and then forgot them utterly, melted a chocolate bar over the course of a day with a fistful of heat and then sometimes licked it off absent-mindedly, other times leaving odd and irregular prints of chocolate on the walls, the banisters, the toilet seat. Windows and mirrors saw splayed fingerprints, and the lines and fine folds of his skin were traced in chocolate.

Tom accepted Sandrine's presence more readily than Clare. He still managed to offer her a cup of coffee at odd times, whenever it struck him that he might have been rude in the lack of such an offer. And while he occasionally asked Clare who she was, he never listened for the answer, as if sensing that Clare knew little more than he did of their situation. While doing the dishes and gazing out at the autumnal blur of colour gradually fading to winter in the back garden, Sandrine sometimes felt a puzzled gaze in the room and turned to find Tom staring hard at her, trying to remember how she had come to be there, who she was, what he was meant to say or do, if anything, at such a moment.

His eyes would barely blink. He would stand in the doorway like this, slightly swaying, silent, until Sandrine took her hands from the sink, dried them, and came over to him. Why don't we go and sit down, Tom? It's too cold for you to stand here in the kitchen, there's a draft from all the windows. Sandrine spoke in her schoolteacher's voice, gently and firmly, looking him squarely in the eye as she would when soothing an out-of-sorts child. Look, the fire is lit, and you can sit and talk to Clare.

He would allow her to move him into the sitting room, near the fire surrounded now with a gate bolted against the wall. He would wind his fingers into his pockets or accept Clare's offer of a biscuit, then spend the next hour engrossed in breaking it into particles of grain that he sprinkled into lines on the sitting room carpet, creating a new design that Clare watched develop with as much attention and which, later, Sandrine would briefly admire before hoovering up.

More often Sandrine would find him standing in the kitchen before a specially built teak spice rack, its doors swung open to reveal a century or so of small silver canisters, each stuck with a label covered in his own slanting, calligraphic hand and indicating not only the spice or herb, but its origin and its date. Tom would pile the lids up in a neat stack until they toppled, but by then he was engrossed in his true project: smelling the spices, tasting their colours on the tip of his tongue, painting them onto his lips. Some mornings he would seem to be concentrating on sweet spices. He would grip freshly shaved nutmeg under his nose, or break a pod of cardamom into sticky beans. Other days, Sandrine was alerted to his position in the house by a sudden spate of sneezes that usually meant the peppers were being examined, the many mills he had fallen in love with at different times lined up on the kitchen counter, small drifts of the grinds in front of them. And oddly enough, no matter what chocolate prints were left on furniture or clothing, the spice tins always remained pristine. Their lids were tightly replaced and they were stowed away from light behind the narrow slats of wood. Sandrine would find that clean sheets and towels crawled with cinnamon and pepper, made to act as dusters of the tins, the lids, and the labels.

Only about two weeks after his return from the hospital, though, Tom refused Clare's usual suggestion that it was time for bed, and lay down in the crimson and saffron-coloured sitting room to sleep. He was not a tall man, but a rather large, big-boned one, with a squat farmer's build like his brother. Watching him lower himself to the floor seemed to Sandrine an eternity of anxiety over which she was powerless. She envisioned herself attempting to stop him, or attempting to haul him up on his feet, but the not-yet-child butterfly-flew through her mind and she knew that this was impossible.

Eventually, Tom lay on his back on the carpet. Once there, he closed his eyes and swam his hands through the luxuriance of carpet pile, his eyelids tremoring with ideas. Clare headed furiously on up the stairs, stomping over the carpeted, creaky boards, leaving Sandrine wondering what to do. After looking at the clock and deciding it was too late to summon Elizabeth for a relatively minor event such as this, Sandrine, kneeling by Tom, murmured calmly to him while she raised his head and placed a pillow beneath his neck, draped a small square of a throw over his legs and settled into an armchair in the hall outside of the room to begin a half-sleepless vigil, listening for floorboards and voices. Clare's footsteps died above her, and Sandrine assumed she'd gotten into bed. There was no sound, only the beginnings of an earnest rain slapping at the windows, drilling at the roof.

Sandrine went in and watched Tom intently for a few moments, and when it appeared he was fast asleep, let herself gaze around the room. She remained fascinated by the house, by its abundance, and in moments like these liked to imagine George and Tobias arriving, to dream up their gasps and delighted reactions. Tobias would love the Buddhas as she did, Sandrine knew. After a while she returned to the hallway armchair and dozed off, sitting with her hands over her belly, her mind dreaming past the drumming of the rain and past the nausea that she was battling.

In her dream she was back in Zimbabwe, and the child was born, shouting, speaking, telling her that she was not feeling well, was feeling sickly and wanted to go home. Sandrine was telling her girl child that yes, they would go home to Ireland soon and her husband was shouting too, saying that he couldn't go to Ireland, that he had no visa. Sandrine woke with a start only when Tom appeared in the hallway half undressed and seemed to be looking for his clothes. It was still raining, harder now. She fought the urge to ignore him and remain in the few moments when she could still remember the dream. But she rose with the sound of the rain thumping irregularly in her ears, and she and Tom found his clothes in the hallway, draped neatly over the walnut stair rails that gleamed in the dim light.

Excuse me, he said politely, there seems to have been a bit of a mix up. I thought I was to collect my suit this afternoon. Is it ready now?

Sandrine told him that it was okay, the suit was ready, and he nodded gravely.

Just as Sandrine got his shirt on, Clare appeared at the foot of the stairs, her eyebrows arched high into her forehead, her mouth a perfect O. Trying to steal my husband! she shouted. She ran – Clare never ran – to Sandrine, snatched Tom's fleece and socks from where they were caught in the crook of Sandrine's arm, and put her slight arms protectively around him. Sandrine retreated to the kitchen, leaving the two of them alone in the rug-strewn hallway, listening to the confused sounds of Clare's sobbing and Tom's surprisingly fitting there theres and the noisy drops of rain slashing at the front door's mottled stained-glass panes.

After only a few moments, the stairs groaned that they had managed to go up, and Sandrine herself sat down and wept. She wept because she had been in the house by the sea almost a month, and the baby was growing and demanding more of her physically. But she had not had time to think of her. Since she had arrived in the house the child had become something physical only. Sandrine might feel the illness of the child in the mornings, or feel the child's growls of hunger as she lay down to rest, but other than that, Sandrine could not bring herself to think of it as a pregnancy. It was like a condition that made her feel unwell from time to time, but one that she had not had time to digest would change and lead to something else, another stage, and another, and another. And the child sensed this; that she was receiving far less of her mother's time since they – that was the fact of it – had arrived in this house. The dream was the way the child now found to speak to her, to let her know that things were going to change. Sandrine sat sobbing, counting the weeks in her mind over and over again. Seven weeks, the first at home, the fourth in airports and the Irish countryside, and this week, next week, all the weeks to come – in a madhouse. What was she to do? Leave? Write to George and tell him what? I am in a madhouse? It's bad for the child? But George didn't know about the child. Sandrine sat sobbing until the thought arrived in her mind that this too was bad for the child, and then she made some tea and toast and tried to hide the rest of her thoughts from the baby. She would talk to the daughter, Elizabeth. She would tell Elizabeth that she could not handle so much at once, and see what she said. In the back of her mind was the anxiety that she was only meant to work twenty hours a week. Perhaps something could be done to reduce her hours, make her compliant with her visa, and allow her to get out to the English classes. Slowly, she rose and followed the ghost of the couple up the stairs, pausing at their door, behind which was a reassuring quiet. Sandrine went into her own room, and, hands stretched over the not-yet-child, fell asleep in the deep darkness while listening to the rain.

᠎   ᠎   ᠎

Elizabeth heard the news of the previous night over the phone and promised to come over as soon as she could. Sandrine did not have to say that it had been too much for her, Elizabeth immediately admitting that Tom would have to go into a home, if only to give Clare a chance to live a more normal life. It couldn't be good for Clare, she said, to be up and down in the middle of the night, worrying about him. And, Elizabeth added when she arrived, I know that the two of them are too much for one person to care for. She looked at Sandrine sympathetically, but the look immediately put Sandrine on her guard. Did Elizabeth know? That she was two people?

Sandrine was not sure what to make of Elizabeth. Most of their dealings so far had been to discuss rates of pay and afternoons off. Elizabeth had asked few questions about Sandrine's life or her purpose in being in Ireland and in this job. Instead she asked whether Sandrine was finding everything that she needed in the house, showed her how to use the washing machine, drew disproportionate maps directing her to shops, and gave her several photocopies of a list of phone numbers – for herself, for doctors, for the police.

But in the weeks that followed, Elizabeth was different, more inclined to ask questions. How Clare was sleeping, what kind of appetite she had, whether she took her vitamins willingly, if she seemed happy. Sometimes when she asked these questions, quietly, seriously, like a child frightened to attention, and in an accent noticeably different from her parents', she seemed to speak through tears. Sandrine, although younger than Elizabeth, wanted sometimes to pat her shoulder as she would her own child's or one upset at the school. It seems strange, doesn't it? Elizabeth remarked one morning as she stood waiting in the hallway for Clare to return from the loo, that in some ways you know my mother better than I do, now. And because Clare appeared a moment later and they departed to visit Tom, Sandrine could not reply, and was glad.

Elizabeth always seemed slightly uncomfortable in her parents' house, and treated Sandrine as if she had more familiarity with the place. She might ask where the sugar was being kept these days, or puzzle her way through several cupboards for anything other than a tea cup until Sandrine pointed to the correct one. Elizabeth knew where basic items were kept, but nothing more. Had Elizabeth not visited her parents before this? Hadn't she herself lived in the house? Clare, even in her forgetfulness, moved with purpose around the rooms. Her hands immediately, if accidentally, found odd things like keys for drawers, a stash of scarves and gloves, old address books; her tiring legs took her up the stairs with practised rhythm, and her fingers twitched the heavy curtains closed with the kind of physical autonomy that was habit. Elizabeth rarely ventured upstairs, and when asked to discover something for her mother on the odd occasion, prowled almost guiltily through wardrobes and presses.

Sandrine initially made herself scarce as soon as Elizabeth would arrive, assuming that Elizabeth would go in and joke with her parents, tell funny stories, pull open packets of biscuits and produce a pot of tea. But she knew after only a few weeks that Elizabeth actually preferred if she stayed. Otherwise, sitting beside her mother on a narrow settee, Elizabeth lapsed into silences, quietly picked up books and asked Clare whether she had read them or not, or simply turned on the television after making her mother some green tea and herself some coffee. This strain between mother and daughter had not been so marked when Tom was at home, but when Tom had first gone into hospital for those few days of tests, Sandrine had noticed a wincing quiet to Elizabeth's visits, and had begun to remain downstairs.

For this Elizabeth seemed grateful. She made green tea for the three of them (even though she herself hated it) and sliced into modest segments the *pain au chocolat* she picked up for her mother. And then she sat talking, mostly to Sandrine, and saying so little about herself that Sandrine realised later that she didn't even know if Elizabeth was married or had any children or what, if anything, she did to make her living. Elizabeth had a quiet way of asking questions and getting Sandrine to spill out a sentence or two in answer before she was aware of it. She heard herself describe her son and her husband, heard her living siblings' names rolling off her lips for the first time in well over a month. Epiphania, Augustine, Gibson, Elizabeth repeated.

Gradually, Sandrine realised that she had, in response to casual questions, revealed the outline of her life in Zim. This outline hung in the room like another of Clare's tapestries, gradually taking shape. The cluster of concrete and wattle houses on the farmland, the school building, the children who were so hungry for anything she could give – food, books, pencils – the basin of sky raining down or vacant of cloud and clear blue. She told of the occasional trips to Marondera, where two of her brothers had gone for work in the sweet factory.

But Sandrine was too fearful and too uncertain of her position to acknowledge her pregnancy, or the fearfulness itself that was bound up in the fact of her being in Ireland on a student visa and not attending any school. She had only paid the fee for her language classes to the school that a Nigerian woman from the first residence had given her when they met on the road, telling her that they would not expect her to show up and would still give her the necessary document saying that her attendance was satisfactory. Sandrine had thus called the school with which she had been in contact before leaving Zimbabwe and told them that this other school would be more convenient. It was a matter of simple paperwork to register instead at this new place.

It was not only that she was undecided about whether or not to trust Elizabeth completely – Sandrine herself also wished to forget, to remain in a realm that was light, unthreatening, simple. And so she told Elizabeth the easy, obvious things: that her son was five years old and had brown eyes shot through with light so that they shimmered like topaz in the sun, which predictably shone for most of the year, that she had been a teacher for three years in a small school on the farm where her husband also worked, that they were extremely fortunate to both have work. It was rare, that two people in a couple should have jobs. She told her that she had been among the extremely fortunate who had been accepted into a private school, and that the fees had been shared among the extended family in the hope that she would secure a job as a teacher afterwards. She told Elizabeth, too, that the work and the food and the sense of security had begun to dry up for them now as it had for many others, hence she was in Ireland. It was an easy narrative, easily told, and one that left out the facts of so much violence, so much heartache, so much loneliness. And with Sandrine's answers between them, Elizabeth could turn to her mother and say, isn't Tobias a beautiful name? Or, doesn't he sound like a sweet boy, Clare?

Clare herself seemed calmed by these snatched hours of tea and polite conversation, sitting quietly, a delicate bone china cup with scatters of pink petals and gold painted rim between her palms, the pattern vaguely Asian, the small bones on the backs of her hands as thin and pronounced as the cup handle. She seemed briefly to forget her urge to find Tom, gazing out of the salted windows at the tops of the sea-blown trees that were shedding. She watched with some surprise the leaves as they skated on gusts out of her sight, occasionally turning from the grey and blue of sky to the heated colours that were this front room and its wall hangings, carpets, curtains.

Sandrine began to look forward to Elizabeth's visits, even after Tom came home from hospital, because they had a suggestion of normality, or of what Sandrine imagined to be an Irish normality: several women sitting together drinking tea and chatting quietly about weather and family and health and news headlines and nothing more. It was a pause for her, a release from one role into another. In her belly, the worry that was the not-yet-child quietened when Elizabeth spoke, and Sandrine felt more hopeful that somehow things would work out, for surely if she could sit drinking tea and nibbling plain, pale moons of biscuits with these two Irish women, she could remain in Ireland. Sitting there in the room with them talking, however superficially, about her other life had the effect of creating a new one. It also created an illusion of retrospect that she did not actually feel. She spoke of her husband, her son, her images of home as past, as some other time unconnected to this one, severed from it. And disturbing as it was in some way to speak

51

of what and who she loved with such distance, it was precisely that distance that granted to Sandrine hope, a future sense of happiness beyond visas and class attendance and silent pregnancies.

So when Elizabeth sympathised with Sandrine for having to care for both Tom and Clare, Sandrine felt suspicious and confused, because it was more difficult to try to conflate the two roles of employee and mere human being chatting over tea. Perhaps Elizabeth had been merely vetting her for the past few weeks, trying to catch her out, trying to learn whether or not she was legal. Perhaps the police had called Elizabeth to enquire if Sandrine was really working only the twenty hours per week permitted by her student visa. Maybe they were aware that she was not attending the school.

Sandrine felt tired all of a sudden, and wanted to lie down. But then Elizabeth said, you know, Sandrine, no one else has been able to stay as long as you. There was always some problem, but both of them have responded really well to you. I knew, really, I knew that my dad couldn't live at home indefinitely, that he had become very demanding. She glanced at where her father was napping in an old brown leather armchair graced with a slice of thin, wintry sun, his head slow-motion moving, falling towards his chest. But I do hope that you'll stay on with my mother here. She likes you. Don't you, Clare? But Clare was gazing out at the leaves and the baring themselves branches, and didn't reply.

Sandrine was, to her surprise, moved. I would be very happy to stay, Elizabeth, she said, Clare and I are getting on very well these days, and I'm happy to help. For a few moments the three women sat in a silence punctuated by Tom's sleep-breathing. Clare staring into the sky through glass and faintly watered eyes. Sandrine lost in the dregs of her beige-green tea. Elizabeth glancing between her mother and this stranger able to manage her, feeling relief and bewilderment to find herself outside their relationship. Her eyes rested finally on her father's oblivion that was growing in the corner of the room as the light sank behind the walls of the house. It would all continue to change, she knew. This ending, it would go on and on so that at some point she would look back at this day and think that it hadn't even begun at this stage. It would be like that. It always was.

᠁ ᠁ ᠁

When Tom moved into the nursing home further down the coast overlooking the cragged rocks near Dalkey Island, Clare was told that it would be best if she remained at home, while more tests were carried out. With the servant? she asked Elizabeth. With a pained look in Sandrine's direction, Elizabeth nodded, yes, and apologised to Sandrine as soon as Clare went out of the room.

Clare was utterly unused to the idea of living alone. This was obvious not just from the stories she seasoned with the names of chefs and chauffeurs and bellboys, but in her manner generally. She was officious, in her best moods, inhabiting a role she had played for the best part of her adult life. She had, after all, in living in a hotel for so many years, lived in public. She would invite her daughter to sit down, to make herself a drink; she would offer fruit or wine or, her own favourite, tiny cups of very strong coffee she had continued to have sent over from Vietnam. She made this coffee herself in a flimsy pot with a filter made of needle-punctured tin she'd bought in the 19th of December market before they'd returned to Ireland, in an attempt to barricade herself from the reality of the return. A French press wasn't the same. She could, in those same moods, idly entertain with anecdotes; it came so easily to her then.

When Sandrine arrived there was still a supply of coffee from Vietnam, loyally sent on by one of the Metropole staff. The fruit remained unusual by Irish standards, with bowls of mangoes and star fruit and papaya – it was so fortunate that Cavistons was just behind the house – but by the time Tom went into the nursing home Clare was too preoccupied to remember to call the hotel for coffee along with the candied corossolier usually available only as Tet approached and which she and Tom still craved. She abandoned her attempts to make up for the lack of fresh dragon fruit, longans, mangosteens and star apples and bought enormous plastic bags of green seedless grapes. She switched from her small fragrant packets of specialty coffee to Bewley's or Nescafé or whatever other instant was on obvious display, and either forgot that her Vietnamese sweets could be ordered or reverted to a child's indiscriminate love of anything sweet, and so gradually bags and boxes of mostly English sweets began to fill the house.

While Sandrine and George had worked and saved for the airline tickets, a chocolate bar had become a treat of which their son would speak for days, and so Sandrine was amazed at the quantities of sweets that Clare brought into the house. A box of jellies the size of a small tabletop rested on the unused end of the dining room table. Another, full of chocolate, somewhat less crude in size, was always on a squatting bamboo coffee table in the sitting room. Near the phone in the kitchen, a pewter dish held the jumbled remains of several bags of mixed sweets and the chocolates that were always left in the box – the ones that neither Tom nor Clare particularly liked but would eat absentmindedly while talking on the phone to Elizabeth: the blackcurrant jelly babies, the pink marshmallows, the lemon creams. If these options were to run out, there were other bags and boxes awaiting opening, stacked unevenly in a kitchen press and still covered in clear, taut cellophane: Black Magic, Quality Street, the odd rectangular box of Butler's or Lir. Beside them were slabs of Fruit and Nut, Wholenut, Bourneville, Rittersport flecked with toffee, Kinder Bueno fingers, Lindt, and crinkly bags of jelly beans, dolly mixtures, toffee bonbons, fruit jellies, and round rolls of Eclairs and Polo Mints and pastilles.

Clare loved cakes and biscuits and *pain au chocolat* and jam doughnuts, on which she would smear butter and more jam. She would cut the doughnuts into bite-size pieces with a bone-handled knife from Thailand, and then spend long minutes spreading soft yellow butter in even thickness on to each piece and topping it with a knife-end of trembling jam. For some reason, whenever she ate doughnuts she was oblivious to everything else. She concentrated exactingly on the buttering and jamming, and then stared out the window while she chewed, forgetting Sandrine was there, her thin, elegant fingers blindly searching the plate for the next mouthful as her eyelids with their almost invisible blond lashes blinked at the view. In those moments, Sandrine saw the fair-haired little girl in her face, the one who dreamed of getting away from butter rations and shortages and the predictable life of marriage and children set out for her and most other girls of her day. When the doughnut was gone, Clare would stare almost mournfully at her plate dusted with sugar crystals and traced with jam – her fine hair swinging against her jawline – and then notice the world around her again.

Right, she would say, there you are.

There Sandrine was.

Despite having experienced so many hotel staff, Clare had never had a servant assigned so specifically to her, never had a servant living in such close quarters to her, and had certainly never had one that presumed to eat dinner with her at the table. She grudgingly accepted Sandrine's presence, and only then because she saw her as a type of servant she had simply not experienced before. If someone, her daughter, had told the truth – that Sandrine was an aide there not only to cook her meals but to keep her from wandering off or setting the house on fire – she would have flung her clothes from the window, thrown her plate onto one of her rugs and then wept with regret at the globs of Bonne Maman staining the beautiful carpet. So Sandrine went along, pretending not to hear when Clare told Elizabeth that she couldn't understand this new class of maid who cooked the meals and then sat down with her to eat them. And really she was a terrible cook, Clare complained.

Sandrine had not yet discovered that Clare, with her decades of absence from Ireland, did not care for the food Sandrine assumed she desired. So they both reluctantly ate boiled potatoes and over-cooked vegetables and various meats broiled or fried, when what Clare would have loved was a bowl of noodles doused with fish sauce and sprinkled with chopped peanuts and fresh coriander brightened to a vivid green by the soup's heat, and what Sandrine craved was a plain bowl of sadze to settle her soon-to-be girl child.

⌣ ⌣ ⌣

While they are seated at the table Sandrine is forced to talk. This is because Clare eats so slowly. If Clare begins to talk before she begins to eat there is no hope of her managing to get much of anything into her mouth. So Sandrine sits there with a full plate of food, the curdled, musty grey smell of potato skin rising and making her feel ill, and she begins to babble, about anything. She learns quickly to talk of things Clare knows nothing about, so that Clare cannot begin a conversation, and so Sandrine talks about her family, about her husband and his hope of being able to get out too some day and come to Ireland with their son, how strange it would be for the three of them to live alone, without other family. She speaks to Clare about whatever news they have seen recently on the television about home: plans for elections, her anxieties that the polls will be manned by Mugabe's teenaged guerrillas again and prevent people voting; how she herself can no longer vote now because Mugabe fears the votes of the Zimbabwean diaspora, and how angry this makes her. She tells Clare about how she had wanted to name her son Morgan but dared not, because anyone from Zanu-PF could then target him for being named after the only hope the country seemed to have at another ruler. She speaks differently to Clare than she does to Elizabeth. She does not dwell merely in fact, does not hold back.

And so she speaks not only about the heat that seemed to shimmer over the whole country as she saw it from the airplane window, tipped towards the ground, about her son's penmanship, about his amazement at her circumstances here, but about her loneliness without him, about her anxiety for him being separated from his mother, and the terrible anxiety that something will happen to him, or to George, while she is here, that the violence that has been moving as unpredictably and steadily as wind will come to their farm, their village. She tells Clare about her brothers' involvement with the MDC, and how one of them, Amahle, had left Mitchell's sweet factory one evening and vanished, no trace left of him except a sighting by a woman across the road who cannot say for sure it was him, but who saw a young man beaten to the ground and dragged, broken-boned, into a pick-up truck. It was the event that ultimately allowed Sandrine to agree to depart since, as a teacher and his sister, she might become a secondary target as so many had. She had to do something for George and Tobias and all the family.

Clare is not attentive. She vaguely listens, but more importantly she eats, slowly cutting up her meat, pushing the softened dull green vegetables aside, forking through a neat mound of white mashed potato, butter drizzling down its slopes. And Sandrine continues to talk to herself while watching Clare, listening to her own voice confirm to none but her own ears that she has a past that is not only another life but still connected to her in the present, the exercise becoming as necessary for her as it is for Clare.

She gets lost in the rhythm of her own voice. This is how it used to be at school when she was starting to learn French and she would read aloud books far too advanced for her level, just to hear the strange foreign words. But she had also done the same with English, when she was a child. She would read Shakespeare's sonnets to herself in the empty schoolroom and marvel at how educated and refined her own voice sounded in the dusky heat of day against the laughing cries of the other children beyond the walls. And when she'd first ventured into Shakespeare's plays, she had carried for months a particular phrase, not knowing its meaning. These are the forgeries of jealousy, she had announced to night-quiet lanes punctuated with the occasional squawls of children. The words had sounded so perfect, so square and even in the air. She had recited them and others, so many others, to herself until something of their meaning passed into her like a miracle. So Sandrine speaks now, using words she would not ordinarily, trying them out. Her son, she tells Clare, is sometimes *incorrigible*, the weather at this season *breathtaking*, her husband's intelligence is far from *trifling*. She pilfers the vocabulary of books. Her longing for home, though, for a moment of her child's arms looped around her neck, tightening, is simply that, a longing that stretches on and on without end, growing daily. There is no word for the elasticity of her desire that now stretches halfway round the world.

When Clare's plate is almost clear – she will not eat any more save perhaps the doughnuts and the *pain au chocolat* hidden under a linen napkin at the far end of the table – Sandrine switches topics. Clare never notices the transition. Sandrine silences her own longings and turns to Clare's. She abandons her homeland and asks a simple question about Vietnam and Clare's eyes shine. Did you like it there, Clare, Sandrine asks, in Vietnam? Clare's fork tinkles against her plate. That, she murmurs, that is the place she would go back to in a heartbeat. Although, she clangs the fork down altogether, it isn't likely that we'll go back at this stage since we're too old for all of that now.

Clare tells Sandrine again, a tiny floret of broccoli that she will not eat still skewered on her fallen fork's tines, about the house in Halong Bay where they took her visiting elder sister and her husband. It was July, you see, she says, and really too early, so we took them up the coast to get away from the heat. And oh the roads! She retrieves the fork, waving it in the air and laughing. Anywhere else it would have been an hour's journey, or two, but there, well, I don't think we ever made it in under seven hours. Getting out of Hanoi wasn't really the problem, although you'd think it would be – but the bicycles really do move out of your way if you honk the horn and just keep moving. But outside of the city the roads ... but it wasn't their fault that the roads were so bad. Those French left such a mess, and then the Americans. Craters everywhere, perfectly round ponds in the middle of fields – children would wash in them! And afterwards no one gave enough money to rebuild or to fix the roads, and the government wasn't interested. I suppose they had enough trouble on their hands. So you just put up with it, the bumping up and down and up and down until you thought maybe you'd scream. My sister did when she saw the bridge over the Red River, all the bits gone out of it from the American bombs. Clare laughed again. But the trip was always worthwhile. You've never seen anything like it. Nor have I. No other place like it in all the world.

When she speaks of the house on the bay for the first time Sandrine can see her there: a house seeming to float above a sea shining like blue glass, its flat sheen interrupted only by the crags and rocky arches that erupted from depths so full of salt that no one could drown; the war-ruins of other houses scattered against the fringe that was the shore; and Clare lying on a deck in a modest one-piece ice-blue bathing suit, the straps tucked carefully under her arms. Clare closes her eyes as she speaks of the heat of the sun, and beneath her flickering lids dances the memory of her body on a slatted teak chair, the brown warmth of wood against her skin. When her lids flutter open again she blinks in surprise at the November shadows that stretch across the table at this time of day.

Fidelma, my sister, didn't really enjoy it, I think. Clare stares up at the ceiling for a moment, thinking. She said that she did, but I know her. She couldn't make sense of it, spent her whole holiday worrying that the war would suddenly start all over again or that the Americans would drop napalm on top of her perm – which probably would have helped it, Clare finishes, savagely, then pauses. No matter what I told her. Really. Ah well, Clare sighs, and put the fork down very gently on the plate. I must ring her one of these days.

Sandrine quickly takes the dinner plate and replaces it with the cake plate of two doughnuts left over from Elizabeth's visit earlier in the day. Clare reaches for one absently, her eyes still shimmering with the memory of the sea and the sun and that other life she'd never imagined would lead to this dreary November and dinner with a servant.

Sandrine walks with the plates to the kitchen sink, pushes the button for the kettle to boil. Clare begins to eat the doughnuts while she is out of the room, in that silence, cutting them into pieces, spreading their sugary surface with butter and raspberry jam, scrutinizing the seeds from time to time, pushing the portions into her open mouth. Finished, she turns her head to the still uncurtained windows, staring at the reflection of herself. She gets up, pulls the curtains over and sits down again, her face a confusion of emotion as Sandrine places in front of her a cup of green tea.

Well, Clare says, licking her forefinger and dragging it across the sugary remains on her plate, perhaps it was worth getting up this morning. But I'm not convinced, she declares stoutly, looking Sandrine in the eye.

c c c

When she arrives the nurse at the desk smiles, and Clare feels inexplicably happy. This receptionist knows her well by now, although that is not the reason Clare pauses to chat to her. The girl is bored, she thinks. She'd rather be out in the sun, if it would shine.

I'm afraid I've arrived a bit late today, Clare tells her. If I'd had my way I would have come this morning, but my daughter was late coming to get me – as usual – and she couldn't find her keys, and Sandrine locked us in then and didn't want to be left alone.

Sure you're here now, Clare, the receptionist says brightly, and isn't that the main thing. Clare nods as her daughter comes in, car keys still in her hand.

Well, Clare, will we go see how Dad's doing today? Elizabeth casts a small, embarrassed smile at the receptionist whom she knows has just heard her mother's complaints against her. Elizabeth knows too that the receptionist knows that something is wrong not only with Tom, but with Clare. The receptionist, more used to such scenarios than Elizabeth realises, simply smiles back and says hello. It is the easiest thing to do. She answers a phone with the same flat goodwill and turns her face towards a computer screen and the small wall of video images from various rooms and hallways.

Elizabeth watches her mother as she strolls purposefully to the door of one of three corridors, watches her press the white button to open the door, watches as she paces her way around corners. She knows her way. Elizabeth feels a slight relief. Perhaps it is her own paranoia, she thinks, perhaps she is projecting her father's senility onto her mother.

They have her father in a chair close to a small television that Elizabeth brought over. It is switched to a news station, a never-ending ticker-tape stream of information running across the base of the screen: headlines, stock index prices, weather forecasts. Tom's hands are still in his lap, his eyes watching the ticker tape loop, trying to follow it off the screen.

Good morning, honey, Clare says. Elizabeth smiles at her mother's Americanism, surprised by its persistence through so many years. I brought your papers. She opens her carry bag by the handles and finds the newsletters from the IPC, the thick inked wads of them. He looks up and smiles slightly, but says nothing.

His eyes search for words in Clare's eyes. And I've brought you grapes. No rambutans or litchis I'm afraid. Unlike the fruits they signify, these words have not disappeared from Clare's world. She puts a small bundle of grapes on the arm of the chair.

Thank you, Tom says with gravity.

Elizabeth smiles. His fingers, long, thin, reach for the green grapes, sort through the smooth rounds until he can distinguish one. The grape escapes from the cluster into his fingers, which fumble towards his mouth but then continue upwards, resting over his top lip. Tom inhales the sticky sweet juice tang of the grape, warm from Clare's bag and the brief car journey, then pops it into his mouth, his fingers shaking with emptiness afterwards. Clare smiles and holds out to him in her own trembling fingers another few pebbles of grapes, encouraging him. Elizabeth begins checking through his clothes to make sure that he has enough warm jumpers, enough pyjamas, and that the zippers on his fleece sweatshirts are not snagging.

When she goes home, Elizabeth will weep softly to herself in the kitchen, wondering if her own husband, should she ever re-marry, will watch her eating in this way in the years to come, or whether she is consigned to suffer the departure of mind alone. She will wonder too whether she really does want a child, and whether the continued desperation to be pregnant and to give birth is not only selfish, but delusional. A child would grow up, she knows, and might well end up as the witness to a similar scene, watching her fade to black in a nursing home. Perhaps it is just as well that she cannot get pregnant, that she and Ciaran are divorced.

. . .

Clare herself never actively wanted children. She told Sandrine this time and again, particularly when Elizabeth had upset her by asking too many questions about what she'd eaten and whether she'd slept. I never asked for her, she'd mutter, never *once* did I ever tell Tom that I wanted children. At those moments she wore a candid hatred for Tom in her eyes. She would throw out his news-letters, toss the grapes to the birds. Damn him. Let the magpies eat them, she'd say.

It was before Elizabeth was born that the plans Tom had been making finally swung into action. The herb and spice import company he worked for had been convinced to expand their busi-ness, and Tom was to be their representative and buyer in America, where there was an expanding market of goods coming up through Mexico and South America. He would be there first, and the prices would be lower than Asian ones, he believed, even considering the cost of shipping back to Ireland. For years Tom had been pouring over fliers and brochures from all manner of markets and stalls and fully fledged companies and corporations, comparing chilli and cardamom and saffron and pepper prices, spending piles of ten Ps calling America to make contact, filing away the brochures of the people he one day intended to work with. And every few months he approached his boss's door with a new set of figures and a new set of brochures, almost pleading with him to see the sense of it. Why import through India only? Why rely on a wholesaler in London who'd already added his markup to the price they were paying? Why, when the prices were so good in America, when New York was such a major port for the pepper trade? Why settle for this, for this ticking over they were doing, stretching their credit not as a way of making interest but because they had to, month after month? And eventually the boss had given in, agreeing to look over the painstakingly handwritten pages with their inked-in-the-margin notes. Tom was ready; he knew that the company would see sense. He wrote again to his contacts in the US, and waited. And gradually it all began to happen. They began to look into renting an office space, into visas and entry requirements, into shipping and export tax regulations, and Tom would come home each day singing with the excitement. The people he had spoken to would become real. The spices would touch his fingers, the scent would go to his head.

Clare had been preparing for two years to go to America. She gave up practicing her French with old school books and read American novels recommended by the Dun Laoghaire librarian instead. She and Tom would talk and talk and talk about what they would do there, how they'd have a picnic under the arm of the Statue of Liberty, buy a car and drive clear across the country listening to the different radio stations. At the Grand Canyon they'd hear their voices echo against the orange and the red and the brown gold rock and laugh up into a sky as deeply blue as hyacinth. They would have money, and a fresh start, a chance to get away from the quiet depression of the Irish 1960s, full of tightening belts and babies and boredom. They would be the success story, the ones who vacationed in California and Hawaii, who returned home – suitcases full of gifts, eyes brimming with health – triumphant.

II

Clare felt a wrenching liberation as she watched Ireland disappear beneath her, the distinctions between fields growing fainter until the mosaic with its brown or darker green lines became only a green canvas and then gave way to a sober blue of the sea and the sky that she had never seen so clear over Ireland, so cloudless and echoing with light. She never felt much like crying or weeping – Clare's approach to the world was dry-eyed unless she had to part from Tom – but just this once, just this once she did feel like it. Clare gripped her hands more tightly on the armrests. Tom smiled at her and put his arm about her shoulders and Clare exhaled deeply in the humming air, exhaled until no more air could be forced out of her lungs. It was over. They had left. She had let go of the last breath of air she had taken in Ireland. From now on when she breathed it would be new air.

As soon as they arrived in America, Clare, encouraged by Tom, began to wander Manhattan. It was so vast and unlike Dublin, full of pavements so wide that it seemed impossible to run into someone else, pavements with chips of mica, so that the very ground she tread shimmered and glinted like a class of magic. So while Tom sat in his new office with only a black metal desk and a phone and arranged to buy spices to ship back across the Atlantic to Ireland, Clare roamed the city in flat shoes, no bag slung over her shoulder, her hands stuffed into deep pockets that didn't betray her fingers fidgeting with the new coins that were thinner, lighter, sleeker than the heavyweight of pounds and pence.

In those earliest days in the city no one spoke to her. She could walk down the street unbothered by anyone saying hello and expecting her to stop for a chat as they had at home. Even as the seasons progressed and she got to know neighbours and doormen and shopkeepers, they only stopped to talk at length on rare occasions. Clare walked feeling free of obligation to anyone, staring or being stared at, but not required to pause.

Clare adjusted with such ease to their new life in New York that even Tom was astonished, since the new business was harder going than he'd imagined it would be. He had all of the hassle of meeting new people, trying to find his way around an already established network of spice and herb trading and shipping yards and tax laws and export forms. Clare had none of his worries, although she sympathised when he came in jaded and fretting, and tried to distract him with tales of her day's explorations. She adored the window-shopping possible in the city, spending hours watching her own reflection shimmying in and out of focus and light. She learned the names of the avenues and felt armed with this simple knowledge that prevented her from walking to the extremes of the island without her realising it. She had been warned by their doorman not to venture above 90th street and not below 14th, to avoid Hell's Kitchen and Chelsea, so she felt safe in the vast playground that remained.

What she found she liked most were the array of carpet shops along Broadway. The way that the complex symmetrical patterns of rugs told tales in beige and maroon, navy and brown, their beauty suspended from brass rods and special wires above eye level as she gazed through the image of herself into the windows. Gradually she made her way into each and every shop, quietly moving through the racks and rolls and stacks of rugs, fingering them with such seriousness that she was left alone by sales staff who variously wondered if Clare, glamorous in her snug camel coat and giant sunglasses and her straight-as-a-yard-stick blond hair that grazed her jaw, was a buyer for the rich and famous or an undercover immigration agent trying discretely to observe how many staff were beyond the counter.

And gradually too, as Tom's work began to pick up, there was money to spend on such things, such beautiful things that made the world easier to walk on, easier to bear, and kept the floors from going hard and miserably cold as they'd been in Ireland. She was very happy in the city full of rugs from everywhere in the world, until several years and seventeen rugs later, she found herself pregnant, and Tom convinced her that maybe they should go home for a year or two now that the business was running so well on its own, and think about what they might do next.

Clare's pregnancy was her excuse not to help with the packing, but really her refusal was a protest. She did not wish to leave New York. Tom took her clothes out of drawers and closets and stuffed them into suitcases he bought on the ninth floor in Macy's. The only things she cared about were the rugs, and so she supervised as her husband rolled them, instructing him, depending on the carpet's depth, whether to role pile up or down, and demonstrating how to tell at which end the weave had begun. Finally he tied them with string and wrapped them with the brown paper her favourite Pakistani rug seller had advised. She'd sat in his showroom on 57th street on the second floor, watching the traffic droning by, disappearing out of her sight just beyond the Alexander's sign, and he'd cut the rolls of paper for her himself and tried to cheer her up – his wife Anjana had even come in with tea. He would miss Clare too, he told her, for she was the only customer not from Pakistan who had returned seven times, and his only Irish customer. Clare signed the last cheque to him for the paper, which he assured her would be delivered that afternoon, and made a mental note to send him a postcard from Ireland, which she never did.

Tom promised her that they would come back, or that they would find somewhere new to go, somewhere new to explore together. He had been happy in New York too, but, unlike Clare, he was ambitious beyond it. His business had succeeded in getting chilli and pepper cheaper than before, and he wanted to act on his success now, further afield. Maybe, Tom thought, they should go to Asia, not to Hong Kong or one of the established trading spots like India, maybe to somewhere like Vietnam, which was so inexpensive because of the trouble with the French and now the Americans. It was the perfect climate for pepper, they'd had a small bit of an industry there before the war, and God were they going to need industry to make money after all of this battling. And maybe it was a good time to leave America for a while, he said to Clare, maybe things were going downhill here with all of these people like King and Kennedy gone and the mood about Vietnam. But Clare was impassive, and unconvinced. I think I'd just prefer to throw up in the morning in New York rather than Dublin, she told him icily.

On the plane home Clare had leaned miserably against the window, the sickness of being pregnant dragging her mood away from her husband, sitting next to her and jotting notes on an Aer Lingus pad of paper a stewardess had brought around. This baby, this is why she was going home. Damn it, she thought, staring out at the clouds and at a sky that seemed to her to darken as they moved towards Dublin.

Clare had known, of course, that she was pregnant, but, she told Sandrine, no one in those days spoke about it, so all she knew was that she was growing bigger and bigger and all for the small thing inside her. She and Tom didn't even talk about it that much. They spoke about the baby itself, yes, in terms of the preparation, purchases of clothes and cots and prams, but never about the experience beyond the usual *how do you feel today?* Aside from telling her what foods had staved off her own nausea her sister hadn't offered much advice, and their mother was several years dead. Neither of her brothers were yet married, and had no wives to offer her advice.

So Clare went through the pregnancy back in Ireland without commentary or analysis, considering the phenomenon a nuisance on the whole, and trying not to think of the ending that she'd heard such vague horror stories about over the years. Even in school they'd heard whispers of how your body tore open and bled and how women sometimes died. Fidelma had had to be knocked out in the end for her first and her second, her stomach bearing a vertical scar that rose almost to her belly button. Clare shuddered with fear when she thought of it. Her doctor hadn't helped on this front and annoyed her because he spoke of her condition as though she were in fact already dying, chastising her one day for walking to his office though it was only half a mile away. He was useless, Clare told Sandrine. In the end Clare ended up having one of those remarkably easy births that other women almost weep with envy over. After two and a bit hours, Elizabeth appeared without too much fuss and feathers and Clare felt surprised and thrilled about how her body had coped with the pain and the delivery.

Elizabeth. The only one, the girl. This was how she was introduced by her mother, who rarely exchanged the definite article for the possessive 'my' that would have softened the child towards her. Elizabeth: the child who lives with us, Clare would say. Elizabeth: the one with the English name. Later, at the makeshift international academy in Vietnam, the other children, so well schooled in international affairs and politics because of their parents' rambling lives around the globe, would ask about this. Your country is free now, so why are you named after the queen of England? Queen Elizabeth, they hissed, no matter how many times she explained that it was a dead grandmother she was called after, not the queen. We're allowed to have any names we want if we're free, she said in reply, but since she didn't feel part of the 'we' she used, saying this was like speaking a language she didn't know.

A little French girl, one of few friends she made that remained in the place for more than a few months, pointed out that there was little difference between her parents and the small community of three or four Englishmen who worked with the UN and lived at the hotel. They even look the same, the French girl shrugged.

She watched her parents, a small spy. What did it mean to be Irish anyway? And what did it mean to be Irish when she lived in Vietnam? Nothing, she told the French girl stoutly.

Mostly Elizabeth played in the hotel and its courtyard by herself, thinking of the family she didn't know back in Ireland, wishing she had a brother or a sister that she could play with in the still-battered grounds of their French-built hotel in Hanoi, a visual leftover of earlier times. These wishes were a sign of a kind of concession on her part, she knew, an admission of something, a near acceptance, a resignation: because there had been a time that she had wished that they weren't going to go to Vietnam at all, followed by a period during which she wished even more fervently – prayerfully – that they had never come.

After considering herself an American child for several years, Elizabeth had become an Irish girl child in Vietnam, with her too pale face, sky-coloured eyes, white-blond hair streaming flat behind her, limbs reddening under the sun and a mind full of the loneliness of being foreign that was more intense than the heat or the monsoon winds.

When they arrived in Vietnam, Elizabeth was twelve. Until then she had little memory of any place other than America, where they had returned – Clare threatening to go on her own if necessary – when she was three. And she had little memory of anything of America beyond their suburban Connecticut home. It had been a compromise to satisfy her father that his child would have space to play in, while still providing Clare with easy access to the city by train. In this America, Elizabeth had left behind a clatter of friends who never asked what it meant to be Irish.

In summer they sprawled in each others' yards, played gentle tricks on unsurprised housekeepers who provided instant Country Time pink lemonade and cookies at intervals, played dress up in their mothers' print gowns and mini skirts and clownish bell bottoms and hand-knit ponchos. They ran like colts through trimmed grass, gathered tinny silvery jacks in their small hands triumphantly, dodged globed pinky-red rubber balls in the school yard, went on class trips where, after singing riotously on the bus all the way into the city and arguing for the back seats which gave the most bounce, they held hands with a buddy while staring wide-eyed at petrified model Native Americans and recovered bones of mammoth creatures whose names they couldn't pronounce.

No one in America asked about her name. Her friends shouted Lizzy! when she appeared at the park in her roller skates with red laces and round blue stoppers screwed into the toes, and she fully believed that after a few more years of pledging allegiance to a flag of always winning colours, she would become a cheerleader, master the art of blowing bubbles within bubbles, and perhaps at the end of it all attend the prom with a boy whose blond down had turned to still soft stubble and who might let her wear his blue and white letterman jacket.

Of a life before America Elizabeth – Lizzy, in her own mind – was granted only occasional, fleeting access by her own memory. When her father sometimes chatted about Ireland to her mother Elizabeth's mind ached with the forgotten. She would close her eyes to grasp at a picture of another garden in whose grass she toddled only inches above hardy lavender blossoms and rose bushes with heavy heads of flowers. That was all the sound of Ireland brought into her mind, coarse green grass, violently swaying flowers and her smallest fists trying to snatch at them. Despite the initial years spent in Ireland, America, for Lizzy, was home: the place of first consciousness, of school, of language. So when her mother, tucking her in one evening, mentioned Asia, Vietnam, asked how she'd like to go there, Lizzy opened sleepy eyes in confusion.

I thought there was a war there, she said timidly, suddenly aware of the gap between her knowledge and her mother's. And that gap widened when Clare laughed and smoothed her cheek. Not any more, and your father wants to go there, maybe, or to somewhere in Asia.

On, like, a vacation? Lizzy stared at her mother. Silence. In Lizzy's mind as her mother ruffled blanket edges the possibility of cheerleading began to dim.

Well, sort of a vacation. He wants to go and see if the business could do well there. He thinks it can.

How long? Lizzy asked. How long does he want to go for?

He's not sure yet. Don't you think it's exciting? Clare asked her daughter.

Do I have to go?

The idea of living with one of her friends sprang to mind. It would be like having a sister. They could share clothes and walk to school together.

Well we wouldn't leave you behind! Clare bent to kiss her.

Why not? Lizzy asked. It seemed a good question. She saw her parents in the morning and evening, sometimes, but spent her days at school and with friends and the housekeeper, occasionally watching TV on rainy afternoons when no one was in the park or on the street with their bicycles. Her parents seemed to exist on the fringe of her life.

Clare's face had changed. Lizzy knew that her mother was no longer interested, that the discussion was over. Lizzy closed her eyes and turned towards the pale-blue wall, the paint colour she'd picked out only a few months ago. She put her fingernail to a bump of paint and tried to slice it off, open up the wall.

In three months, Clare said. When you finish school we'll leave here and go home for a holiday, and then you and me and Dad will fly to Vietnam.

Go home where? Lizzy asked. This is my home.

Home to Ireland, Clare answered. I know honey, I know you don't want to leave your friends, but you'll make new friends. Lizzy turned on her back to look up at her mother. She knew her mother was lying, knew she wouldn't make new friends.

Lizzy tried again the next day when her father came home. That's where the *war* was! Her voice rang around the house in a glassy waterfall of sound.

The war's over, sweetheart, her father said.

Not long over, she shouted. We learned about it in school – I know! I'm not stupid! Why are we moving? Dad, why? Why do we have to go to Vietnam? Why can't we at least go somewhere where I can talk to people?

But they'll speak a lot of French in Vietnam, honey, and a lot of English too. The country is changing.

Elizabeth stuffed herself into the corner of an armchair with her thin fair arms hugging her waist and started to cry. Her shag of blond hair trembled around her chin. What are you going to do in Vietnam anyway? Buy rugs and pepper from starving people and send them to Ireland?

Elizabeth. Clare interrupted but didn't approach her.

She and Tom both stayed back from their seething daughter.

Can I stay in the US? Elizabeth demanded. Please, Dad? She ignored her mother. Please can I go to a boarding school? Near my friends? Or – she was crying so hard now that her voice was catching in her throat – or can I go to Ireland and live with Aunt Fidelma? Please? I can go to school there, at that little place around the corner you showed me where the kids were playing in the yard.

Tom looked at Clare and Clare looked at Tom, and Elizabeth caught the exchange. I get it, she shouted, standing up. You've already talked about this, already decided, probably I'm already enrolled in some stupid Vietnamese school because I'm too young to go to boarding school so far away by myself, right? Right? She screamed now, even though Clare was waving her hands frantically and gesturing to the kitchen door, behind which Gina was preparing to go home for the night. I don't care if anyone hears! Elizabeth shouted. I'd rather stay here with Gina anyway than go with you! And she ran out of the room.

Clare tried to soothe Tom. Once it's all set up and you don't need to be there we'll go home and she can go to a nice Irish school and she'll be fine, she reassured him.

Lizzy's friends sympathised. What do your parents want to go there for? they asked, without knowing exactly where they were talking about. Lizzy wasn't sure either. Why don't you just run out of the airport and come back here and we'll hide you? Jennie said. It would be like Anne Frank, and we could take turns bringing you stuff.

They spent hours planning this escape that they all knew would never happen. One girl decided much more practically that they should do something special before Lizzy went away, so they saved up their allowances and went to see *Cats* on Broadway, one of the girls' mothers acting as chaperone. On the way in, some of the girls reminisced about seeing *Annie* when they were younger, about how by intermission they'd all wanted to be Andrea McArdle or the other girls who got to sing and dance and get paid and have great lives. Lizzy listened to them and wished that she were like Annie, an orphan. She even wondered hopefully, trying to stare out of the train at the nothingness of the tunnel, if she could have been adopted. Maybe it was all a big mistake and she wasn't actually related to these two crazy people who wanted to move to such crazy places in the world when they had a perfectly nice place to live right here. The life the girls had in the orphanage didn't seem so bad to her, really, because they had each other. She'd go to Vietnam and have no one.

Lizzy was only a fraction as excited as the others by the time they got to the theatre. During the intermission she went back up the carpeted stairs of the theatre with her box of Dots still full, and the second half of the musical seemed trite while she was in this mood, a whole lot of waffle with syrup and bologna with mustard, as Gina liked to say. And Lizzy knew that if she didn't have to leave soon, if she wasn't going to go away from all of this America that was dancing and singing below her, the cats crawling and looking so stupid with their fake tails, she'd have enjoyed the performance as much as her friends. She glanced down the aisle at their faces, which were rapt and open mouthed, smiling. They would stay like this, and she would change, become something else. The big day out in the city – Jennie's mother took them to TGI Friday's afterwards and the waiters were really friendly and cute and they all got Death By Chocolate Sundaes – was just another disappointment for Lizzy. She left her programme on the train and cried when she got home.

We'll write to you, her friends promised, and helped Lizzy to pack up her room. Jennie even stayed over the last night in the house. She brought two sleeping bags because all the blankets in Lizzy's house were gone and they were going to spend a final few nights in a hotel in the city so that her parents could shop and buy presents for people in Ireland. They sat up half the night with flashlights Jennie had had to bring over from her house, eating Crunchy

Cheese Doodles and marshmallow fluff together, their fingertips orange stained and sticky, slipping down the stairs to the fridge for a drink and finding it empty except for half a quart of low-fat milk and a hard half a loaf of Wonder.

Are you happy, Jennie? Lizzy asked her friend as they drank the milk back up in her empty room. I mean really happy?

Yeah, I guess, Jennie said. But I'm, like, well, I never get to do anything, like, exciting, you know? You do, she shrugged. So in a way it's kind of cool.

Lizzy stared at her in the torchlight. But I don't want to do anything exciting. I want to stay here. With you guys, and go to high school.

Maybe, Jennie said, trailing her index finger inside the jar of fluff, maybe you can come back here, later on. Then you'd get to do the exciting stuff but you could come back. We could be room-mates when we go to college, and we could have parties like my sister does. And this possibility, that someday she would indeed be old enough to come back here on her own, startled Lizzy. They spent the next two hours talking about what kind of furniture they'd have and what kind of boyfriends they'd like, and then they fell asleep with the almost empty fluff jar between them, their lips glossed and shining with sugar.

After Jennie was gone, though, Lizzy started feeling that the dream of returning was a long, long way away. They'd spent their two nights in the hotel that angled over Central Park and was full of businessmen and women dressed in sweaters sprinkled with rhine-stones who smiled too tightly at her in the elevator when she rode up and down by herself. She was only twelve. She'd have to be at least seventeen, she figured, to come back on her own. At least. She sobbed on the plane, so hard that her father experienced waves of regret looking at her small body doubled towards her knees. He patted her arced-over shaking back. She wriggled to get away from his hand and kept crying into her hands and her Jordache-clad knees.

It's not so bad, Elizabeth, he said to her quietly. Mom'll want to go back to New York, just like the last time, you know. So cheer up. But Lizzy didn't. She'd gotten her hopes up before that something would change, that they wouldn't go at all even, and so she stayed hunched over in crash position for as long as she could bear to and then curled towards the window, refusing the view and squashing a pillow against the pulled-down grey plastic sheathe.

A stewardess serving dinner had noticed the child's body bent over itself, then saw her sit up, eyes swollen, cheeks salt-streaked, and brought her a tray with a roll and a small square container of tuna fish and a carton of orange juice. Thank you, Lizzy whispered. Her parents, on the other side of the aisle, were asleep. She ate slowly, thoughtfully, thinking that this was the last American meal she was to have, even if the orange juice did taste funny, kind of tinny and unsweetened compared to her regular Tropicana. And maybe the movie was the last American movie she'd ever see – who knew? So Lizzy stayed awake, forcing herself, holding her eyelids, and watched *48 Hours*. When the movie ended and she found herself in the dark-humming silence punctuated by dinging calls to the stewardess, she cried again, and would always remember it as a flight of tears.

III

They had come before the end of the monsoons. The wind and rain would begin all at once, like a scheduled duet. Lizzy grew to know when it would begin by watching the pregnant clouds hunching together and flattening the sky, lowering themselves with a menacing, sick-yellow light. As soon as the rain began, this light was washed away and the world became a shimmering, glistening grey. The hotel workers tried to usher her inside, urging her away from the edge of the veranda she chose each evening, but Lizzy loved the rain. It was the drama of the day, this falling-to-earth sky, and so she sat on a white painted wooden chair with her feet propped up on the edge of the veranda's decorative bamboo wall, her toes in the storm.

The rain had a certain heat to it, the warmth of clouds that had basked in sun from early morning. Lizzy watched it trickle between her toes, which were brown and thin and full of bone. Often her mother, woken by the incessant trill of the drops against the roof and windows, appeared in the archway of the doors that led back into the hotel, leaning her body against the left-hand side to watch as well. The first time she had come after a maid told her worriedly that the little girl was out in the rain and would she perhaps listen to her mother? Clare had said yes, though she knew that really the maid would have had more of a chance at this task, but, forced into it, went in search of her child.

When she saw Elizabeth, barelegged, toes wriggling, the focus of her eyes lost somewhere in the green and grey of the garden that graced that side of the enclosed courtyard in the centre of the hotel, Clare smiled and felt the nearest she could to a spontaneous affection for her. She had to go ahead and ask her to come in, interrupting her solitary reverie because of the staff's concerns, but really Clare wanted to leave her be. She seemed happy, sitting there, so wistful too, and so utterly separate from her mother. Would you not watch from inside, Elizabeth? Clare said after a moment. Her daughter jumped, the toes curled. No, she replied, still startled. She turned immediately back to the rain, wondering if her mother would stay and nag for a while. Rather to her surprise, Clare stayed but said nothing, folded her arms across her body and gazed out at the rain herself.

It became a routine, of sorts, in the early weeks. Elizabeth grew adjusted to her mother's silent presence, sensing her still-sleepy arrival in the doorway. Had Clare sat beside her, drawn up a chair, attempted to make conversation, Elizabeth would have taken her book and retreated to her bedroom window of their upstairs suite, against which the rain wasn't as immediate. But Clare said nothing, and Elizabeth remained on her perch, and gradually, after a day or two, ceased to worry that at some point her mother would try launching a conversation. It was the closest she would ever feel to her mother, those half hours in the strangely dimmed daylight of a monsoon's afternoon sweep across the city and suburbs and countryside, the silence and the damp and the plummeting air of the rain between them like a gauze curtain. Years later, in her parents' home in Ireland listening to the end of a rainstorm, Elizabeth would catch her mother's gaze resting on her and know that Clare too knew that it was those moments that had been the most real between them.

Clare tried explaining to Tom the light and the noise of these afternoons. The rains continued in a path across the city, but often he was inside somewhere and emerged smelling of Saigon cinnamon and lemongrass to find the roads glazed with rain, sometimes swimming with it. Drains would be blocked and children waded home from school in knee-deep water filled with sewage, plastic bags and cigarette butts. Motorcycles drowned and bicycle wheels went slowly, churning and spinning out lines of water from the spokes. He couldn't see how such rains might also be devastatingly beautiful. They wreaked havoc, damaged homes, crops, made people ill. When he returned to the hotel at the day's end and Clare tried again to explain to him over dinner the treacherous beauty of the open sky, Tom laughed. Stay here some afternoon, Clare urged him. And you'll see. Isn't it worth seeing? Clare turned to her daughter.

For once Elizabeth didn't come back with anything but her own voice. It really is Dad, she said simply.

Clare nodded at her husband. You see, Tom? She smiled at her daughter. It will be your loss if you don't. It's just so peaceful somehow.

⸱ ⸱ ⸱

That pause in the courtyard while the rains fell was the only peace she had. It wasn't that Elizabeth was afraid, exactly, but she found danger everywhere: in the faces of the people she saw from the windows of the hotel if she watched from the hallways as her father left in the morning, in the faces of those who gazed in at the car that took her and two other hotel children to the hobbled colonial school building each morning. There was talk of a new international school to replace the defunct Lycée Albert Sarraut, but Elizabeth was not hopeful about anything happening quickly enough for it to matter for her. She remembered fragments about Vietnam from America, remembered hearing news reports about MIAs and demonstrations by ex-soldiers who walked around in jungle green and who wanted their friends' bodies back. She knew the Billy Joel song about Vietnam because her friend Jennie's father had been here during the war and liked Billy Joel and they used to listen to it and liked the noise of the helicopter slicing its way through the stereo at the start of the song. They'd giggled when he sang the word 'playboy', because they knew all about what that was from the stash in Jennie's father's desk drawer. It had been a long war, she knew, and Jimmy Carter – did he have something to do with Vietnam? Or was it Nixon? – didn't like wars and she liked Jimmy Carter because he seemed nice and he had a daughter near enough to her age, and her school had a guinea pig in the kindergarteners' room called Jimmy Carter after him. These things she remembered, and sensed that to be American in Vietnam was not a good thing.

Because she knew that the Americans were not that long gone, and felt that it would do her no good to tell the polite hotel staff that she had been to school in America, Elizabeth spoke only when absolutely necessary, aware, for the first time in her life, of what an accent could mean. And that her accent was different from her parents' puzzled the staff, and made them enquire in a friendly way of the child why that was, and made Elizabeth worry more.

When she was a little bit older – and not much, only fourteen – Elizabeth would refer to the hotel as 'the compound'. An old French colonial mansion of a hotel, it had grown from its beginnings and been extended and shaped around a courtyard which the permanent residents' rooms overlooked. The courtyard contained a pool and deck chairs and a bar and palm trees but also the trappings of a European garden: rose bushes, dwarf lavenders, patches of lawn edged with red bricks and potted geraniums.

She had spent most of the time hiding from the heat, the first year, and so the courtyard became her haunt. Her mother trailed after her with sun tan lotion if she stepped out of doors, and so to keep this annoyance at bay Elizabeth began carrying her own, smearing her coltish limbs, pink and feathered with blond hair, with the thick white cream, watching the streaks left by her hands and fingers absorb and disappear, leaving her palms sweaty and slippery. And she stayed out of the sun when she could.

At the pool's edge the ex-pat women daily gathered in perfect and shimmering bikinis, their skins as weathered as pelts, smoky with the years of exposure in this and other courtyards. And the sheen from their skins was like the shimmer from the flat stomach of the pool, each glimmeringly flirting with the other for prominence. Clare often joined them in a more modest one piece, her fair, soft Irish belly glimpsed only rarely by the sun. She was the odd one out, not as effortlessly glamorous as the others, her daughter thought, too pale and white and glowing next to them. But like them she wore perfectly shaped sunglasses in brown tortoiseshell and floppy straw hats, only a few dong at the market, and had her toenails painted to look like beguiling little shiny candies that matched her ten fingernails.

Partly to avoid having to sit with her mother – while knowing that her mother was equally eager to enjoy their conversation without her – and partly to avoid the sunburned taut feeling she still remembered from a few childhood beach days, Elizabeth would sit under an umbrella at the far end of the pool. She sat armed with books and schoolwork and kept sunglasses on so that she could eye anyone approaching and look busier, if necessary. And every so often, once every hour if it was coming to summer, and oftener if the hot months were bearing down on the city, Elizabeth dumped the books and pens off her lap, slid the sunglasses from the bridge of her nose that was slick with cream and sweat, and threw herself into the pool's deepest end.

She never announced these leaps, just flung herself in, sometimes in a much-practiced dive, sometimes in a more desperate, suicide-like jump that brought her feet to the floor of the pool and allowed her a few seconds of seeing her hair drift past her eyes before she leapt to the sky again. And what she did in the water depended upon her entry. If she dove in, Elizabeth became the diligent member of the high school swim team she might have been in Connecticut, her narrow frame hurtling towards either end of the pool in a frantic way, racing no one, back and forth back and forth back and forth not counting and not stopping, her arms tossing themselves forward like darts, chopping the pool into sections again and again, catching sight of the hotel at odd angles as she sucked in breath secretly, under the curve of her arm, until her chest heaved and she'd hang on her end of the pool looking up at her towel, spent. If she dropped in like a forsaken puppy to the tiled bottom, Elizabeth sprang into a series of water-slowed handstands, back flips, forward rolls, playing all by herself the game she had played with friends at the local pool as a kid, pretending to be an Olympic gymnast doing floor exercises, executing routines with pointed toes and arched feet and strong hands.

The French women and her mother grew quickly used to these displays that, unlike almost anything else Elizabeth did, utterly lacked self-consciousness. It was as if Elizabeth in the water resumed being Lizzy and was satisfied with some basic sense of herself. As she drew herself out of the pool, always at the deep end and never by way of the ladder that brought her to the feet of her mother and friends, Elizabeth, like a mermaid on land, grew awkward again. Her slight body with its angles and joints and tight skin coiled itself in towel, sought flip-flops and sunglasses, a book to prop before her face. Her grace hid itself in her age.

And at that moment of transformation, it was Clare who watched her. And Clare wanted to be able to communicate to her daughter something she could not, to say that she was beautiful in her awkwardness, beautiful on her own down there at the opposite end of the pool under her lone umbrella, and Clare would think this every year for almost five years, watching her child turn into a woman whose skin was brown and who in her youth occupied an entire side of the courtyard and left the aging, sagging class of women – some mothers – at their own end to gaze at her. Lizzy avoided the sun as they avoided shade and a too-direct, too-near comparison with Clare. Until she left Vietnam, Elizabeth perceived sun as something other people shared together and that she had no part in.

Elizabeth was unsurprised by the hotel's attempts to recall Europe in the courtyard gardens, but still found it disturbing when her mother and other European women would have a declared gardening day and arm themselves with small shovels to add lime trees, orchids, lilies, the anxious gardener running out of breath trying to dig all of the necessary holes at once. Because if she left their rooms and their windows (one of which had a window box that was the garden below in miniature, tended to by her mother) and crossed the hallway and peered out of one of the hallway's windows, the sight was so different that she couldn't reconcile it. She began to dream about these two worlds, the control of the garden on one side and the chaos of the streets with their cyclos and cracked, fragmented sidewalks on the other. It's like going from France to Asia in three steps, she told her amused father, who repeated this comment to other adults in the hotel, particularly the journalists, much to her embarrassment.

She knew that there had been widespread poverty in America, but, she reasoned with herself at the age of fourteen, she had been too removed from it in the comfortable house of the Connecticut suburbs where people parked their boats in the driveways next to BMWs. Here, in Hanoi, it was different. Besides going to school until early afternoon, Elizabeth seldom left the hotel because her parents refused to let her. It was too dangerous, her mother told her: she couldn't just walk the streets by herself. So Elizabeth's initial view of Vietnam was an indoor one, the gaze of a teenager from a window, unless she was with either father or mother.

She gazed down at street vendors and traffic that rarely thinned, at people bathing babies and children in basins at the side of the road, at the roof tops that were cobbled out of tin and concrete and wood and tiles, a mosaic of recovered materials. From the window she heard the calls of those selling everything from pomelos and sweet sops to baguettes and boiled water, and she heard the cries of children as they tumbled and fell to their knees. She saw mothers impatiently trying to cook dinners while comforting babies, saw now and then the stir caused by the arrival of a Viet Kieu back home from abroad, or by the presence of an expensive new Honda on the street. And quietly, as the years passed, Elizabeth's gaze became unfocused, full of longing for someplace else, for somewhere that she could walk freely, and in all of those hours of window sitting and street gazing, Elizabeth decided that regardless of what her parents said when the time came, she had to go to university in America.

School was dull in Hanoi. Few westerners had returned yet – the country was only just opening up again – and so Elizabeth's class was comprised of children older and younger than she was, Korean children and Swedish children and Australian children. A girl named Genevieve who had lived in Vietnam her whole life but insisted she was French and a pair of British siblings, whose father was involved with the UN effort to remove landmines, were her only real companions.

Since the three of them didn't live at the hotel the friendships were strictly confined to school times, which could themselves be disrupted by power failures or flooding or the return of a teacher to Europe. The word was that there were more foreign children, but they were being tutored privately until the much-talked-of

United Nations International School was built. The Russians had their own school, though, and hopefully, Clare told her daughter, the new school would start soon and she could go. Rumours announced that more and more business people would be arriving from North Korea, from Sweden, more Australians too, and Viet Kieu who'd want their children's education to continue in English. In the meanwhile, under the tutelage of two French women and a Swedish man, Elizabeth's French dutifully improved so that her father brought her the occasional translated contract when he found a strange word. But overall she felt an increasing desperation about remaining in Vietnam.

Months passed, the rains began, and Elizabeth peppered her father with questions about when they were going. We're going to stay about another year, he told her flatly after avoiding the answer for an hour. Elizabeth turned away, retreated into her own room and slammed the door.

The only real break in the monotony was the arrival of new guests, most of whom didn't stay long. There was a young Australian man doing some sort of research into oil reserves or something, who came one week out of every month and who had a sister back at home about Elizabeth's age. Sometimes he'd bring her something from Australia, a stuffed koala bear, once, or a magazine, or a Toblerone from Sydney duty free.

An American man arrived at the hotel with a battered suitcase, perfectly cut Hong Kong suits that draped elegantly over a prosthetic leg, and a haggard look. He had returned to try and find a woman he had known during the war, he told everyone who would listen, and showed a few shabby photographs in black and white of his 'lost wife', as he called her. Elizabeth, sitting by the pool each dry afternoon with a book, was a captive audience for his heartbreak, and over the years she grew used to the arrival of such men, because, in time, their flow increased, and the looks became more haggard and the suits less elegant.

Then there were French colonial families who couldn't stay away, but simply had to visit again and see all that had happened and get their clothes made at the same time, perhaps flying home again via Papeete. Old women whose hands trembled and glittered with jewels told Elizabeth about Hanoi before the war, how beautiful it had been, describing the opera house – still being renovated – lit up while cars arrived for a performance. They told her how serene and lovely the lake was in the mornings when the vendors were just beginning to sell baguettes and pho, side by side. At that hour the grass glistened and everyone stretched and performed slow moving exercises while gazing at the water, which hadn't been polluted in the way it was now. And then it all became ugly, a woman with a strawberry chignon sighed to Elizabeth by the pool one afternoon.

Early on, when her parents were shopping, Elizabeth went out of the hotel on her own for the first time and made her way up the street, aiming for the river. Despite her feeling that she knew the road from so much sky-down gazing at it, it was different here on the ground. She had only seen the roofs of the shacks, their scrap metal undulating like rusted waves. Down here, outside, she could see what was in them: vendors of all kinds selling everything from French pastries whose icings sweated even in the early mornings to radiant ao dai that flapped in any slight breeze.

One old man had a cracked mirror suspended from a kinked, discoloured wire, and offered haircuts with a battery-operated razor inherited from a dead American soldier. A crowd of begging children and women and old men gathered behind her like a train. Several children younger than she was held up plastic bags of sugar cane juice to her and shouted, you buy, Russia, you buy. Elizabeth remembered what her father had said, that since *doi moi* began, some of them had to try and raise money so that they could go to school. School wasn't free any more. But she had no money with her, so it was useless.

As Elizabeth walked by the children, a group of men hunkered around a pot of steaming pho turned to stare at her. She looked uneasily back at them. One had only one leg, and another was missing part of an arm. His stump shot out at a strange angle when he pointed at her and said something that she didn't understand. Elizabeth paused to stare at the surprise of the wounded end of his arm and then turned around and hurried back to the hotel entrance, where one of the cyclo hawkers who knew her father called out Di dau? Where you going? No go out, go home. He sprayed cigarette smoke towards her. By the time she pushed open the door and stood in the quiet of the lobby Elizabeth's heart was pounding, her eyes swelling with tears, and sweat was spreading across the small of her back, her palms, her forehead. She bolted up the carpeted stairs to their rooms and hid herself at the window, looking again at that which she had now seen for herself. For several weeks, even when her parents asked her if she wanted to take a walk she refused, terrified that she would be confronted again by the stump-armed man. What amazed her as an adult thinking back, though, was the fact that she did eventually continue to go out, increasingly on her own, and especially when it rained, which meant that the city quietened as people scurried for cover. Bicycles, motorcycles, pedestrians all seemed to shift to the roads' edges during the downpours, which left wide swathes of road for her to walk in.

The relentless rains reminded her of the scent of spices and the sound of her father's voice as he had told her stories back in America. Remembering as an adult, she knew that this hadn't happened very often. For all of Elizabeth's avoidance of the fact, it was her mother who had nightly read to her in a calm, quiet voice, no matter what the tale or character, and her mother who would never hesitate to read the entire book over again if requested. Reading aloud Clare found the easiest of all parenting tasks, since it was scripted and could not be marred with silences and tensions. But Clare never made stories up, and Tom did, on the rare occasions when he had found himself alone in the American house with a daughter driven indoors by rain.

So what do you know about allspice, Miss Elizabeth? he had asked her one Saturday afternoon. He had been sitting at the dining room table poring over invoices when she'd slumped in with the glum look of a seven-year-old with nothing to do.

Nothing, she said sulkily.

Well, Tom told her as she fiddled with a tartan placemat, rolling it up and trying to fold the fabric tube in three, it's the only spice native only to this half of the world, the only one. And it's called allspice – why do you think? he asked her.

Elizabeth frowned at the placemat, thinking hard. I don't know, Dad, she told him, and went back to rolling the mat.

Well when Europeans came along and tasted it they couldn't figure it out – to them it tasted a little like cinnamon –

I like cinnamon, Lizzy piped up. Cinnamon toast the way Gina showed me with butter and sugar. Yummy!

Yes and it tasted like cinnamon but also a little bit like nutmeg. He looked at her for signs of recognition. None. Do you remember when we went to Jennie's house last year on Christmas Eve and her mum had that drink I gave you a sip of, eggnog?

Lizzy nodded uncertainly. With the raw eggs! she said suddenly, a picture of the glass jug and the frothy yellowness clear now.

That's the one, her father told her. And on top there were little brown flecks, and that was nutmeg.

How does it come, like that? In brown flecks?

No, allspice is from a tree that can grow enormous, bigger than our apple tree, taller than our house.

Oh, Lizzy said. Look Dad it stopped raining, she shouted, and ran out of the dining room towards the front door to grab her roller skates and float down the path towards the gate and her own world.

Years later she forgot the roller skates and the seize of joy they brought her. What she recalled as she strolled through supermarket aisles and happened upon herbs, or as she baked bread or chopped vegetables for salads, were the spices and her father's voice, so seriously interested in his subject.

Elizabeth knew little about her father's early life until her mother, ill-advisedly in a fit of fury with her newly teenaged child in Vietnam, declared that Elizabeth simply had no idea how lucky she was, and how hard her father had worked to give her the kind of life that she had. She had never wanted for anything, there had been a housekeeper to mind her, more than enough clothes and any food she desired, toys to beat the band, unlimited books and more travel than most people did in a lifetime – and she was only thirteen and living in a hotel.

And Clare was correct, Elizabeth had no idea. Elizabeth heard little of her father's life before his marriage to Clare in the big grey church in the suburban Dublin village that Clare had grown up in. Elizabeth knew hazily that they had married only after Tom had saved enough to secure a home for them in nearby Sandycove, where Clare had loved to swim as a child, the windows opening towards a swelling winter sea. It was a new, modern house, with an upstairs and down for themselves alone, but the huge windows were hung with the same white lacy foam as all of the neighbours' were. The door was made of a fancy frosted glass, bevelled and curliqued so as to obscure any figure beyond, and was surrounded by stained glass panels that admitted irregular coloured light that bounced off the wooden floors.

They had splurged on the walnut throughout the house when the carpenters recommended it, the dark radiance extraordinary in the light. The house was so immediate to the sea that the window-panes caked with a gradual salt from November on, and close enough too that, when the curtains were drawn, a magnificent light leaked into the front windows from the sky and the sea's combined blue, a lemon-coloured light that pierced darkness and sea salt.

Tom's morning walk was limited here to a quick pace along

a green that gave way to the sea. He had driven tractors all of his boyhood, he told his new wife, and if she didn't mind he'd prefer not to drive to work like a boyo with his bales of hay. Much better to be driven, and dream his dreams while the bus rolled and tripped its way into the distant city centre. And so, like the house windows, the panes in the black Morris Minor grew crystals of salt over that first winter, and were only erased on the occasions when Clare scrubbed them off with warm water and a cloth before they visited her parents in Dun Laoghaire for a Sunday roast or his brother in Arklow for the odd birthday tea, and until she herself learned to drive by reversing up and down the abbreviated drive onto the coast road.

Elizabeth knew these things because they were part of the general mythologies that evolve in families, how Clare learned to drive or why they couldn't see through the windows or how they came to move from Sandycove to America. Like most teenagers, she was uninterested on the whole, particularly so because the country of which they spoke was so foreign to her. She heard their stories of Ireland cynically. If they'd been so happy in that house that first winter and the next then why be so mustard keen to dash away to America? Why not settle down with your bedroom suite of mahogany and your stretch of back garden and snatch of a front one and your expanse of sky and the endlessly rippling horizon of sea? Elizabeth didn't believe in their happiness, because if you were really, really happy, Elizabeth thought, you wanted to stay in one place, to not leave, to not abandon the crust of the shape of happiness that was place.

She was told nothing of the paucity of happiness before the marriage, before the house, before the urge to fly and conquer great mountains of dreams had seized them both so utterly. She didn't know Ireland or its damp or potato rot or violent prayer or the desperate lack of space that one could feel in the presence of a family. For their child they created stories and images of Ireland that were acutely happy. And so for her Ireland was not a home or even a real place merely unfamiliar to her, it was the imaginary geography of her parents' delusions.

For most people, love of a particular place was a thin, taut disguise for love of a particular person, a child, a lover, or a ghost, an idea of someone. Lizzy experienced her passionate attachment not to Ireland but to America while she was in Vietnam, for a ghostly reason – a ghost self that would not come to adulthood as she had intended. All other places, but particularly Ireland, as the place of her parents' birth, kept her from this idea of herself.

It amazed her that so many people flew away from their places of birth and made other homes. It was so complicated, the shifting of populations, because there were so many reasons and so many ways that those moves happened. There were those like her parents in search of adventure and wealth, those who were forced to flee from some dreadful circumstance, those like herself who were simply brought along for the ride. She would not become one of the ones who stayed, she knew, she could not stay in Vietnam.

Monsieur Philippe was an old man, maybe eighty, Elizabeth thought, and he told her he'd lived in Hanoi for six decades and that he'd never go back to France. Many of the other guests and residents seemed to avoid him though he was an evident favourite among the staff, and Elizabeth, despite parental warnings, continued to speak with him. It was a way of practising her French, learning odd Vietnamese words, since Monsieur Philippe, as all called him, cursed a lot, even if he was in a fancy suit and tie, and used odd old phrases. Her favourite was *Khó lam. Có buon*: 'Life with great difficulty and sadness'. There was something hard and defiant about it that she liked, something resigned that made her feel perversely strong. After he taught her this saying she used to recite it to herself sometimes when she looked out of the windows and felt miserable. All of the people below her, they knew that phrase too, but for them it was much more real, Elizabeth thought, and yet it was still life.

Monsieur Philippe was the one who told her too not to say *no*. But in exceptional cases, he said, don't say *no* if someone is trying to sell you something or offer you something you do not wish. Say *chua*, not yet. The Vietnamese, he told her seriously, are masters of this kind of language, indirect, subtle. It is a kind of poetry, that avoidance of honesty. And as an adult, Elizabeth would reflect that that same subtleties of language, the ability to talk around the truth, applied to Ireland. Perhaps it was why her father had done so well in Vietnam.

While he talked the old man chain smoked Gauloises Blondes that his daughter in France continued to post, month after month, even though Elizabeth was pretty sure she'd seen them for sale around somewhere, and certain that the officials would make him pay such high tax on his packages that it could not be worth his while. Other than this, he had no contact with her or any other family.

Et pour quoi? he'd tossed a hand into the thick air when Lizzy asked him why he didn't keep in touch with them. What for?

Even your own daughter? Lizzy pressed.

Ah, that's her choice, you see. She is from here – she's Vietnamese – and all she wanted was to go to France, get away from here. So I got her the passport and the papers when she was fifteen – she came here to meet me on the last day before we went to collect them – and she promised in return to post me my cigarettes. The old man paused, took a sip from a thin glass of iced coffee thick with condensed milk. And she has never broken her promise, he continued, setting the glass back down on the table, or written anything other than my name on the label. She is happy this way, as am I.

What about your wife? Lizzy ventured after a moment, watching him open a fresh packet of the cigarettes with firm, muscled hands.

Wife? He looked at her. Has the hotel not informed you of this already? He smiled. I never married. We ran off together for a while, me thinking that it was like Romeo and Juliet, Abelard, James

Joyce, love until the death. Alas, no, it was brief love, made impossible by the nature of that moment and our different cultures, ages, and now I alone await death. Once he mentioned death Elizabeth, only fifteen, started watching him, waiting for it to happen as he walked away. But he not die that afternoon or the next. He was still there when Elizabeth finally left.

Monsieur Philippe became a sort of grandfather figure. Most afternoons they sat and talked for a while. I know you find it hard here, he announced one day as it approached Christmas and Elizabeth had taken refuge in the lobby from a chilling, drizzling rain that came in from the river. It is hard to be young and to be in a place you do not wish to be, he mused, perhaps harder than when you are an adult. And I know it is not much consolation for you, but it was much, much worse not so long ago, before *doi moi* began, before this place was redone. Oh, it was just dreadful. Now, the rat, on occasion – then, all the time, while you ate your lunch, while you collected your post, everywhere the rat. People were hungry. After the war, nothing to eat for many people. After the war, the joke was, Hanoi sends a telegram to Moscow. Send money! it says. And Moscow replies: Tighten your belts. Hanoi wires again: Send belts!

Monsieur Philippe chuckled, then considered his cigarette. Desperate people, spending all of the family's money to get on a boat from Quang Ninh to Hong Kong, and the army allowed to shoot at them! Everyone applying for jobs in Siberia, East Germany, Czechoslovakia, trying to get away, get food, sending back everything they could get their hands on, blue jeans, mirrors, irons, crazy things to send through the post, but all so that the family could sell them, try to get some money for food. Only slowly, slowly, did the rice come back, only when they realised they could not spend all of their money on weapons and armies, could not keep fighting all of the neighbours. All of that waste in Kompuchea, he shook his head, and trying to stand up to the big bully up north. Now, it is all changing. I know, I know, for you it is bad, it looks bad all the time, but it is getting better. America will lift the trade embargo, more businessmen like your papa will arrive, and all of these computers will change Vietnam, make people less hungry.

Monsieur Philippe looked at Elizabeth, who was staring seriously at him. He laughed. Funny child, he smiled. I should not talk with you so seriously, of all these serious things. It is because you listen to me. We will speak of something else. They will be selling glitter soon for Christmas Eve – remember how incredible it is to see it all over the streets the next day, all of the cracks and the paths covered in with tinsel. And Tet will come soon after and there will be mume blossoms and we will eat bánh ch'ung and hear the firecrackers exploding all over the city. The blue haze of smoke over the old quarter. All the sellers, the packets of tea, the flowers, and it will be warm again soon enough.

Elizabeth returned his smile, but in the early mornings as she prepared for school and watched the streets from her windows, she could not think of glitter and rice cakes. She stared at the lithe bodies of small children who trailed hopefully down the damp winter streets collecting tin cans to sell, at the old men with only a few betel-stained teeth, at the backs of women bowed under the bamboo shoulder poles on which hung baskets of bread or roasted corn that sent steam into the air. It would never end, Elizabeth thought each morning as she listened to their calls.

᠎ ᠎ ᠎

When the second summer came they flew back to Ireland, and when they stepped off the plane Elizabeth almost cried from the cold and rain and also from relief. She was free. She could walk to the shop alone and buy anything she liked, didn't have to worry if she didn't feel like getting dressed for dinner and going to a dining room, didn't have to worry that the lights would flicker and fade each evening as the power failed in district by district of the city, didn't have to brush her teeth with bottled water or keep her mouth closed in a shallow bath, didn't have the spectacle of the staff running through the marble foyer after rats that were all but impossible to keep out. Ireland, she thought now, was not so bad, and she was surprised at her own concession, the way that she could have shifted her thoughts in the time since they had left Connecticut.

IV

Vietnam was different when they went back. Or at least Elizabeth imagined that it was. She found herself looking out of the windows differently at the yellow and grey buildings, wondering what Irish people might think if they saw the man with no legs offering to cut hair for passersby with his American army razor. Or whether they would like sugarcane juice, or what Irish girls would make of an ao dai instead of their school uniforms.

As she peered out at the streams of motorcyclists and bicycles and cars – there seemed to be more and more cars, many more than when they'd arrived a few years ago – through the window of the car on the way to school, she reminded herself of the words that so many uttered: it could be worse. But even though it was an easy thing to say, an easy enough thing to repeat to herself, she didn't really feel it as a possibility. How, really, could it be worse? At least, since it was September, it wasn't so hot, and the rains hadn't really started yet. The humid mornings gave way to a buckling of the sky by mid-afternoon, brief storms like tantrums, the air before the rain thick and heavy with the pollen of jasmine, camellia.

And at least the same people were in the hotel. Monsieur Philippe still drank his iced coffee each afternoon, smoking his French-mailed cigarettes. And there was a new school finally, a real school, with tuition costs more than fifty times the average Vietnamese family's income. The shocking thing to Elizabeth was how full it was, full of all of the other foreign kids whose parents now let them emerge from behind their walled-in lives. It was better to have a school, but it wasn't great, by any means. She still couldn't go for quiet walks, couldn't sit by the sea wall and eat 99s after dinner and speak casually to groups of local teenagers who found her foreign and intriguing. She couldn't wander in and out of shops full of things she wished to buy. But – she told herself resolutely – it was getting better. The heavy Czech motorcycles were giving way to sleek little Hondas, and new houses were going up at West Lake. The school gave her some company of her own age on a regular basis, even if the company was as shell-shocked at this turn of event as she was: international kids with extra pages added to their passports that were full of purple and green and red stamps whose ink leached into the surrounding paper. It could be worse, though, she told herself. *Khó lam. Có buon.*

In late October, her dad and a few others had planned a holiday, had decided months and months before to rent a boat and go up north a little bit to Halong Bay. Her mother wasn't going, choosing instead instead to fly to Singapore for a long weekend to shop and visit a former hotel resident. Clare said she'd wait until after Christmas when it was cool enough in Hanoi to don sweaters – then they would head south to Vung Tau outside of Ho Chi Minh city and spent a month or so at a villa owned by a retired politburo man who had been heavily involved in setting up the pepper trading and who simply liked Tom for the business he was bringing to the country. Pepper was becoming increasingly important to Vietnam. Clare added that under no circumstance was Elizabeth going, either; she could stay in the hotel and be minded by the staff. But Elizabeth, on finding out that another child younger than she was meant to go, pleaded and pleaded. Let me get out of Hanoi for a few days, Dad, please take me, please get me a travel permit too, until he finally acceded and the time came to pack her bag.

The journey to the boat was the usual nightmare when one travelled by car, and Elizabeth swore she would never forget it, would never manage to survive such a trip again. Her dad had been told that it would take two or three hours, no more. The five businessmen and the two children piled into a van as the sun was spreading its heat over the early morning city. Her dad patted the driver, also their guide, on the back and away they went.

It was okay for the first few hours, but once the sun was up, and once they all realised again that within miles of Hanoi the roads, as such, had stopped, and dirt tracks began, a quiet heat rash settled over the van. Two of the men were newly arrived, only in the country for a matter of months. One was from England and the other Australia, the Englishman with some charitable organisation trying to set up adoption services for Vietnamese babies to be brought to the West, and the Australian a new appointee to the off-shore oil interests his country had been developing over the last few years. Both of them exclaimed over the state of the roads, over the heat persisting so late into the autumn, and the others sympathised casually, so accustomed to it themselves, inured to their shirts sticking to their backs, to sweat rivering their foreheads.

After a while, no one spoke, not even the eleven-year-old son of her dad's friend. They were stopped once and asked for their permits, which they duly produced. The silence continued in the van. The driver spoke to the police, gesturing. After fifteen minutes of animated conversation during which the driver grew more and more agitated and careful, Elizabeth's father interrupted. How much? He produced dollars and the permits were returned. At noon they stopped at a tiny shop, where Elizabeth's dad broke the news to the new fellows that they were only half way there, and also sighted the beach over the hill, to which everyone walked silently for a dip to cool down. In their shorts and t-shirts they waded into the relentlessly warm water, and then returned to sit in wet clothes that dried all too quickly in the oven of a van, the droplets streaming on the vinyl seats and dripping slowly onto the floor. It could be worse, Elizabeth muttered half to herself and half to her dad, making him laugh.

That's my girl, he patted her leg. Good thing your mum didn't come along, what, Queen Elizabeth?

Dad, she leaned against him and said it quietly, her sentence lost under the motor of the van, when are we going back to Ireland?

Tom gazed out of the window at the disappearing parentheses of the hills and put a hand up to the roof to steady himself as the van turned down another sandy, pocked stretch of road. It was the first time in a long time she had called him Dad; he knew this was important.

Well, hon, I'd like to stay here a few more years. I think if I give this business another two years we'll be close to making Vietnam one of the biggest pepper players in the world. Things are changing here, and they'll keep changing, and the cities will get bigger, and they'll rebuild and have new airports and new industries, and I'd like to be a part of that. I imagine that in the not-too-distant future Vietnam could be not just one of the biggest but *the* biggest producer of pepper in the world. We could even get trademark on the types of pepper we're growing.

He was speaking to her as if she were an adult, and she knew that she just couldn't cry now, at the prospect of having to stay in Vietnam indefinitely.

Isn't there a way I could go? Go back to Ireland? Live with Aunt Fidelma? She asked quietly, again, afraid that if she let loose the conversation would stop, and the possibility of getting out of this place disappear.

You're only sixteen, he said simply, almost sixteen. We don't want you to live alone yet. Fidelma, well, she's out and about and busy with her own kids, and they're down the country, and neither your mum nor I feel comfortable at the idea of you being on your own a good deal.

What about next year? Elizabeth asked him, the tears coursing down her cheeks and meeting rivers in the streams of seawater dribbling down her neck from her hair. I can get the international baccalaureate by then and go to college. I can't go here.

For a long few minutes her father said nothing, just held her hand as they lurched drunkenly along the road.

When you're seventeen and you've finished school, he said slowly, okay.

Promise, she said to him.

I promise, Queen Elizabeth.

Promise what, she pushed.

That when you're seventeen you can go away to college, if we're still here.

And what about Clare? Elizabeth wanted to cover all of her bases.

I'll talk to her.

They said nothing then, but when Elizabeth turned to look out of the window with new eyes she didn't let go of her father's hand.

When they finally reached the village where they were to pick up the boat, it was almost dark, and they were all glad of the small guest house and the prospect of stretching their legs out of the sun and didn't give a damn, as Tom said quietly to the other men, about the beautiful sunset flowing colours into the ring of islands off the coast. They ate bun cha and goi cuon together on a wooden porch at the back of the house, waited on by a husband and wife and their two small children, who expertly folded the salad rolls in the kitchen, visible from the porch, as they ran low on the platter.

Elizabeth whispered to her father that it was awful that the kids had to work, but her father whispered back that in many ways they were lucky, since they'd managed to take over one of the French colonial houses and had a home and income. The annual income was still only a few hundred dollars a year, her father said, and the poverty was worse outside the cities. They were relatively lucky. So it could be worse, much, much, she answered back solemnly, tapping her nails on the side of the coconut she was drinking from. But Dad, you know, it's still messed up that we come here and they have to do this. She eyed the girl who was about her age removing the empty pho bowls.

After dinner Elizabeth went up to her room, which was connected to her father's by double doors that had once held glass panes but whose squares were now filled in with thin slats of dark wood. These she closed over and then perched herself by the window with a book, which she didn't read, gazing out instead at the dark and considering the fact that she would, finally, be leaving.

᠂ ᠂ ᠂

One of the American men who returned every six months or so with a more haggard face and less hope of finding his child had offered to bring her a book on American universities. What the school had was limited, especially since most of the other kids would go to Europe to study. The Korean kids would be sent to England, the Swedish kids, like the Australians, tended to go home, and some of the really wealthy Vietnamese kids, sons and daughters of high-ranking officials or of Viet Kieu who'd made loads of money in France, would go to Paris or London. Only another one or two were interested in the US.

Elizabeth had been sitting by the pool telling him how that was really what she wanted, to go and study back in the US. I don't know where, though, she said fretfully. It's hard to find out about anything like that from here. The teachers only know about universities in France and Australia and Sweden 'cause that's where they're from, and most of the others are gonna go back there. I'll have to wait until my dad has to go to Hong Kong again, maybe. You know that other soldier guy, Jack, who was here last month? Well he told me you could get these books like an encyclopaedia of colleges. I'll have to get my dad to try and find one.

I'll send you one when I get home, her friend told her, taking a pen and a diary the size of a packet of playing cards from his inside pocket and writing, in a small, careful hand: College Book: Eliz. Metropole. And then, looking at Elizabeth grinning and hearing her declarations of thanks, he added, I'd like to think that my kid will go to college someday.

This type of thing did not happen only the once. To many in the hotel, to those whose lives had somehow bound them to the heat and noise and monsoon mud and political uproar and the continuing sense of disembodied history that was Hanoi and Vietnam, Elizabeth was a surrogate child, a projection of some-thing or someone. She became a distant niece, a long-lost cousin, the child of friends, the teenager they knew.

This made Clare nervous. When the book on the US univer-sities appeared, she seized on it as an indication that these men – there were so few women, really, in the hotel, excepting the French – were aiming to seduce her daughter and whisk her off to the States, entice her with books or promises of an education. But Clare's protests were met with cold stares from Elizabeth, and no words at all beyond don't be so crazy, who else am I gonna talk to Clare? Since Clare couldn't answer this, the question produced an oddly tingling silence between them. Tom steered clear of the subject most times, knowing that his daughter did indeed lack company, and knowing too the promise that he himself had made to her.

Elizabeth pored through the college guide. Then began the process of deciding where to apply, making photocopies of her *relevé des notes*, filling in sent-away-for application forms, and hoping that the hotel photocopier wouldn't break down just before she needed to send it all away. Gradually the pile was reduced, and Elizabeth gathered herself into her room with a cluster of pens, trying very hard to force some essence of herself and her life into the cramped hand poised around the nib, thinking about how her life had changed in the last five years, how she had changed, but also how much Vietnam had changed. Then it was a matter of waiting.

One such afternoon Elizabeth sat and gazed out of her window to the street below, where she could see Thu, one of the maids, buying litchis on her way home from a man eating a bowl of pho. Thu was laughing as he put the squat grenades of fruit into a small brown paper bag, twirling the corners tightly and dropping it into her hands before returning to his bowl, lifting it right up under his chin like a cup. He too was laughing, waving with his free left hand as Thu climbed on the back of her moped and covered the sleek cap of her hair with a helmet. There were so many more mopeds now, and more of the sporty-looking Honda ones instead of the Eastern European imports from twenty years ago, still zillions of bicycles, but now more mopeds and cars too. And there were more stalls on the streets; you didn't see those mad lines like five years ago with everyone queuing up to buy cigarettes or vegetables or anything at all. They'd even just about finished repairing the Opera House, putting the sidewalks back together. There weren't as many communist posters everywhere any more. At last month's Tet it hadn't seemed so much like it was everyone's one chance in the year to eat and have a holiday. It had felt more like a real celebration, with the peach blossoms stuck on the back of every bicycle and moped, all of the confetti and glitter snowing through the air for the whole holiday, the restaurants packed with laughing, chattering families whose voices were lost beneath the drumming of firecrackers.

The school had organised a Tet night for the students and it had actually been loads of fun, the atmosphere different now. It had felt different in Ho Chi Minh city too, when recently she'd flown down with her parents for a few days. While her dad had met with exporters, she and her mother had sipped iced coffee at the Rex and wandered around, amazed at the enormous industry of everything. They had spent a small fortune when they visited the Saigon-Intershop supermarket, which took dollars only and stocked western products rarely available in Hanoi. Clare had laughed at Elizabeth, who told her she almost wanted to buy even Pampers and Huggies, just because they were there. There was no doubt. It was all changing.

Elizabeth felt in her pockets for dong, suddenly craving litchis. Walking down the stairs, the inky notes in her fingers, she thought about Hanoi. It was all so familiar to her now, the caverns that yawned in the middle of certain streets, the jagged paths, the glass shards stuck into the tops of walls around old buildings that had been used as prisons, the new ice-cream parlor on the lake where if the electricity failed for long the customers and staff all ended up in a laughing frenzy to eat all of the ice before it melted. She'd become accustomed to streets full of water in July, August, September, drains stuffed up and choking on old newspapers and cigarette butts, everyone wading to work. The children, despite their parents' curses at the annoyance of it all, still rang out a splashing enjoyment from the floods.

And now she'd leave and go to another new place where she knew no one, where there was no pho and French bread and dragon fruit sent up by room service for breakfast and no green bean candy and no revamped and gleaming hotel lobby full of the lonely and dethroned, all of those who could not live like the rest of the western world, in their own homes with their own families, taking care of themselves. Wordlessly, she paid the litchi man – she'd watched him selling fruit for months now but didn't know his name – and walked back the few yards to the hotel, hearing him resume his now twice interrupted meal, swinging the bag of fruit clutched in her sweating fingers. She would miss the coming summer, the preposterous burst of sun that was morning, the unbearable shimmer of afternoons. She'd be half way round the world, back in the modest warmth of the Irish summer and then, finally, when it was time to start college, in the waning, late summer sun of the land of her childhood.

The light in Ireland, in the States, would be different, Elizabeth thought, and instead of going in she sat on the steps of the hotel, to the side, and opened her bag of litchis. No one paid much attention to her because of the doorman at the hotel, standing somewhere behind her in his suit. The adult vendors knew he'd send them away, although the kids did begin to swarm towards her to point at her blond hair that flapped like birds' wings. When a few minutes later her mother was rolled up, cradled in a cyclo, her mouth, like so many Vietnamese women's, hidden with a white mask, Elizabeth waved and the children stared into the cyclo. Clare stepped out, thanking the driver, handing him the notes, and turned to her daughter. Coming in? she asked. I'm shattered. It's been quite a day. She didn't seem to see the children staring.

Just thought I'd eat my litchis out here for a change. Want one? Elizabeth reached her hand out with the yellow-pink ball balanced on her palm.

I'd love one, Elizabeth, but I couldn't possibly sit in the sun any longer. Coming? I'll buy you a Shirley Temple.

Elizabeth laughed, but got up and went in. Now that she knew she was leaving soon, she found that her mother was bearable, the conversation not so stiflingly annoying. They walked through the lobby together, pausing at the desk so that Clare could retrieve the post. *Et pour mademoiselle*, the porter smiled at Elizabeth, *rien que ça*. His hand stretched across the stretch of black marble was brown and smooth. Elizabeth saw the return address and felt herself redden under his gaze, under her mother's. *Merci*, Phuong, she smiled, stuffed what she hoped was an early college acceptance letter into her pocket with the leftover dong. So I'll see you at dinner, okay? Elizabeth's feet pivoted towards the stairs, poised to race.

What about the litchis? Clare asked, trying not to laugh.

Oh! Sorry Clare. I forgot. I'll take one more – she twirled the bag open – and you can have the rest. Okay? Elizabeth smiled, passed her mother the bag, and, already lost in the world of the unopened letter, failed to notice her mother's expression soften to something she might not have recognised as she carried herself up the stairs.

ϲ ϲ ϲ

On her last night in the hotel they had dinner down in the restaurant instead of in the room of their suite that had served as a sitting and dining room. Elizabeth and Tom ate roasted fish with lemongrass, chilli and nam pla. Clare refused the hottest of dishes and Elizabeth and Tom teased her, together, bullying her into a taste just to be able to laugh at her pantomime of needing water to cool her mouth, claiming that she didn't like too much heat in the evenings and could only manage it in morning pho. The French have their wines, the Vietnamese their sauces, Monsieur Philippe says, but some of them are clearly wasted on you, Clare. Elizabeth giggled. People stopped at the table to wish Elizabeth bon voyage and Daniel, the French maitre d' and sommelier, joked that now she'd finally have to learn how to cook, because the chef refused to send her room service to America. When the table had been cleared except for wine glasses and her father had lit his daily cigarette, Elizabeth sank back and gazed across the white tablecloth at her parents.

He's right, you know, I can't cook. I've barely been in a kitchen for five years.

I'll show you a thing or two myself, Tom nodded. Do you remember when I made you mole poblano when you were small?

No, Elizabeth shook her head.

Yes you do, Elizabeth, Clare laughed. I'll never forget it, coming home from a day in the city and your father had made you chicken –

Turkey, Tom cut in.

Turkey with chocolate and God knows what else, Clare finished.

You loved it, Tom told Elizabeth. You helped, stirring the pot, getting out the almonds, the cinnamon, the chillies.

I remember, Dad. Elizabeth smiled. She didn't add that she remembered the story he'd told her about the dish's origin, about a nun somewhere in Mexico, and how it was a mix of American and old Spanish ingredients. It was good, she told him. I guess I liked spicy food even then.

Yes, you and me, Elizabeth. I don't think your mum had learned to appreciate heat at that stage, had you? You ended up making grilled cheese later that night, didn't you? Clare nodded. Well, Tom sighed, smiling, you can learn to cook spicy food for yourself, Queen Elizabeth. And you'll never be short of pepper, I'll make sure of that.

Elizabeth smiled across the table at them, this nice pair of people with whom she was chitchatting about mole poblano. And yet on some level she didn't care what her parents said tonight, whether they kept the conversation light and friendly like this or proceeded to advise or even ignore her. She wouldn't live with them after this. Elizabeth watched her mother slide an ashtray towards her father's elbow, saw him pat her hand and briefly rest his own on top of hers. They'd never divorce, she knew. The separations that would occur were far more likely to occur between parents and child.

Elizabeth sat in her room that, once her things had been packed and shipped, had already returned to its former state, a nice enough hotel room, with white waffle towels piled neatly on a rack, suitcases and bags in a heap at the door. There was nothing to do in the room any more except watch the bits of TV that were of interest to her. And she didn't want to watch TV. She thought hard about Ireland, standing there in front of the window, and, remembering the cold and the wind and the rain, decided that, on her last night, she'd sit outside, in the courtyard, eating litchis, feeling heat, watching the bats' flight as they swooped down low over the pool's underlit blue surface.

ᴄ ᴄ ᴄ

From the moment she stepped on to the Lao Aviation plane that would deliver them to Hong Kong, where another plane would carry them above the now familiar mountains towards stopovers in Los Angeles and New York before a final swoop towards Dublin, Elizabeth experienced a lightheaded happiness that almost panicked her. Even the Californian smog seemed dreamily opalescent, a muted rainbow of sun colours dozing over the city. And the arrival in New York – the sight of buildings she knew she would soon be living amongst – was thrilling.

Elizabeth clutched the undersized pillow to her body, wanting to cheer as the Americans did upon landing, to clap like a child, suddenly shy because for so long she had felt that she herself was American, and here she was. She felt that she would cry if she moved, and couldn't bring herself to clap after all. In the airport, in the few hours before their flight to Dublin, Elizabeth wandered while her parents drank coffee in a bar near the Aer Lingus gate. Don't go far, Clare cautioned her daughter gently, too tired to use an assertive tone that would have received a sarcastic reply about how much more dangerous Vietnam was compared to an American airport. But Elizabeth, startled out of her own habits and glossy-eyed from sleeplessness, just nodded and walked off, regarding other teenagers' clothes, wondering if they were starting college, wondering if she looked different to them: too tanned, too out of fashion, too thin and awkward to wear body-hugging tank tops, sneakers with rows of neat white laces, woven friendship bracelets that looped ankle bones.

She roamed through duty free, ogling the makeup, and eventually stood in front of glass panels, watching the dull, clouded sky swallow planes one by one by one in endless chains, while another squat flock of clouds spun out another chain. You couldn't see the buildings of the city from down here, only cloud and the colour grey, but still it was wonderful, a covering like a lid to keep the city from taking over everything, from spilling over on itself.

On the last flight, Elizabeth finally slept after watching the clouds over New York engulf her own plane. When she woke it was to a lightening sky and the realisation that really they had left Vietnam, and that a part of her life that she'd found interminable was actually over. And this was so reassuring and so strange at once that Elizabeth did not protest at anything her parents proposed to her in the four weeks of their visit. If her father insisted that she accompany them to see some old friend in some tiny, wet village, Elizabeth went. If her mother suggested that she would need copious amounts of awful woollen sweaters for the New York winter, she let Clare buy them and stack their shades of earth and leaf in a new suitcase. This too would end. She could feel it.

She could easily endure this wet July with its rain and seaweed-smelling winds that poured in through bowed wooden window frames at the front of the house and that were so different from Vietnamese winds. The winds would not be hers in a month, nor the villages full of pubs and geranium-planted window boxes and empty churches and nothing else. The family friends would be lost to her again, would remain in these places with the milk bottles huddled by the doorstep, the foil caps sometimes nicked by cheeky magpies, daring cats to get the cream. The sweaters would not be hers but would remain a canvas of Ireland in the new bag until she carried their soft bulk to a thrift store in New York. And, in some ways, the parents too would no longer be hers. They would leave her in New York in her own person and return to Hanoi, to one less room in their suite, to one less factor in their days.

Elizabeth drifted through the vacation with this sense of philosophical finality, dreamily, wordlessly letting her mind sift its way through what she considered 'lasts' – the last time her mother would buy her clothing, the last time she'd attend a family dinner. She bundled herself into cars and houses and restaurants with her parents, their relatives and friends, wrapped herself in Clare's chosen sweaters to ward off the cold.

For relatives and family friends she provided hundreds of answers to hundreds of questions about her schooling and her new college and how she was and whether she was excited. She chatted, smiled and was endlessly polite. When they called in to people's houses she ate the offered slabs of speckled fruitcake, dense brack, yellow madeira, and cherry cake. She drank Barry's and Bewley's and Lyons and sometimes felt her heart pounding when the last of a pot had been drained into her cup, the caffeine flowing through her body like its own blood. She got used to people calling her love and darlin and missus even when she just met them for the first time and was pretty sure she'd never see them again. She got used to smiling and smiling and smiling so that aunts and cousins and uncles and neighbours told Tom and Clare that she was a lovely girl, now, a lovely girl, and weren't they blessed with her, weren't they? Teenagers now could be a terrible nuisance, they could indeed, but weren't they only blessed with Elizabeth?

And it was curious for Elizabeth to see Tom and Clare, whom she knew had often despaired of her in Hanoi – her silence, her slamming of doors – nodding yes, that she was a blessing, Clare even reaching out to touch her shoulder a few times when they stood at front doors saying their farewells, their clothes and hair and bags wild and flying with a cold summer wind.

Only towards the end of the month, when her flight to New York was becoming a looming reality and she wondered which of her parents had her passport, did Elizabeth feel an acute, starved longing come over her body for heat, for the ripe air of mid-summer afternoons in Hanoi. This startled her, as it would continue to all her life: that she could involuntarily yearn, physically, for an intangible such as heat. After living in Vietnam, Elizabeth would continue to go through phases when she craved heat, the way that others wanted to cram their mouths full of the sweet molten darkness of chocolate. She would feel a desperate urge to experience the sun seeping into every pore of her skin, to keep her eyelids down and see only the faint but solid orange colour of the eyelids themselves full of sun. Ireland did not satisfy this yearning, though Elizabeth rejected the thought that first time out of the flat surprise that she could miss anything of Vietnam.

ᴄ ᴄ ᴄ

Elizabeth would return to America several weeks later with a suitcase full of clothes from halfway around the world made to fit her particular body by seamstresses barely older than she was, and a hope that stung the back of her throat. In America, she would return to herself, pick up where the child Elizabeth had left off. Still brown-skinned, overdressed by Irish summer standards and uncomfortable in so many layers of clothes that she was not used to, Elizabeth suffered through attempts to convince her to abandon the idea of America and to remain in Ireland.

And so, on the plane journey that she had dreamt of for so many years that it seemed surreal, Elizabeth pulled the airsickness bag out of the seat pocket in front of her and started her first letter of independence. *Dear Tom and Clare*, she wrote, *thank you for letting me go.*

V

Sandrine is learning about the limitations of narrative. She writes to her son of the things she sees and does, and to her husband she writes other things. Nothing things. How today she is beginning to think of the verb 'to be' differently – because here in Ireland, it does not seem possible for her to just be, and for her own voice to be heard – and remembering how as a child she pestered her father for a definition of the word 'the'. *Dear George, I remembered today asking my father to define 'the'.* It is one of her fondest memories now that she has retrieved it; his hands on a dictionary darkened by the oils of his thumbs and forefingers, the beige threads of its woven cloth cover untwining, and his laughter at her confusion. What is *the*? A series of letters that point to something assumed familiar, known, understood? A word that defines being in some way because it points to things or other words that we assume also exist?

Her father and the dictionary together could not answer her. *George. Do you think of these things?*

She thinks differently here. Here she has no story. She feels the pressure of other stories hemming in on her own, so much so that she is absentminded, thinking constantly of gaps. When she arrived in Ireland, Sandrine had thought that some story of hers was beginning; she could even hear herself at some imagined time telling the tale of how she had gone to Ireland. But in the reality of Ireland, the reality of a foreign land, that was not possible, not immediately. The story was not yet hers.

There seems to be no place for her in this country. People stare, snigger, or turn away. At worst – at least, so far, this has been the worst – there is the cursing, the spitting, the murmuring, the feeling she has of being threatened when certain people pass her in the streets. They deny her, and she feels it. Sandrine feels, increasingly, that she is denied. Her story depends on collaboration, something that she, on her own, cannot supply. She is dependent upon some level of acceptance and that is not forthcoming. The telling of incidents at the end of each day over tea, the passing of information between neighbours, the recitation of prayers as a child goes to bed – these things seem to have lost their place here. There are no rituals with which to make her life vital, so that she lives in memory and at a distance from the realm of the real. Here she forgets, begins to forget rituals that were before too commonplace, unnoticeable, consumed by the everydayness of their existence. She wants to describe these feelings to George, but the sentences begin to break down.

Here. Away from you. Away from our son.

When she first become pregnant with Tobias, she used to imagine life without George. When he left for work so early in the morning, walking through the doorway and stepping into the world towards the fields that he would plow and harvest with the other workers, Sandrine would feel overwhelming loss, wondering where the day would take him. For a few minutes she would feel this fear creep over her, stand in the concrete box of their home with his memory, his scent lingering, before she would be able to answer to herself and begin to prepare for her own day at the school. In all those mornings of small farewells, during which she would gather herself and compose her face before turning around to face his parents and her sister-in-law, Sandrine never imagined that it would be she who would leave for a place like this, and say larger farewells.

Is madness contagious?

So she writes to her husband. He knows nothing of her days except that she lives with Clare, who is mad, and whose husband is also mad, but madder, in a home. He doesn't know that, in the hours when Clare visits Tom, Sandrine wanders the small roads around the house, the small paths that curve past the sea, much as Clare does when she manages to get out unnoticed and head uphill to find Tom. He doesn't know that Sandrine reads the books on the shelves that belong to Tom and Clare, reading more than she ever has in her life, simply because there is the time and there are the books. There is no company, no sisters to visit, no children to mind. George doesn't know that the school to whom she had paid a high fee simply prepares for her attendance certificates at the end of each month, which she collects on foot during a time when Clare is with Elizabeth. He does not know that she is not actually in school and defying her visa.

He does not know, either, that she wonders about Irish people's reputation as friendly and welcoming and holy. It is true that for all Clare's eccentricities, she does not bat an eyelid at Sandrine's *foreignness*. But the rest of the country seems to, in radio debates and newspaper columns. Sometimes Sandrine wonders if another country, even England, might have been better, since in England there was, at least, a sizable population from Zim already.

Beyond even these things, George does not know of the new fear that their son will grow to see them go mad, that he will visit them in a state-run Irish hospital or home and feed them, if not grapes, then bananas, or soft, stringy mango pulled away from the flat hard stone. Sandrine is horrified thinking that if they all move to Ireland, she and George will be forced to spend the ends of their lives in a nursing home, away from their children, gazing into the middle distance, not knowing each other. George doesn't know that so often Sandrine wonders if she is already gone mad, wondering again like a child what 'the' means, that so often too she thinks that the money of this new life is not worthwhile, that if their son has new clothes and a new school later on it doesn't matter as much as the fact that she does not see him in them, that she is forgetting how to define fundamental words, that she is forgetting how to love.

There are moments when she fails to know him, her husband. In these moments the agreed-upon stasis of sorts that is making a life together collapses, folding in on itself like a piece of furniture rotten with age and overuse. They are moments of intense despair and bewilderment that stretch into hours and days when she is not certain of the depth of reality. Who is this person in the letters? Is he the image she has created, something that has taken shape in her mind, a kind of interaction between her own way of thinking and these words on the page? Or had he created this image of himself in words? Was he responsible for his image, or was she? Sandrine turned the letters over in her hands, searching for something beyond the letters, the spacings, something else of him, something to make her remember: something tangible that she could feel, taste, like bowls of smoking nhedzi from morning-fresh mushrooms, something to keep in her mouth, like the mealy solidness of roasted groundnuts.

But the trouble was that she was at the final stages of a kind of chronic forgetfulness that began in over-familiarity and the preoccupations of parenthood, and was ending in absence. Had she not, at times, felt the need to be free of him and all of the family? She had gone out of their home and walked by herself to the badly defined edges of the village, where houses broke down and stuttered. There the detritus of their lives spilled into the fields and hills as so many deserted the countryside for the hopes of work in the sprawl of cities. She would stand amid the confusion of deconstructed shelters and consider the horizon by herself, imagine herself standing on that line against the sky.

Had she not feigned sleep on occasion rather than rouse herself at his touch, the heat in his soft, thick fingers too much against her skin? Sometimes she endured sex silently in the night with her eyes gazing upward into the darkness, listening to the sounds of the household settling down to sleep around them. In fact she had done this many, many times. Perhaps, then, she had forgotten him while still at home, when Zimbabwe was more than a string of letters on a map of the world framed in Tom's study, more than the microphoned noise of a reporter's delivery of a story on the television, more than the blue-black ink slurred over a postal stamp that cried home.

Their relationship had changed when her brother disappeared. Everything had. Since Amahle had gone, she had not wanted to touch her husband. There had been two miscarriages during that time, when Tobias was two, the blood sudden and thick, her body seized by brief labours. There had been nothing to bury, but Sandrine still felt their spirits with her at times, the two small creatures who had gone, she hoped, to be with Amahle and comfort him on her behalf. It had changed everything. She was surprised at her own mind, the way that the grief for Amahle and her grief for the babies had entangled so profoundly. She had pushed George away, with harsh words first, but after the second loss his mother had ordered him to give her time.

The plan for her to go away had revived everything between them – but had she, in fact, finally agreed to go away because she had already departed, in a small way, in her heart? And now, now here she was pregnant, so sure that this one was going to hang on and make a proper appearance, and she was thousands of miles from George, thousands of miles from those who would comfort and help to sustain her through the birth.

Sandrine stared at the letters and, in her silent desperation, wanted to clutch at something more than paper. Her son in her arms would satisfy this, relieve her of abstractions. And when she felt this – the physical absence of husband and son from her life, her parents, her sisters, her last brother – Sandrine was overwhelmed, and the letters, mere paper, were transformed into some beacon on which she had no option but to train her gaze.

She had started going to the church when it was clear that Elizabeth and Clare intended to stay with Tom for more time than it took to have a cup of tea. It was a heavy, grey stone building, cavernous and cold, with lacquered wooden pews and deep red missals, and it was always almost empty. Here and there, in a shadowed corner, in the front rows, the last, and before certain statues, were scattered handfuls of regular attendees, mostly frail, grey-haired women with bent backs and large leather purses with brassy zippers and buttons. They knelt on stockinged, swollen knees, the heels of the solid shoes they favoured in navy and black leather scuffed and polished to a dull buff. The tacks on their soles became visible, sometimes gleaming when the sun plummeted into the building through a high up, dusty window. Some held rosaries, the round noise of the cool beads cracking, ghostly words edging from their moving lips. The few men were angular, their frames folding into physical prayer like splinters of wood, long and hard, joints crackling, their hands boned and pointed.

Sandrine inserted herself into this dark, chilled, echoed silence, the youngest person by decades, and felt a sense of relief. Here, amid these men and women who prayed bowed-headed and closed-eyed, she disappeared. And no matter how different the church, how marvellously marbled compared to those at home, no matter how quiet, she was with God again; she felt it. And so unlike the others Sandrine sat with her head back, her eyes tracing slowly the arches and the statues and the bent heads and the vast emptiness of the pews. And she prayed this way, by gazing – for the words of the prayers seemed too loud, too sharp for this quiet that settled in her mind. And God did not mind. She could feel this too.

Sandrine usually left before any of the services began. She could remain in the church for an hour or more in the silence, but the mass itself seemed an intrusion into her privacy and into the privacy of the old men and women. She had always enjoyed services at home, and she had been told that Ireland was a religious nation, and that she would find it easy to fit her own beliefs into those of her adopted country. But she didn't find Ireland at all religious. There were no young people at the services, no spontaneous eruptions into prayer, no accompanying the celebrant at his prayers, and the priest, a faint man whose robes swayed from sloped, uneven shoulders, spoke into a microphone that sent his voice unnecessarily into shadows and holy places, into crevices and built-up dust.

His voice was forcefully present in the building that housed perhaps twenty people and had been built for a thousand, and this depressed her, as did the lack of music and the droning murmur of recitation that lacked all diction. Even the sound of the chain attached to the thurible as the priest's hands moved, the *chic chink chic chink* that Sandrine loved, could not override the depression, nor the heavy smoke of the incense. After one service when she'd taken communion and faced a watery distrust in the old priest's eyes, Sandrine decided to go and stay only on her own terms. No one ever spoke to her or noticed her there week after week, and so gradually Sandrine felt a familiarity grow that she had with Tom and Clare's house.

Between the church and the house were stores, gardens and walls that also became familiar. There was a fruit and vegetable shop with sacks of potatoes on the path on dry days and crates of waxed green apples that glimmered in the sun when it shone, a sandwich shop whose staff stood under the awning in the frequent rain to smoke, their white kitchen hats sagging in the damp. She liked to pass the front garden packed with rose bushes so carefully pruned by a middle-aged man with a wilting face, and then to take the short cut in between two houses whose trees kissed overhead when the wind blew hard from the sea and breached the barrier of the houses.

Walking home one day through this white-walled, pebble-dashed passage, Sandrine startled herself with the realisation that she now walked thoughtlessly, without needing to pay attention or worrying about getting lost. She could now just walk and get there. This was her life. She lived here in this Irish seaside suburb. The shock of this, on a damp Sunday morning – Clare was visiting Tom with Elizabeth – was great. She paused her steps and a panic gathered in her belly, which she tried to settle before it reached the not-yet-child.

Her son was living thousands of miles away and she was here. Her husband – was he exhausted with his life of working and minding their child without her? Was the rest of the family coming to resent the extra help they had to give? Was her mother-in-law and sister-in-law, her own sisters – were they replacing her in Tobias's heart? Was the money she was sending not enough? She watched the water pooling off the path under her feet for a moment and walked on, trying to recover thoughtlessness, holding the child in her belly. Two strangers eyed her suspiciously as she plodded past. One of the men spat on the ground as he strode past and said something to his friend that Sandrine did not catch immediately but heard in afterthought: *fucking asylum-seeking nigger.* The shock of it. Tears started to her eyes in an instant. It turned her stomach and left her unable to speak.

She had hurried back to the house afterwards, aware that it was indeed her refuge, for Clare and Tom and Elizabeth were all, in a way, foreigners too. She has shown them pictures of her son, of her husband, has increasingly told Clare everything. She tells her that evening about the two young men, speaking in an open, broken way of her fears, knowing that her story will be swallowed up by inevitable fractures in memory.

Clare recalls nothing that she says during their dinnertime ritual exchanges, and Tom fails to recall even Clare. It is inevitable, the fraying of the mind. She is fighting against it all the time, praying to God to preserve her memory, to make certain that he preserves George and Tobias's memory of her as well. And she knows, instinctively, that prayer is not enough, that she must work, all the time, to make sure that her mind remains alive.

When it rains – and that is often – while Clare is out with Elizabeth, Sandrine sits in Tom's study. He had not used it much since the return to Ireland. Dust settled on everything, filling in the carvings and crevices of the Buddhas that were hidden among the bookcases. When she first came, she avoided cleaning the room whose curving windows pushed into the garden and stared hard at the sea through woody stems of gnarled old lavender. From reading English novels she believed there would be uproar if she entered, that it was Tom's private preserve. This wasn't the case, though. Clare traipsed in and out, the door was open at all times, and Elizabeth often disappeared to discover a book she could not locate in her own home. It was Tom himself who had avoided the room, his mind too crowded already to take in a space of books. Clare remarked to Sandrine once after Elizabeth had gone with several volumes under her arm that the books were rotting on the shelves and it would be better if someone took them away to a library or a school. When Sandrine asked in those first strange weeks if she might borrow one herself, Clare reacted with surprise. Of course, that's what they're there for. Lucidly, as if the madness had been banished.

So Sandrine ventured into the study. She came to think of it as the room that most contained her in the house. It was not her room, for no space in this house could be truly hers, but it was enough to contain her. In it she could disappear into a labyrinth of words. Mostly there were works of histories to do with spice. Histories of America, France, Vietnam, ancient history, books on the spice trade, on gastronomy, on the history of food usage, the history of spice in cooking. Endless rows of magazines and brochures and pamphlets about spices were stacked on the lowest shelves, special numbers of the International Pepper Community.

There were also a few books on Africa. Not on a specific country, but on the continent, and one on African cookery. She read those first, about Leopold and Rhodes, ambushes and gold, ivory, the gathering of her country into a named realm. Afterwards she read several of Tom's cookery books that told of the use and history of spices. And it was only then, not after reading the books on Africa, that Sandrine felt something close to betrayal.

She had known before, of course, about the European colonisation of Africa. The mess at home was due in large part to that history, and she knew it better than most. She still remembered vividly the emotion of the stadium in 1980, the band whining out 'God Save the Queen' and the tear gas that made her weep as if with emotion. She remembered viscerally the hope of that childhood day, and the long way they'd come on buses just to be there, to see it happen. Then the hope quietly withdrew as the Fifth Brigade rampaged and money and petrol and security seemed to dry up. She knew the colonial history, knew about the 'discovery' of Victoria Falls – this, in many ways, was why she was here. But she had not known that so much of what had provoked Europe overseas hundreds of years before was the simple desire for spice, and she knew, now, that that same itch had led to the beginnings of empire that had ended, ultimately, in Africa, as the last land mass available to the expression of those compulsive desires.

It cost her a wry smile, to learn that James I had once been king not only of England, Scotland, Ireland and France, but also

Puloway and Puloroon, all for the sake of nutmeg. Cinnamon from the forests of Ceylon had been so costly that a Roman centurion would have paid six years' wages for a pound of the finest grade. The Dutch, to prevent smuggling, torched clove groves on all of the Moluccas but Ambon, and to prevent anyone else from growing nutmeg, treated the shrubs with lime.

Prices were kept high by staging bonfires of spice that, like the clove fires, sent plumes and wreaths of intoxicating, heavy fragrance into the air while the population looked on and were drugged by scent and desperation. For those who might risk the flames and snatch a few hot nuts into their hands, the penalty was death, and so such bonfires raged while the perfumed oil ran in the streets. And invariably in these accounts of pepper and nutmeg and clove were the casualties, the slaves taken on board ships or tossed overboard without provocation, the natives overrun, the lands ravaged. Sandrine wished she had not read the books. She regretted her knowledge of spices and all that they represented.

After a week of avoiding the study, Sandrine returned to it one night after Clare had fallen asleep on a sofa, lights out, curtains drawn, the fire casting its fluid glow on the room that was full of those same colours of fire. Sandrine picked up a book on Irish history and read some of that, distractedly listening for Clare's movements. It seemed so incongruous to her, sitting there, to think that this family whose own country had been swept through many, many times according to the book – this family had been involved in a business that itself swept through other lands. Sandrine frowned at the pages. Why had she started thinking this way? It did her no good, she thought – except that the anger kept her mind alive. She closed the Irish history book and looked around again. But it was too late. When Clare reached for the apple-wood pepper grinder, Sandrine's mind drifted towards mutiny.

．．．

Steam rising from tender green grass newly touched by sunlight: the shimmering, buckling air just beyond the glass. His fingers touch the windowpane, surprised by the rigidity. He had expected water.

That was his experience of the world now. He was peering at it from above the surface of a vast pool, watched it moving, contorting beneath the surface. He was surprised by what he saw. The drift of steam from the grass as the winter morning sun set itself down in long, thin beams, bodies in motion in the space around him, moving to what purpose he knew not, bodies seemingly at rest, reading or eating or sleeping – but Tom had discovered that nothing is ever still. He watched one old lady all afternoon asleep in her chair, her dry lips parted as if for water, and he saw her moving. Her chest, the rib cage haunting her dress, the dress itself, the fabric creasing and uncreasing slowly, everything moved. Even her still lips, they moved, the breath breaking through in slow, steady turns, whispering her hair into wisps. Nothing was still.

After that period in the factory of learning about the spice trade, he had become a man given to patience, given to careful watching. Once his turn had come, he had found this patience to pay off, particularly in Asia where there were rituals to buying and selling. Now he found himself, here towards the end of his life, still slow, tentative, gradual. It was the way of the farmer bred into his bones, the need to persevere, to go along, keep at something, quietly, quietly. He watched the old lady sleeping, and he watched a plant on the windowsill. It was green, and he watched it grow. From day to day it changed and somehow he managed to sit still enough for long enough to see a leaf stretching itself, or a flower crouching in the shade of the curtain before straining itself towards the light.

He never touched the plant. It was too marvellous, too curious, and he was too afraid that if he touched it, it would wither, like his hand. Something had withered his hand, and he thought, vaguely, that if his hand touched the plant it too would distort and look like a Picasso plant and not a plant he would always want to look at, just as his hand was no longer a hand he liked to look at. It was even faintly blue.

Picasso. Picasso was on his mind today, the name, mostly. He'd seen some of the paintings in museums over the years, but that was about all there was to his knowledge. Picasso, he whispered to himself (he didn't want to waken the sleeping old lady, it would give him one less thing to watch should she leave the room). He didn't question why Picasso was in his thoughts, nor how he knew somehow that Picasso had painted, in blue sometimes, and distorted. He had passed the stage of questioning his own mind, and didn't know it.

In the early stages, he did question. If he turned to his daughter when she came in and said, casually, unthinkingly, Hello Queen Elizabeth, his mind suddenly jumped into anxiety – who was that? Why did he refer to his daughter that way? Why could he not remember? He would say not another word then, his mind steeple-chasing while his eyes were still on this image of his daughter as a queen. Dad? he would hear. Dad? Would you like a cup of coffee? Dad? And his eyes would grow with tears behind his spectacles and he would bat her hands away like tennis balls.

It was not like that anymore. When Elizabeth stood before him she was no longer a queen. She was a woman he sensed some connection with, although it was not an instinctive one. He did not see her and feel that she was somehow a part of himself, made up of something he had parted with in lust, love, fear, loneliness, desperate hope. Who knew which night had seen her birth begin?

He watched her as he watched the plant and the old lady, quietly, as part of the new scenery of his over-water life. He noticed her hair that had once reminded him so fondly of his wife's – flat, even, sunned, smooth and soft – growing or becoming shorter, noticed when her nails needed to be cut, indistinctly saw her eyes behind glass through his own eyes behind glass, and thought perhaps he knew her. *Dad* meant nothing to him, but he gradually ceased batting at her hands that attempted to touch him. Her hands on his head were like his own on the windowpane, attempts to see, to live, instead of watching a life.

These were the normal days, the ones of watching, watching, waiting for something to change. Waiting for himself to change, himself to become something that was not what he was now. And this was easy, to sit and wait for himself to become. But there were other days, when he would wake in a fog of memories that drove him to moan and call out names the nurses did not recognise. There were days when he was seized with the desire to go, telling the staff quite distinctly that he had a meeting in Hong Kong and if they were good and called him a car quickly, he would send them a photograph of the bay. Surely they would like that? No? Then a photo of the koala bear from the zoo? All women liked koala bears, his daughter had … He would gather together old magazines, newspapers, sometimes even the doctors' clipboards, prescription forms, and would tuck the lot under his arm, ready for his meeting. He would fret over his lack of a pen and threaten the youngest nurse that if she did not hand over hers at once he would have her fired, warning her that the company would never use her again as a secretary.

On such days the head nurse would come flying down the hallways to the site of the argument and would gently steer him to his meeting. I'll take you, Tom, don't worry, the others are already inside. When she had gotten him into a chair in front of the window, he might ask for a sweetie, like a tired child, or a handful of litchis, would lapse into quiet with the sweet wrapper or with a tissue that he gradually wore away to shreds. But not always. Sometimes he might curl his head towards his knees and let the wracking sobs seize hold of his body, knowing momentarily that it had been a hoax: there was no meeting, there were no more spices, and there was nothing left to do but to wait it out.

Elizabeth's hand on her father's cheek, on his head, a time beyond childhood tugs on the arm that he has submitted to her touch, that she has offered it. Beyond the time on the mini-bus going to Halong Bay, it is the only time she has touched him with affection. It seemed a long time since her face had felt the shock of his whiskers against her cheek. His stubble had now passed the stage of wiry tension, had relaxed into age. She weeps with her fingers in his greying hair and thinks of all of the childhood that lacked such touching.

His hair is softer than she expected, thinning, and the scalp pulses like a newborn's. She senses this pulsing in her hands. He is living, his mind is moving, and he is looking up at her with surprised, glazing green eyes. Her tears are for nothing. There is nothing to weep for, since he is unaware, gazing at her crying or laughing with the same indifferent emptiness in his look which seems always surprised now, because everything lacks for him the context of memory.

When she lets her hands fall back to her own body and his eyes fall away from her, Elizabeth thinks of all of the moments when she might have tried to touch, and pulled or was pushed away. A nurse who comes in to deliver a squirreling of pills squeezes her upper arm consolingly, pulls a tissue from a box with a practised deftness, and shoves it into Elizabeth's hands. Elizabeth watches the nurse, doesn't hear as she repeats phrases and sounds to convince Tom to swallow the now fragmented pills with a slug from a straw full of juice, and she wonders if her father too had such memories: the memories of non-touch, almost touching, wanting to touch. It is impossible to ask those questions now. Elizabeth had thought it a stereotype. The things left unsaid.

Elizabeth remembered a friend telling her that she had stared into the coffin of her own mother and thought then of all of the silences of their lives together, at the breakfast table, in the car. At the time, Elizabeth had not understood, but now, watching the shade of her father, his body ebbing the way of his mind, she felt distinctly that her own situation was worse. This prolonged silence, having her father's physical presence there still, the possibility of her saying the unsaid and having him stare blankly at her, she felt these things as a violence to her thoughts. Her friend had had to reconcile herself to the impossibility of imparting words only once, but she had to reconcile herself to this impossibility daily.

And it was happening not only with her father, but with her mother as well, and that relationship was more volatile, more dangerous, somehow. With that teenaged trip to Halong Bay, she had achieved a sense of almost adult-like camaraderie with her father. In those hours of overheated containment in a bus that wended its way through the landscape like a zipper, her father had, she felt, accepted that she would become an adult and needed to establish some self beyond the one that was itself contained and overheated in Vietnam.

The same sort of shift had never happened with Clare, except in the last weeks in the hotel before she'd left for college and the weeks that followed in Ireland, and that was only because Elizabeth knew she was about to get away. When Elizabeth thought of her mother, tried to feel the warmth that her ex-husband had spoken of in his family, she failed. She didn't have cosy memories of baking smells or birthday cakes with pronouncements hand-scrawled in sugary ridges as Ciaran did. Clare had been a good mother, Elizabeth couldn't say that she hadn't been, but she had been a formal mother. She had taken on the shape of motherhood without wanting to fill it. And Elizabeth, as an adult now, couldn't blame her for this. She was certain that millions of women had been forced into motherhood by chance and constructs and had shadowed their way through the process with a sense of despair, even if – most of the time – they were comforted by love of their children.

To offset the lack of the memories of stereotypes, Elizabeth tried to retrieve different memories of her mother. What appeared in her memory was the time they had witnessed the monsoon, sitting and standing apart on the porch of a strange house in silence. Elizabeth thought now that her mother's standing there was appropriate, the exact symbolic act of Clare's way of mothering: standing in the background, removed, but there. And this was a comforting idea, to think that even if she recalled a cool kind of removal, still Clare was there. And anyway she could not say that her mother was cold, exactly. Elizabeth remembered too that Clare had shed tears each time she departed from Tom, and daily saw her mother's bewildered grief at the separation from her husband – she was not cold.

Perhaps, Elizabeth thought, Clare's heart had been too taken up by her husband, and for Elizabeth this was somehow comforting instead of debilitating or hurtful. It meant that she could look at her mother and feel a certain sense of understanding, since she herself imagined such love to be an ideal, one that had failed in her own life and one that she felt unhopeful of recovering. Clare had loved to excess this man, Tom, who had waved his way into her life from across a street.

c c c

Elizabeth couldn't tell whether or not it was raining. The grey air beyond her windows seemed to move and tremble. That grey trembling was part of her life now. It was in the air beyond her office, in the office itself, the hallways. Her days felt grey and were marked by corridors of cars that lead from one zone of her life to another: the corridor between here and home, home and her parents', here and her parents', and the more recent traces to the nursing home, the hospital, the doctors' offices. She pictured it from the air, sky down, this zigzagging car-light-streaked passage of time and place, pictured how her corridors crossed so many others, their paths all lines and circles and repetition.

And there was that other life she had just glimpsed in an email from an old friend whom she'd written that her dad was unwell, the lines she had never imagined before. On several continents, they traced their lives' lines with exhaust fumes, lost pennies, receipts, the occasional flicked cigarette butt – that was if Jennie still smoked; everyone in America seemed to have quit. They left these traces, these phosphorescent glows of themselves in the world all the time. Jennie's life had continued as hers had, but Elizabeth had not thought of her in a long time.

This was odd, really, because for so long all she had wanted was to return to that world. To be American, to call herself something. Irish had always seemed funny. When she had learned to think of what she was at all, as a child, she had been living in America. On St Patrick's Day for school her mother had given her dozens of postcards from Ireland (all of places Elizabeth had never been) and tourist posters her sister Fidelma had sent over from the travel agency a friend of hers ran. Elizabeth learned about the Doors of Dublin, picked her favourites among the reds and blues and greens with bronze gold knockers. She learned about the grey squares of Blarney Castle, which frightened her unspeakably and gave her nightmares about hanging upside-down and kissing wet cold stone that not just kissed but sucked back. She learned vaguely the names of Irish counties and knew which ones her parents were from. On the postcards were puffy sheep and donkeys with slow, sad eyes and tumbling ruins of cottages trying to grow into the shape of houses in the middle of gorse and inexplicably purple heather.

She carried the posters through the school hallways awkwardly, in a plastic tube that boys with names like Ted and Chad snatched to sword-fight with, just like Luke Skywalker. At show-and-tell she vaguely answered questions about Ireland: it was an island; people spoke Irish there, and English; people were farmers, but not all of them, they did other things too, like her daddy.

Other students in the class had Irish ancestry and for them Elizabeth's mother had given her tiny clip-on metal green shamrocks rimmed with gold paint that made the others so jealous that the following year Elizabeth had been armed with thirty instead of ten, all purchased by her Dublin aunt with her mother's money, and thirty small children who all called themselves American but whose parents or grandparents or great-grandparents were from Russia or China or Germany or Mexico or Ireland all wore shamrocks on their t-shirts for the day. For the teacher, there was a doll's bouquet of real, live shamrock carefully padded round and round with wet Bounty paper towels and bought from the balefuls flown in from Shannon, in part to fill a Waterford bowl for the President, then Carter.

Elizabeth's idea of Ireland was constructed out of those St Patrick's Days, the photos of too-green grass and tumultuous seas and cottages and animals she never remembered having seen, despite pictures of her as a baby on her uncle Alan's farm with white splotches of sheep in the corners of the photos.

And because the first teacher had been so gentle and kind with her as she stood so small and all of six at the blackboard, Elizabeth initially felt a kind of pride for the homeland she didn't have any familiarity with. It was something she knew that her friends didn't, something special about her. But the photos on the John Hinde postcards were very different from the ones in her parents' albums, the ones that were stacked heavily on the bottom of the trolley that held the TV.

Those had pictures of weddings, including her parents', outside grey churches and the men wore tall black hats like Abraham Lincoln and the women wore hats that were all different shapes and different colours, even though you couldn't tell that from the black and white photos. You only knew because your mother or father told you so. There were other pictures of people on pebble beaches and of farm buildings stuffed to the gills with hay, a couple that her dad had told her were his brother Alan and sister-in-law Mary waving at the camera from beside a gate beyond which was grass and hill, but not green. Grey and shades of grey.

It was all black and white, and no matter how many times Elizabeth asked and was told what colour the hats and dresses and scarves and shoes had been, Ireland in her mind stayed black and white and grainy and sometimes even out of focus. Still it was something kind of nice, Ireland, something that was in their house not only in the photo albums but in the way her dad talked sometimes and said something like 'sweet Jerusalem' that no one else's parents said. 'Sweet Jerusalem' was also part of Ireland. There were also some books on Ireland, big, thicker-than-pancakes history books, and even though Elizabeth thought them too big for her yet, they were already hers too, because they were Irish and so was she.

But at the end of that first year in American school, the end of the first grade, they had a history lesson on how America had become independent. This meant how America came to be America, or how it was born, the teacher said. They'd all been learning about the colonies for a month or so, and Elizabeth had been very taken by the Indians and people like William Penn, whom her history book showed strolling down the unpaved streets of Philadelphia with loaves of bread under his arms. Then there'd been Benjamin Franklin and they'd all drawn pictures of him with his keyed kite and understood that lightening was dangerous and this was why we didn't put our fingers into plugs or bring a radio near the bath.

The teacher had saved up the lesson on independence until the last week of school because the Fourth of July was only two weeks later. For Elizabeth it had been a relief to finally know what the Fourth of July was for, since her friends had been talking about what they would be doing and, when they asked her, she had to shuck her shoulders and put out her small palms in imitation of adults' helpless gestures, and say that she didn't know.

St Patrick's Day began to pale by comparison. As Elizabeth walked up the driveway after the school bus pulled away, she was almost in tears. Their housekeeper, Gina, provided milk and the usually forbidden Oreos (Clare didn't like that they turned Elizabeth's teeth and tongue black) and the promise that she'd inspect Elizabeth's teeth after brushing and heard the whole story.

You have fireworks, Gina, Elizabeth said seriously, twisting an Oreo apart and eating the sugary cream off one biscuit, and we have *shamrocks*. We have those old songs my dad sings that are sad and about creepy things like dying people, and postcards of cows and stuff (here Elizabeth's notion of St Patrick's Day ran into her general notions of Ireland) and you have 'I'm a Yankee Doodle Dandy' (which the class had learned at the end of the day). Elizabeth gloomily put an entire cookie into her mouth and didn't even care if her mother appeared and saw.

But sugar, you live here now, and you can be American if you want to be, Gina said. That's what this country's all about. Like what the Statue says, what my papa always said to me: 'Give me your huddled masses, your poor ... ' Elizabeth was confused. You go see the fireworks and I'll get you a little flag and you drink lemonade with your friends and you'll be American, honey, if that's what you want to be.

I guess, Elizabeth sighed, but she did feel better at the prospect of a little twirling flag and forgot to brush her teeth. And Fourth of July had been absolutely magical. There was a little parade that went down the main street and girls with batons that they flung up towards the sky and caught again and then turned into spinning silver flowers. When the band marched by where Elizabeth and her parents stood, one of the drummers who knew her dad winked at her and did a special twirl of his hand and an extra thum-thum-ti-thum rose from the drum skin. Clare gave in and bought her a pink cotton candy cloud on a paper stick and Elizabeth's flag from Gina made a brilliant noise in the breeze and Tom barbequed chicken in the backyard later on when the parade was over. When she went to bed that night, her flag under her pillow, Elizabeth felt happier than she had even at Christmas.

ᴖ ᴖ ᴖ

As she left her office building and walked to her car, facing the corridor to home, Elizabeth watched an elderly man (surely even older than her father) in one of those ubiquitous uniforms, near to that of a garda's but without the same mark of officialdom, not so bronzed with trim or buttons. He was crossing the expanses of neat grass, weaving his way between the flowerbeds of Stephen's Green in the rain. She almost stopped. It was raining and he was walking slowly. He stopped before she did, though, and in the distance she saw him lowering his arm slowly to the ground. His fingers finally fastened on a bit of silvery paper and he straightened. He turned and wove his way back, close to her path, gave a slight saluting gesture and smiled, the plastic sweet wrapper in his arthritic fingers, the rain beginning to stream over the jutting balcony of his hat. She felt herself smile wanly. Perhaps if her father had had something to do, some small sense of responsibility, the doctors' words might never have been uttered, the nursing home might never have presented itself. If he'd continued exporting pepper and remained in Vietnam, refused the familial – or was it national? – sentiment that ultimately brought him back to Ireland. In her car, she tried to imagine her father in a uniform picking up litter or living out his final years in Hanoi and knew that it was impossible to think this way, to imagine alternative worlds for herself any longer.

It had become similarly impossible to imagine herself in America. The projections of childhood and the ideal of belonging had diminished. Not as soon as she had returned for university, not within the first year or two when she had relished her freedom and had been overwhelmed by the newness of it all and overtaken by the desire for various lovers, but slowly, after that, the realisation had broken that she was not American, would never be, didn't wish to be – that it was a failed experiment. She knew more of Vietnam now than Connecticut, more of Ireland than Vietnam.

She drove slowly. It was raining now, properly. The sweep of all of the red brake lights through the tearing windscreen was like stilled fireworks, the colour shattered and reflecting in the droplets. Elizabeth became Irish slowly, without noticing. One evening, in a restaurant with her parents and her boyfriend, Ciaran, shortly after her return, she ordered a pasta dish with sun-dried tomatoes. Ciaran roared laughing, for suddenly, without being aware of it, she had shortened the vowel, softened it. Other words followed: *basil*, *garage* – vowels swelling and accents shifting. And then there was the gradual accumulation over a period of months of new words. I'm grand, she heard herself saying to Ciaran's mother's offer of more tea. The word 'sure' began to creep into the starts of some of her sentences; she bought a *biscuit* tin and stopped buying cookies; she started calling Swiss cheese Emmental. And with the new vocabulary came a new life of petrol and shops and PRSI numbers and gardaí. And the old life, of subways and markets and social security numbers and cops gradually faded from her life.

She had met Ciaran in a pub and almost right away moved in with him into a flat he shared with a Pakistani surgeon who was about to abandon his Armani suits and his Irish nurse girlfriend to return home to be married. Their shared coffee table was stacked with manuals for different surgical procedures, most of them cosmetic. The first few days, after both the surgeon and Ciaran had fled into the droning traffic, Elizabeth would curl up on the couch and pore over them, aghast at the photographs of peeled-back skin, the revelation of messy bone and the rivers of veins, arteries, tendons, all alive with colour. Only when the phone rang or the light changed in the small room did she drag herself away to the newspapers, the online job sites, looking for work.

And the work came surprisingly quickly, just as the feelings for Ciaran had, because it was that time in Ireland when the Friday *Irish Times* was fat with job prospects, when every shop seemed to advertise work on hand-written signs in windows, when every affair seemed to begin with a grand explosion of passion that would never diminish. Within two months she too was throwing herself into the debacle of Dublin rush hour, frantically running after lumbering buses while digging in pockets for exact change, fumbling with the heavy, unfamiliar coins.

She hated Ireland every morning when the bus failed to stop, or failed to turn up, or when she was jammed up against a group of teenaged boys in misleadingly respectable school uniforms calling passing men faggots out of the rain-steamed windows, or sniggering about an African woman's old-fashioned dress or amusing themselves by changing the ringtones on their mobile phones for twenty minutes. Everybody they discussed was a fucking eejit or a git or an arsehole or a right cunt. Elizabeth would grind her teeth until her jaw hurt and sometimes, early on, would ask them to lower their voices, to stop shouting obscenities at people or she'd call the police (this never had any effect) or to turn off their bloody phones: this was a public space and people were entitled to a bit of quiet. But her still American accent just made them laugh even more and garnered startled looks from other passengers who threw themselves into Maeve Binchy and June Considine and Deirdre Purcell, or rubbed viewing holes in the steam on the windows and stared disconsolately at the rain.

Within a few months Elizabeth found herself just as quiet as those other people, and the bus rides became a kind of ride through teenage anarchy, breaking or broken male voices carouselling around the upper level of the bus, female voices twanging raucously and graphically. And like everyone else, Elizabeth breathed out when the bus driver (God help him, Elizabeth often thought, stuck with them day in and day out) lurched to a stop. Twenty, thirty of them, their own little mob, all traipsed down the aisles with enormous bags jammed full of who knows what (it couldn't possibly be books, Elizabeth told Ciaran viciously) and scarred with permanent markers – Amy loves Neil, Robbie 4 Ever, Slipknot, Fuck Off My Bag!, Marilyn Manson – and clumped down the three steps in impossibly platformed black shoes and hundred pound runners. As the bus pulled away and everyone shuffled in their seats and glanced up from their paperbacks, Elizabeth gazed after them, standing there in their uniforms. These uniforms puzzled her immensely, because they flattened out the possibility of identifying the kids as one type or another. Ultimately, Elizabeth realised, everyone with white skin looked the same to her. They all seemed to wear the same clothes, to speak with the same accents.

It had been in telling her parents of a huge row she had had with Ciaran about skin colour – the last straw as it turned out – that she had first noticed her dad's decline. Ciaran had been reading the paper and telling her that he really did think they had to do something in Ireland about all the immigrants coming in. Jesus Christ, Ciaran, Elizabeth had exploded. Seriously? The row had lasted for hours, evolving from her irritation and feeling of shame at his racism to his fatigue with her sense of world citizenship until eventually they got to the crux of things: the no-baby-on-the-horizon fact, the infertility, and the falling-apart marriage.

Elizabeth, feeling it was too late to arrive at a friend's, had fled to her parents' house and found them sitting at the table sipping coffee and eating biscuits. She told them everything. Tom had looked up after listening gravely and said, I'll fire the bastard, Elizabeth. He won't work for me anymore. Clare had laughed, that's one way to put it, Tom, but Elizabeth can't *fire* him. Of course Elizabeth can't fire him, Tom returned, sure she's only a child and I wouldn't ask her to take care of business.

Elizabeth had been startled out of her grief and sat staring at her father, realising that something was changing, that his mind had begun floating free.

c c c

Sandrine stares at other Africans when she sees them. They do not speak. They exchange glances on the bus, on shopping queues, in the road. Sometimes there is a slight nod or a tiny sign, imperceptible almost, a flutter of a smile. Sometimes she wants to return to her other language, tempted by a face in the road. As they pass, Sandrine wonders where they are from, if she cannot guess, wonders what their experience of Ireland has been so far.

Some of them are refugees, others are the asylum seekers so scorned. They shop in Aldi, travel together in an aimless manner, hoping for the refuge that is not a given, seeking place. Many are neither refugees nor asylum seekers. They are like her, having come to attend school, to go to university – quite a lot of nurses and doctors in training – or to simply make a better life. On occasion they are pregnant, the women's bellies bulging with their soon-to-be Irish daughters, their European sons. There are already many small children in second-hand prams with rust diseasing the chrome handlebars, their hair combed into tight pigtails with brightly coloured bobbles from Penney's, others toddling down windy roads reaching their arms overhead to hold their father's warm hands.

It is, when she thinks of it, the women who look hopeful. It is their bellies, after all, that contain the promise of belonging. The men are thin, their eyes are thin on hope, full of a strong suspicion. They hold their children's hands and lead them without knowing where they themselves are headed. Sandrine sees them in banks and post offices on occasion, their frustration with the language, with the mores that are so different to what they have known.

The men sometimes shout at a bank teller who will not cash a cheque, who cannot open an account with the identification shown, will not bend the rule that requires electrical, gas, phone bills as proof of address. I am living in a residence for asylum seekers, she hears a Nigerian shout one afternoon when she is lodging her own cheque, how am I supposed to have a bill for electricity? The woman ensconced behind the bullet-proof glass is immune to such questions. She wields the power of regulation. You tell me, how?

The women do not shout. Their faces garner distress in such situations, or they might walk quietly out, steering a pram or a child through a door that most often is not opened for them and which might, in fact, be deliberately closed in their faces. Sandrine finds herself opening doors all the time now in such instances, even leaving the queue, losing her place if necessary, just to show humanity. And when she returns to the queue, it is with the sensation of being watched now by the Irish around her. They watch to see if she too will be turned away, fumble her words, struggle with the door.

There are many who are outside of all of the categories of expectations. They have qualifications useful to the Irish economy, they are nurses, radiologists, teachers, doctors or professors. They appear the loneliest, the ones who gave themselves up to come here. They have bank accounts and homes and have lived here for decades, some of them, have children whose voices are traced through with local accents and who have never known Africa except on Sky or National Geographic. And they are anxious to seem separate from the others, from the refugees and asylum seekers, bogus or otherwise. They sense the growing hostility in the country and are afraid. They do not open doors either but check their wallets distractedly, thumb their mobiles for messages.

And Sandrine, with her bank account and job and swelling stomach and false certificates of attendance and the uncertainties of the future, does not know to which group she belongs.

She does know that it doesn't matter how she perceives herself to fit in. What she feels, how she might work to become part of this new society, it makes no difference. Sandrine has been spat and cursed at, has peered with shock into women's faces as they have sneered at hers – she expected better of women, and has been disappointed. At moments the desire to commiserate with another black Zimbabwean is overwhelming. She knows from the news that instances of assault are on the rise, the country is increasingly angry about *non-nationals* and there is a referendum coming up that scares the life out of her.

It affects other people who have moved here, too, and so she stares at anyone she suspects is an immigrant. Filipinos who have been recruited to staff the hospital wards with nurses, who bustle past her in their uniforms on the way to work. Russians, cheek-bones protruding, the pale skin around their eyes ringed darkly. Romanian women (where are the men? Sandrine wonders) who sit on the pavement unsuccessfully hawking copies of *The Big Issue*. When Sandrine buys herself a copy for the first time, she finds herself staring downwards into the face of a child who has climbed into the folds and lap of his mother's teepee-shaped skirt, which is red with yellow and blue and white embroidery hemmed with black. He is about her son's age, and has an adult look of fatigue, has pulled the hood of a cheap, sweatshop-produced fleece around his head so tightly that all she can see are swimming brown eyes, the tip of a red nose, pale lips. The woman thanks her, and every time she sees the women with their bundles of children tied to their breasts and bellies, perched on walls or leaned against bins or, like the first time, pushed against the ell of a path and building, Sandrine looks to see if it is that child, the first one – and it never is.

What shocks Sandrine about Ireland is how the newspapers and the television reports would have her believe that *non-nationals* in the country are all alike: Filipino nurses robbing jobs from Irish ones, Romanians selling the *Big Issue* because they all must be homeless dole-grabbers, Nigerians committing crimes. The news ignores altogether all of the *non-nationals* who are, actually, living and working and raising Irish children: Filipinos, Romanians, Russians who have been here for a generation now, whose children converse in English and Irish outside the school gates – whose children are *Irish*. She has seen this in Zim, the way Mugabe has increasingly argued that only certain people may be considered true Zimbaweans, has encouraged violence between those of different ethnicities. The media coverage in Ireland of foreigners seems similarly merely to stir anger.

Now there are also Chinese people around Sandycove and Dun Laoghaire. In some ways Sandrine thinks that in a superficial way the Chinese are luckier than any of the Africans, the Russians or Romanians, because people here seem to like their food and tolerate their presence better as a result. There are Chinese restaurants and takeaways everywhere. (And many Indian takeaways, but not so many Indians, Sandrine notices.) And hundreds of Chinese people seem to put their hope into the promise of a Chinese restaurant of their own some day, complete with goldfish in a wall tank, starched white tablecloths, wooden chopsticks that would go largely unused, a gold-painted Buddha to mark the entranceway.

She talked to one middle-aged Chinese man on the queue at the post office in the first few weeks after she'd arrived, when he boldly asked her where she was from, practicing his English. That is what he wanted, what he said his friends wanted, to own a restaurant. His friends and he were crowded into a flat, saving money to send home or to return on a glorious holiday to their left-behind families. One day, in a few years, the Chinese man told Sandrine, he would send for all of his family, and his father would cook in his restaurant and they would eat duck every day. Sandrine nodded, thinking of her own imagined returns home, the slaughtering of a goat, the warm nuggets of sadza in her fingers, the wilted greens of muboora, rape, and the sweet tang of naartjies, the juice running down Tobias's chin.

Being Asian or African here is a sign, she thinks. Others, she sees, do not realise this. To many Irish it is a sign of danger, a sign that their culture is changing, evaporating, even. As a result Sandrine seeks out the other signs, other black and brown and yellow faces. They may not speak, but that in itself is a sign, she tells herself, of a quiet resistance, since they would have to speak in a language not necessarily their own, the language of their adopted, if temporary, homeland.

In the house, at the place she now calls home, Sandrine tries to stop thinking about these things. She tries hard, conscientiously, to be. To be with Clare, to be herself, to forget about being black, using pepper, holding a door, to forget her longing for simple white maize. Clare is forgetting, and so this makes it harder for Sandrine to forget. Someone must remember, and it must be her, for now. But still she tries, sitting with Clare in the mornings that are so dark now.

Clare has found a new occupation. The fine wool, spare balls of which she accumulated to repair carpets and rugs if they frayed, winds around her fingers in loops and strands in a knitting of the mind. The ball at her feet diminishes, occasionally startled into the air as her fingers tweak at it. And while it diminishes, shrinks and dances on the carpet, the other ball, the new one, takes shape in her hands, becoming something firm and real that Clare can hold on to.

What kind of place would the world be, she suddenly asks Sandrine, if we couldn't laugh? Clare grips the wool between her palms and smiles faintly. Sandrine does not say that she wishes she could laugh at the absurdity of the ball of wool being unwound and rewound into another, but cannot. It is too solemn an absurdity. Sandrine thinks of the stupidity and ignorance of the young white women who had looked down their noses at her earlier in the week when she walked to the shop for milk, and she says to Clare, yes, it is important to laugh, to realise the madness of the world. She says it unsmilingly, though.

If she were able to laugh, it might bring Clare perilously near memory. Clare has been sitting there for an hour or more after breakfast, which, because her hours are so irregular, occurs at no particular time of the day now, winding wool and awaiting Elizabeth's arrival. Elizabeth will take her to Tom, to what she persists in believing is the hospital. The television is off, but she gazes at it anyway – her distant reflection hidden from her among the objects in the room – and occasionally chats while Sandrine wipes tabletops and Buddhas with a damp cloth.

I was talking to Michael Collins, she informs Sandrine, suddenly again – all conversation is now sudden. Do you know him?

No, Sandrine tells her, although this is not true. She has been reading a biography of his life, and Clare has probably seen it lying on the table, likely spurred to some faint memory that now rears into life, shapes itself in the front rooms of her mind.

Well, she says, I was talking to him. My mother would do anything for my father, she continues, and my father would do anything for Mick Collins. And that was the way it was, and the way they had to get on with things.

Is your coffee gone cold? Sandrine asks her. Clare, would you like a hot cup of coffee? I can make it fresh in the press from Vietnam.

What I need is to find Mick. I keep telling everyone and no one helps me. Daddy told me he'd be back to see us. Clare laughs, then frowns.

Then he must be on his way, Sandrine says, reshelving some books whose spines were hidden away, the leaves yellowing in the air.

Yes, Clare murmurs, yes, and settles into another silence during which her lips part and her eyes pool.

Sandrine does not tell her husband when she manages to write that it is getting harder to talk with Clare, harder to weave the logic of language. After these weeks that have moved autumn into winter, Sandrine can no longer idly chat, but feels instead the oppression of the changes taking place in Clare's mind. Sandrine's own knowledge – that Tom is dying, that he is on a drip, unable to speak, to eat – is also oppressive because she cannot share it with Clare. Despite her daily visits to the home, despite Elizabeth's daily attempts to ready her, Clare speaks of Michael Collins, but only rarely of the anguish Sandrine senses she must feel. So while Clare speaks Sandrine busies herself with dusting the relics of Clare's past with Tom, which is, in a funny way, Sandrine supposes, just what Clare is doing.

How do you describe the private anguish of the period before grief, particularly when it is an anguish that ebbs between forget-fulness and realisation? Clare's knowledge of Tom's state shapes itself into an uneven spiral of memory that has collapsed time. She is both getting married and is married, has finished working for the fabric importer, and speaks of her parents as a child and as an adult. There is no linearity. Time is like the massive knots of wool that pool around her feet, unstraightened, without aim. Time feels like a trick, a riddle that she can no longer solve. Through the gauzy confusion a few things remain, Tom prime among them.

When Clare believes Sandrine to be out of earshot and begins talking to Tom while winding her wool, Sandrine is ashamed. She is an eavesdropper on the most private of moments. Tom, Clare says, her fingers paused in the web of beige threads, sure you're still my favourite, even if you aren't up to much these days. You'd better be on the mend soon, she says stoutly, beginning to wind wool again. And then – but Tom, please God you'll be home soon, because I don't know where I am any longer and there's something about the weather and the light that is full of death and you know I always said I wouldn't want to live if you died. We should never have left Vietnam, Tom, we should never have left. I didn't know that then, Tom, did you? I thought it would be okay, but it wasn't. It wasn't. We left here for a reason, didn't we? We should have stayed in Vietnam. At that, the wool is in her lap and curling like snakes around her fingers, and she begins, quietly, to weep, saying only to herself, *Vietnam, Tom, Vietnam.*

Sandrine attempts to hold her; it is no good. She will not be comforted. She waves Sandrine's arms and hands away and, still weeping, climbs the stairs, the wool in a tangle behind her, caught on a button, a finger, catching under doors. Sandrine is left in the darkening light of a gathering rainstorm. She herself is sick of rain, weary of dusting to keep busy, full of grief for Clare, spilling over with trouble about her child. Her children. After a feeble thump of a door, Clare is silent upstairs. Sandrine sits down.

It rains. I am sitting in the glass conservatory that juts into the garden. Everything is wet and green. There is no sign of the neighbour's marmalade cat, who sneaks in here sometimes when it is dry, to curl up in a bed of heather and blink lazily at the few birds. But it is too wet for the cat, and too wet for me. I, like the cat next door, sit by a streaming window and watch the weather.

I don't know if you have ever seen rain like this, Tobias. It is unlike our storms, which are sudden, fierce, with the lick of lightening behind them. This rain is continuous, cold and thorough and hard. It pelts the glass above me like your hands on your painted drum in early morning.

Your letter gladdened me. Your handwriting is so neat and smooth, like the nape of a neck. I am glad that you continue to play cricket, and that you have so much enjoyment in your cousins' company. It is wonderful that you enjoy school, and get on with your father. He is a good man.

Here Sandrine breaks off and stares out of the window. Nothing is happening. The rain continues to slice air and needle the panes of glass. She thinks of her husband, the good man who cares for their child. Staring through the rain, with the awareness that, while she wrote, Clare sleeps upstairs as much separated from her own husband, Sandrine can't go on. She lets the pen slide from her fingers until it rests on the rug laid over the wood, pointed towards the glassy shimmer of water on the windowpane. There is no difference, really, except that she still has memory of the separation. Clare's remembrance has faltered into a constant stalling, Tom is left with only the tracings of a life outside his private mind. And her own husband's? How on earth did he see her, now? How did he cope with the distance, the gap that was now their marriage?

ᴄ ᴄ ᴄ

The medicines were no longer working. This was clear to Elizabeth when she gazed at her father in his wheelchair. There were no more walks in the morning on the strong young arms of nurses, only the lift from bed to chair and then from chair to bed. The staff spoke to him in the same cheerful manner, although he replied less, only occasionally gathering his eyes into a focus. He no longer looked up when she came in, alone or with her mother. And she was beginning, more and more, to come alone.

There was nothing for her to do in his room. The floors were spotless and his clothes always clean and even ironed, the few pictures dusted, the plants watered. There was nothing here of the horror stories of nursing homes. It was expensive, draining away her parents' lifesavings at an astonishingly hungry pace, but what did she mind? Tom himself was always clean, and often his socks matched his shirt. A thick fleece might be zipped over the slight, shrinking bubble of his belly. Someone even continued to use his treasured razor blade, usually locked away like a valued trophy in a drawer, to scrape the soft, thin hair from his chin every few days. So Elizabeth could do nothing of use, and her visits became a sort of meditation on family and their family and all that had happened to him, to her mother, to her.

She would come in, sometimes with a book, and she would greet him, sometimes only with the resting of her fingertips on his shoulder that announced its bones now, and sit down opposite him in a chair near the window. When she had nothing to say for too long, she would begin to tell Tom one of his stories, the only one among his favourites that did not involve spices, the one about the Armenian flag. It was one of Elizabeth's favourite stories as well. She had loved when, at some function that took place during the day time (if it was night she was not usually allowed attend), she would hear her father's voice begin. Did you hear about the Russians and the Armenian flag? The listener would shake his head and smile in advance. At this point her father would seek his cigarettes in his pockets and, with a match, light one. This story was, for him, worth the using up of his daily ration of one cigarette before dinner.

The Armenian flag, he'd begin, has on it an image of Mount Ararat, which the Armenians regard as a symbol of their homeland. Mount Ararat isn't in Armenia, though, since the Turks have it on their side of the pitch. So the Turks took it into their heads to complain to the Soviets that Armenia was using a symbol of the Turkish homeland on their regional flag and should be stopped. And the Soviet thought this complaint over and sat in silence at his desk. The Turks said nothing and felt satisfied. The Armenians said nothing and felt uncomfortable – they didn't even have a bloody homeland and were now going to lose their flag as well as everything else. And then the official stands up and walks to the window. It's night, and he stares out at the sky. Finally he says, still facing the window, I seem to remember that the Turkish flag has a moon on it. Yes, the Turkish ambassador says, puzzled. Well, says the Soviet, you don't own that either.

Then her father would replace the cigarette between his lips and twitch his eyebrows like Groucho Marx and the listener would roar with laughter.

Elizabeth, child that she was, loved the story simply because she knew that no one could own the moon. The first time she'd heard it – overheard it – she hadn't known what Mount Ararat was, but she knew the moon, and that was enough. Now that she was an adult, she had learned to appreciate the story differently, and she told it to Tom, trying hard to replicate the gestures that had belonged to the tale when he had told it. But he didn't react. Maybe she told it badly. Or maybe he'd heard it one too many times. Then she would try some of his spice stories, reminding him of how funny she'd found it as a child when he'd told her that the great Ramses II was buried in his decadent tomb with peppercorns up his nose. Or about how Columbus had been given a coat of arms that had nutmeg on it because it was so valuable to Ferdinand and Isabella. She even went to the library and found the passage in Herodotus's *Histories* about how the Arabs acquired cinnamon:

> *They cannot say where it comes from and where in the world it grows (except that some of them use as an argument from probability to claim that it grows in the parts where Dionysus was brought up). But they say that the sticks which the Phoenicians have taught us to call 'cinnamon' are carried by large birds to their nests, which are built of mud plastered onto crags on sheer mountainsides, where no man can climb. Under these circumstances, the Arabians have come up with the following clever procedure. They cut up the bodies of dead yoke animals such as oxen and donkeys into very large pieces and take them there; then they dump the joints near the nests and withdraw to a safe distance. The birds fly down and carry the pieces of meat back up to their nests – but the joints are too heavy for the nests. The*

nests break and fall to the ground, where the Arabians come and
get what they came for. That is how cinnamon is collected in
that part of Arabia, and from there it is sent all over the world.

But he did not react to these tales of his either, or to his favourite names, grains of paradise, zedoary, spikenard, malabathron and the spice it was said that Nero had made extinct with his greed for it, silphium of Cyrene. And so, like her father, she would gaze out of the nursing home window at the changing seasons witnessed in the sea and in the small flowerbeds of the courtyard. The flowers sank down and became a shrubbery of evergreens, and then remained like that until the deep frosts of winter came and killed one or two plants; then there was a bald brown patch of frozen earth, quickly filled.

One afternoon she watched as a gardener dug out one of the frost-snatched shrubs, a small heather like those in her mother's Irish sea-garden, so unlike the potted orchids that ranged Clare's windows in Hanoi. Its fronds withered, brown and spidery, the heather rested on the gardener's fork while he replaced it with another, larger, healthier one.

That is just like us, Dad, she said quietly. He said nothing. He too was staring out of the window. There's an empty room down the hall, she continued, dreamily. And someone else will come and bring their parent in, unpack clothes and photos and bring a flowering plant for the windowsill, and feel their life cracking apart because they have to leave that parent there in the room and go away. And then the room will not be vacant; it will be full of the forgotten memories of someone else. And if a memory is forgotten, how can it be a memory any longer, Dad? You don't remember and so you have no memories, nothing at all. So there is no need for a child to feel that terrible cracking apart, because there is nothing remembered. And really it is the child that needs the room and the flowering plant and the silence of the window to stare through.

Elizabeth turned to her father, whose head was lolling towards his chest. In his right hand he clutched, tightly, a bit of his shirttail.

I don't think I can come any more, she said.

And she told him this each time she came.

· · ·

I have lived with Clare for eleven weeks now. It has been almost twelve weeks that I have been here. Tom has been gone from the house for six weeks, it has been eighty-four days since I have seen my son. I am fourteen weeks pregnant.

Sandrine tells herself such things each morning, because she is beginning to fear that she too will lose her capacity to remember. Clare does not remember to eat, she does not remember to go to bed. She remembers only that she has parents (even if she does not recall that they are long dead), a husband in hospital, a daughter who puzzles her, for Elizabeth too is drifting out of the core of memories necessary to Clare's survival. And she remembers Vietnam. Everything else has been swept away as inconsequential. There has been a swift and sudden cleaning away of the mind, a reduction of her experience to the most essential things only. If she spent half a year in an utter depression watching from a clouded window the rains driving off the Irish Sea, desperate to get back to the States, she does not know this now. If she wanted, once, nothing more but to remain in a quiet bed with Tom and kiss his eyes, his lips, his earlobes, consume him with want, this, too, has been forgotten, swept aside by something more powerful even than the love that had determined the facts of much of her life. Clare has forgotten, she no longer forgets.

Sandrine watches this. She sees Clare drifting as if to sleep, making her way to another realm of consciousness, literally losing herself, leaving off watches, rings, a once beloved necklace, shoes, socks. One morning, Sandrine knew, Clare will arrive down the stairs with nothing of the externalities of herself. She will stand at the bottom of the shallow stairs on one of her own carpets and her skin will tense against the cold it will be subjected to. Naked, Clare's breasts will collapse under their own slight weight, onto a rib cage that takes on the shape of that phrase, eerily delicate. Her spine will be marked by the sharp ridges of bone, her skin will seem too softly thin to cover the undulations of ribs, too papery for the experience of nudity, the potential dangers of a body bruising against doorways and furniture. And yet, Sandrine knows, this will happen. As Tom shed his clothes like a child in protest, so too will his wife. It will be another step towards something, a sign of a further change wrought in the caverns of Clare's mind.

But Sandrine is also changing. Her body begins to forget its old shape, and to remember another. The child begins to show herself, minutely, with a push outwards into the world, making space for herself already. Sandrine hides her underneath one of the two thick Irish sweaters that Elizabeth presented her with as a Christmas gift from the family, and lets her out only in the evening, in bed. There, lying on her side in the wintry dark, Sandrine speaks quietly to her. Even this early in the pregnancy, she is longing for extra time, knowing that there is too much at stake – she needs another term of pregnancy, another nine months, another year.

Sandrine thought that once she had settled in she would make telephone calls to find out what to do about her child and how to make sure that she would not be deported. She had these thoughts back at Deirdre's house when she had found out that she would have a job, with money and a place to live. For the few days Sandrine remained there before moving in with Clare and Tom, she had walked the quiet country roads that spun like a broken web from Deirdre's home and felt quietly sure that everything would be alright. She would be happy here, her daughter would come and she herself would be allowed to stay. In not too long a time, George would arrive with their son and they would be a family in Ireland.

When she'd first arrived, the leaves of beech hedging had been golden with the gathered and stored sunlight of the year, edging to orange. In some moments Sandrine thought she had never seen anything so beautiful as the colours that littered the roads, the wild ash trees berried with taunting red and the fallen acorns that rolled and clattered on the road in the wind. All of the indications after one week were good, so good, in fact, that already she imagined a quietly self-satisfied return in several years' time to her family, laden down with chocolate and new clothes and of course her daughter, whose English would be charmingly different from her elder brother's school English. She would return with money enough for a new house, for their children's education, perhaps even enough to build a bigger place for their family. She would carry vitamins, medicines and stockpiled school supplies. And even as Deirdre drove her towards Tom and Clare, drove her in a blue Volkswagen towards that imagined future, Sandrine had felt a lightness, a sense that the triumph had already occurred, and she pictured a carefree drive five years from now, her family in their own car watching autumn throw down its leaves to winter.

But once Sandrine was in the house, these ideas changed. The reality of her situation forced simple images of happiness to the edges of her mind. She was a servant in someone else's home, did not feel free to use the telephone, and did not know where to begin looking through phone books. Tom and Clare didn't have a computer, and so she was without links to a larger world when she had arrived in Ireland. And there was also the hostility in the air, which she hadn't felt in rural Wicklow, simply because – she now knew – she hadn't seen any people.

Sandrine felt an uneasiness, a kind of bodily fear she had never experienced before. Back at home she had worried about her son, about money, food for her family, the life of her country, the arrests taking place, the oppression and corruption – these things she had known since a child herself. But here, even though she had food enough and clothes and the shops were always stocked and the petrol stations open and the police not obviously corrupt or dangerous, it was different, and because it was different she felt afraid. She didn't know how to act. She lacked all familiarity with the ways of this country. Sandrine didn't know how to respond to the sniggers and daily slights she experienced walking down the roads, whether to angrily put people in their place or to turn the other cheek. The racism surprised her, on the one hand, because for some reason she had naively thought that it wouldn't exist in a country that had experienced such persecution itself. On the other hand, white people treating black people badly could never really surprise her.

It was all made so much more complicated by being not just African in Ireland, but pregnant. She didn't know what they might do to her. Lock her up? Take the baby from her when it was born? Put her on a plane to face her husband, who still didn't know about the pregnancy? And so instead of calling someone, even an anonymous hotline for crisis pregnancies like the ones she occasionally saw advertised on the rear end of a bus, she put it off, and continued to put it off, even though the girl was pushing her way into view, because those hotlines had not been set up for her, and she knew that.

Part of her reluctance must have come from meeting Ling, the young woman from China who worked in the shop around the corner from the seafront houses. When Sandrine would run in for a litre of milk or some extra doughnuts for Clare, Ling was always at the counter ringing in the purchases. Slight, with shiny black hair that swung with her movements like a curtain about her face, she spoke next to no English, but had obviously learned the symbols on the register for meat products, sweets, and newspapers, swinging the scanner into effect with perfect ease. She had also learned numbers, which she recited easily. She barely nodded at each customer, just called out quietly, next please and thank you. One morning several weeks earlier, Sandrine found Ling outside the shop in the drizzling rain, with one hand to her clammy forehead, looking pale. Sandrine asked if she was all right and, embarrassed, she smiled shyly and nodded. Are you sure? Sandrine asked her. They were about the same age, surely. A smile almost floated across the young woman's face as she hesitated. Pregnant, she blurted out, her newest word.

Oh, said Sandrine, forcing herself to smile now while Ling did. But their eyes caught and the smiles began to droop. They stood with blank faces, staring at one another, foreign.

Very dangerous, Ling said quietly. Pregnant. She shook her head and gestured to the shop, the rain, Ireland. No good, she said. Sandrine said nothing. I go, Ling said, pointing to the glass door of the shop. Thank you, she added, and smiled slightly again, leaving Sandrine in the gathering rain that would later give way to a downpour.

She was right, Sandrine knew. It was dangerous, it was no good, this business of having another in your body. It was no good calling anyone or doing anything about it. No good could come of it, not here, not when the country was debating who belonged, who was Irish, who could become *new Irish*. But the child would come, here. When she gathered herself and entered the shop to buy the milk, the young woman was back behind the counter, her hair misted with water. Sandrine felt ill now, the sweat beginning to burst like stars on her forehead. The young woman eyed her, scanned the milk, took the money, said thank you, next please, but her eyes had drifted to Sandrine's and then down towards Sandrine's belly. And Sandrine, milk in hand, nodded to herself, knowing that something had just changed for her, as she stood outside the shop getting wet. She would no longer think hard about what she should do. She would do nothing. She would wait and see.

VI

The March day was overcast and suspiciously warm. Elizabeth had been giving her parents' grass, much abused by the salt spray of the winter storms, its first cutting since before the previous summer, aware that her mother was wandering to the windows every few minutes to see what the noise was. Clare's face appeared Mars-like at the window over the sink, frowning. Elizabeth waved, Clare smiled then, waved back, and turned away. Elizabeth did another lap past the apple tree her father had not quite managed to cut down, its mottled greening leaves next to the gangly dried wintry violet hydrangea that had never been pruned. When she turned she spied her mother staring vacantly through the glass of her eyes, through the doors, over the blush of soon to be pink camellias, beyond everything. Elizabeth waved again and kept going.

With her back to the windows, Elizabeth's smile collapsed. Her fingers tightened around the handlebar and the beginnings of blisters grazed the rubber grips. She ran the back of a hand along her forehead and let the machine idle.

It was like that now. She often felt the need to pause during some activity, as if to remind herself that there had been another life once, different to this one. There had been a time when she didn't have to think about her parents slipping away. There had been a time when she had thought of the narrative of her own life as only beginning and that beginning involved getting away from her parents, the beginning of some story of her life. And that narrative, Elizabeth had been sure, didn't involve being alone. It had included a husband, children, some perpetuation of self and family, some giving way to another generation. Not now. Her parents were slipping, there were no children, and her husband was now an ex-husband. One generation was not making way for another.

Something in her own body refused continuation. There was only her, stuck, feeling the need to pause because everything else seemed to be pausing before a final stop. As she urged the mower over a last odd triangle of long weeping grass and headed to the corner of the garden, once the site of a flourishing compost heap, Elizabeth heard the door opening. Sandrine smiled and held a glass of water out to her as she tipped out the small bucket of shorn green fragrance.

Tired? Sandrine asked as Elizabeth took the glass and smiled her thanks.

Just warm, she answered. They stood in silence as Elizabeth drank. Her mother was at the windows again, moving between rooms, her eyes unknowingly trained on her daughter.

The doctor should be here any moment, Sandrine said gently.

And when he'd gone, the doctor had left Elizabeth with only that one word. All of her language seemed to have been reduced to a penultimate silence. She inevitably held the one word in her mind, but it was also in her mouth, the physical presence of syllables like marbles. It was a word that did not need to be spoken. Sandrine, when Elizabeth emerged from the study with her hands faintly grass-green and a few daisy petals buried in her hair, knew, and said nothing. She just took hold of Elizabeth's stained hands and compelled them into her own. With their hands together, Elizabeth could think more clearly about what this word meant – that her mother would go the way of her father, and that her father was dying.

⌣ ⌣ ⌣

In the end it was sudden, in the sense that death is always sudden and breathtaking, even for those left behind. Tom had been in the home long enough that his supply of international spice trade newsletters had begun to provide the nurses with their nightshift reading material (Tom would have been pleased to know that several were, for the first time, learning about pepper), and short enough that Elizabeth still got the nurses' names mixed up.

It had come to this: to near-daily nursing home visits, to the infinite detail of the body. Tom had not eaten, but had had three small, white boxes of high protein, strawberry-flavoured drink. They had to be poured into a plastic glass, since he kept thinking that the flexible little straw attached to the box was a cigarette. Tom had not released his bowels in two days, and so one nurse suggested that they not give him so much of the fibre-rich drink. Tom had refused his ground-up pills in water, and his hands had shaken violently for several hours, making his heart race. In the way that new parents shift casually and unknowingly into a semi-obscene vocabulary about their child's urine and shit and farts and burps, so Elizabeth matter-of-factly found herself talking about her father. The other obscene vocabulary – of death itself – remained obscured to her.

By the next week, her ruminations were about Tom's inactivity, his sitting in a chair all day in a stupor that had dawned on him one morning like a character in a Beckett play. Elizabeth only bought the papers if she was going with her mother. She knew that, otherwise, she would hold them too tightly in her own hands and then discard them in the lemony, sunlight simulacra of the common room. She took, instead, to sitting before him or next to him by some window, pointing out the movement in the monkey puzzle trees that the wind effected, the trills on the water, the occasional glimpse of a fat, sleek seal.

Look, Tom, do you see? See how the branches are bowing down and then coming back up? She had taken to calling him Tom again, which made her feel extraordinarily apart from her father. But her father had been 'Dad' for only so much of his life. He had been 'Tom' for much longer, and perhaps would respond more to this word.

He didn't speak. His eyes might sometimes follow her fingers as they traced the air before the windowpane, and often she wasn't sure if he saw only her fingers, or the pane, and failed utterly to know that there was anything beyond. It was a slow movement; his eyes were filling with liquid substances Elizabeth had never seen before, bluish, whitish, clear. His blinks were becoming more rare and purposeful.

She didn't cry when she left, or when she got home. When anyone asked, she would say she was fine, and felt fine mostly, only under the weight of something she could not name other than time. Because this visiting period would end, she knew, would solidify itself into an end. And after there was still Clare at home, wandering and looking for Tom in closets and cupboards and bathrooms, and finding instead chipped porcelain dishes with pink vines, skeins of rough twine, hairbrushes with missing bristles, all of which kept her occupied for a few minutes before landing in some other odd location in the house, under the leaves of a plant, in the refrigerator, in her bed.

Elizabeth was thinking about this one evening in March, not long after cutting the grass, staring out of the kitchen windows while she and Sandrine prepared dinner for Clare and themselves. Sandrine was chopping an array of vegetables into bright-hued pieces: carrots and red peppers and sheer layers of onion that would deepen a stew, and Elizabeth was washing the morning's coffee cups and any utensils Sandrine had finished with. Thinking about the weight of time, how she had seemed to close her eyes and awoken to a life in which her parents had aged thirty years, in which she herself seemed to have suddenly aged. Her eye lingered over small grey hairs one recent morning as she brushed her teeth, her golden hair shimmering slightly silver in one spot, and she realised when she looked at a photo of herself from college that she looked, then, very, very young. Her friends' children were edging towards double digits, and she still had none. Yet she could stand and do dishes while her parents were fading in other rooms not too far from here, busying the moments during which nothing happened, waiting for those rare moments of crisis when one could actually do nothing.

Then the phone rang, and a moment arrived on a wire, and the cooker was turned off (Sandrine remembered to do this), and the car started.

Tom's breathing had become irregular, his skin seemed to expand as his frame contracted, and the flesh hung in ripples around his bones. The doctor had been called and had inserted the drip into his arm, peered under his eyelids, and then shaken his own head slowly, glancing at the nursing home staff in a sign that they were to speak to the family.

Elizabeth was there, sitting by the bed as Tom slept, or appeared to sleep, but actually was dying. She didn't know what to say, so she sat. She occasionally brushed her father's forehead with a damp towel or with her lips, holding her father's yielding hand. The nurses and the various carers were in and out, adjusting the drips, feeling his skin, swabbing his lips with water. They seemed to speak loudly in some quiet place, their voices echoing off of the metal rails of the bed, the chair legs and the empty walls.

So used to death they were, Elizabeth thought. And not callous, like a professor in college who had spent his career teaching about Nazi Germany and still wept on some days. Like that, these nurses saw death every day and still felt it, or at least had the subtlety to realise that others still felt it. She wanted it to be over. And then she remembered: she had forgotten her mother. She'd rushed out of the house and just left Clare and Sandrine behind to await news.

Should I ask my mother to come here? Elizabeth asked a nurse suddenly.

That's up to you, the nurse said gently, gripping her shoulder for a moment before turning aside to focus on Tom.

I think I'll go get her, she told the room, and her father.

When she returned, the nurses eyed Clare nervously. Clare herself was somehow aware, perhaps because it was so dark outside, and cold, that this was not her usual visit to what she still called the hospital, where Tom was still having 'tests'. Sandrine followed tentatively behind because, in the weeks that Tom had been gone, Clare had begun to cling to her, to feel afraid when she was absent. Sandrine's presence was what she relied on now.

Hiya Tom, Clare said loudly when she came into the room. She bent down over his forehead. Hi hon, she said, her thin fingers resting lightly on his skin, brushing back a few fine wisps of grey hair. Then she burst into tears.

Oh Tom! she stood there shaking, a thin sweater twitching about her slight frame. Elizabeth started towards her and found herself pushed away. It was Sandrine who, slowly, moved again towards Clare.

Hold on to me, Clare, she said clearly. You just hold on to me and I'll hold on to you and everything will be okay, she said softly. Everything will be okay. You hear me?

But he's dying, Clare's voice was muffled by Sandrine's embrace, but the words edged themselves into the room, into that stinging, sterilised silence of the tiled floors and electric yellow-white light.

God is with him, Clare, Sandrine said simply, without a pause. God is with him, and he'll help you. Just hold on to me, and I'll hold on to you.

Elizabeth listened to this, her eyes closing against the unnatural light of the room. How could this woman, whom her mother had only known for, what, three months, how could she step in like this, so capably? And why couldn't she, Elizabeth, do this? What kind of a daughter was she? There was Sandrine, her dark skin glowing in the electric light that made the rest of them look like her dying father, her thin arms wrapped around Clare's hollowed middle. Her hands, her fingers with their small bands of thin gold and their rounded nails, were perfectly able for such a moment. Why was that? Elizabeth felt no resentment, only a deep bewilderment that a woman who had been a stranger to them only three months before now stood at her father's deathbed comforting her mother. How did this happen? And what did it say about her, about Clare?

Elizabeth had unconsciously bowed her head and closed her eyes as if at mass, as if trying to imagine what that kind of piety, that kind of humility and stillness was like, the result of Sandrine's mention of God. And gradually, while Elizabeth listened, Clare's sobs lessened.

Now, Clare, Sandrine said, Tom will hear you, and he will be very disappointed. Here you are, she smiled, talking to me and ignoring him! That won't do at all.

Sandrine drew a tissue from her pocket and dabbed at Clare's eyes and then, like a mother with her child, dabbed once on her nose, an exclamation mark. Clare said nothing, mashing her lips together in a crying child's imitation for a smile on command, and then turned back to Tom. Sandrine's had been a mother's gesture, one that both women instinctively understood. There in the room that was by day inhabited by the ghostly old people of the home, her father dying, Elizabeth was thinking. Her parents would both die without becoming grandparents. She herself would die without becoming a mother.

The night passed slowly. Elizabeth convinced Sandrine to go home to bed and to take Clare. She sat alone in the semi-darkness (the nurses had turned off all but one strip of the lighting), without a book, without a newspaper, sometimes holding her father's hand, sometimes pacing the room, sometimes staring out into the corridor after the ghostly steps of night nurses in other parts of the building. She wanted him to die, because that was what was going to happen, and did not want to be there when it happened, but she didn't want to be away either. What if her father died while she was stuck in morning rush-hour traffic on the dual carriageway, her mobile phone to her ear, or listening to Newstalk or Marian Finucane or a boyband on 2FM? What if that was the last she heard of her father's life? And what if she was here and had to call Clare, wake her up in the middle of the night to say, it's over, or he's gone, or he's dead (how would she say it?), and what if it happened during Clare's breakfast?

It was like being on a plane, on a plane to Vietnam after a holiday away, all of those hours and hours stretched out in front of you like a ribbon of road you were forced to walk one step at a time, toe to heel. Nothing to do, nothing that could possibly distract from interminable time, sitting, waiting, watching the clock.

The building ached every few minutes, different parts of blocks and plaster and timber moving invisible fractions. She took to listening to these aches, to the hum of the light, and to the unpredictable breathing of the man in the bed: a crack in the air, the flicker of a light, the withholding of a breath for a few seconds too long. Elizabeth waited. After it seemed that Clare and Sandrine had been gone for hours, she began to wonder if it was worth it, this whole thing. Sitting here in a room about to be a morgue. The life. Had it been worth it? She moved closer to the bed, lifting the chair so as not to make any noise.

Dad? *Dad?* she said softly. His eyelids were drooping half way over his eyes like careless curtains. She moved her head so that her gaze met his half gaze. Dad? I'm here with you. Can you hear me?

The self-consciousness of it galled her. What was she supposed to do? Come out with a speech, a kind of modern monologue about how much he'd meant to her, how she loved him for the small things, like ordering her books that flew from America to Vietnam? Like letting her go back to the States for university? Like never, ever saying anything about grandchildren? Because he'd always insisted that of all the spices, pepper was ultimately his favourite, because it was a democratic spice, used by everyone, everywhere, which had made it cheaper than all the rest since the middle ages?

You know that I love you, Dad, she finally said. You know that, and I am with you. You hold on to me, she said slowly, and I'll hold on to you. She stared hard into his eyes through her own tears. Dad, she added, do you remember the story about the Turkish flag? That's what I loved about you, that story. You wrote it to me in a letter once, when I was in the States, my first term in college. You wrote it down and told me that I was the moon, you were the Armenians, or something like that. And that you couldn't stop me from going to the States, because I didn't belong to you. Dad. Elizabeth closed her eyes and leaned her head on the edge of the bed with its thin cotton sheets pressed around him and lay like that, waiting.

с с с

The confusion of the day would have been too much for Clare. People coming up to her non-stop, saying they were sorry, saying they had loved Tom, saying that they could not believe it. Clare would have looked at them and would not have known who they were, these women with sober grey silk scarves and muted cashmere coats, men with trimmed moustaches he had once worked with, or played football with. Clare would have stood still and listened to them because she would not have known what else to do.

Sometimes the confusion was too much for Elizabeth. She wept without realising it, and her tears fell on to her green silk blouse and left dark, distorted dots of wet. Then she would find that she was crying and feel surprised and stop, but her mother would not have been able to stop. Elizabeth cried when she thought of her father, and stopped when she thought of her mother, brought to attention again by the strangeness of her mother's absence on this day.

Many of her father's relatives were no longer living, but there was his brother Alan and his wife. They were so old-looking now, Elizabeth thought, her eyes filling again. She didn't recognise her cousins, who were adults she unknowingly passed in town, perhaps, or in shopping centres. They had fled farming, leaving their parents' land and the relentless rhythms of lambing season. Elizabeth thought of how she had wanted to stay where she was and know them better, all those years ago. And for all of that old longing, Elizabeth wept.

At home, Sandrine would give Clare sweets every few minutes, soft toffees or chocolates that she unwrapped and placed with her smooth fingers into Clare's knotted ones. Clare would not know what had happened. She would have forgotten the night at the nursing home, Elizabeth thought. And yet at other moments Clare seemed to know. She knew. She seemed to imagine the varnished wooden box and know that Tom was in it and wasn't getting out again, and for full minutes at a time would harrow the house with her sobs. Oh Tom, she said, over and over again, Oh Tom. Finally Clare's voice would die out. Sandrine's hands busily unwrapped sweet after sweet, the cellophane wrappers crinkling like eggshell in her pockets, and then there would be a slight sucking noise, like that of a baby latching on to a breast, and then the relief of silence.

The priest continued on gently, pressing on to the finish, while Elizabeth tried to contain the feeling of rolling grief that overcame her body: the need to rock, to move, to do something to release or contain it, she wasn't sure which. A final blessing, an arc in the air, a conducted, orchestrated movement of hands, a choreography of grief. And it was over.

᠃ ᠃ ᠃

After the funeral, Elizabeth drove to the house. Clare was not crying. She was sitting quietly by a window with a rug over her legs. Elizabeth talked to Sandrine about her own parents.

It is very different, Sandrine was saying quietly. It is not like here. My father is not very old, but he seems very, very old to you, if you see him. This is because, I think, of his work. He was a farmer, like my husband, George is, on the same farm. Every day, early in the morning, he got up before the sun rose, and he went outside to feed our animals before he went to work on the farm.

What kind of animals? Elizabeth asked.

Goats, mostly, Sandrine said, her neck turning to the window so that she could watch the white clouds with their dark underbellies flow by. He had a few goats, and then he grew some maize in the garden, and sometimes some vegetables for us as well. But it was very hard work, she trailed off.

That kind of work takes its toll, Elizabeth agreed, equally quietly.

They said nothing for a few moments. Elizabeth tried to picture Sandrine's parents, wondering whether she looked like them. She had seen photos of the boy, and one of Sandrine's husband, but that was all.

Will you go back, Sandrine? she asked suddenly. Do you want to go home?

Sometimes – Sandrine hesitated and then began again – I would prefer to stay here, Elizabeth, she said. I can make a good living here, maybe in a few years I can teach again. I would like that, very much. It is no life at home, she said. So I would like to stay, and eventually to have George and Tobias here. *I would like to stay.* It was strange to hear her voice saying this so clearly.

And can you? Elizabeth pushed. Is that okay?

I hope so, Sandrine sighed. But one doesn't know with these things. It's in God's hands.

Elizabeth thought of the bent backs of her aunt and uncle in the church, how they'd driven, slowly, all the way up from near Arklow. And Elizabeth felt sorry then, and blurted out: you've been great with my mother, Sandrine, a lifesaver. And with Tom too, she added. I don't know what I'd have done without you. I'm so glad that you came, even though it must have been so awful to leave your family.

I carry my family with me, Sandrine said, her voice quivering. And Clare has become my family. I didn't get to know Tom very well before he went to the nursing home, but Clare is my family.

⸱ ⸱ ⸱

Sandrine patted her belly every morning now, saying hello to the not-yet girl. It was the one moment of her day that felt isolated from all of the others, the one that stood out when she returned exhaustedly to bed and thought things over. For that one moment (sometimes only a few seconds, if she heard Clare moving around already), Sandrine lay still with her baby and dreamt about all of the life in that one little bed. She could feel her moving now, a little bit, the slight tremor of a turn, the slightest hint of an elbow or a foot protesting at the small space. She would smile and then think, okay little girl, here we go again.

For the rest of the day it was different. She did not exist with the girl alone. There were other people about, Clare, Elizabeth, sometimes doctors or Fidelma, who visited more frequently now that Tom was gone. Mostly there were other people in her mind: George and her son. And they were always absent in that first moment, when she was alone with the baby and had not yet remembered her husband or her already existing child. During the day she thought guiltily of George and considered, again and again, how she would tell him. Dear George, she would think, I am pregnant. But that one phrase, so simple and stout, produced such anger in her that she didn't know what to do. He had not written her back. He had not answered her letter, and so did not know about the baby. When she did sit down to write to her husband, it was of the mundane, everyday things, the things happening with Clare.

Dear George, she began, watching from her seat at the dining room table as Clare nodded off in front of the television. *Dear George, Tom has died. The funeral was yesterday and they are very sad in the house. It made me wonder about my own parents. How are they, George? They tell me they are fine and keeping well, but you tell me: how are they? Is my father in good health? Does he want anything? And how is our son? There were children at the funeral yesterday, I hear, distant nieces and nephews not much bigger than Tobias, I think.*

Tobias will be almost finished with the school year by now. Is our son happy to be on holidays soon? I will send him something, a book or a little thing, with my next letter for when he finishes school. How is the weather, and how are the crops? I hope you are not working too hard. And here she would stop and sign her name, carefully.

But this was not the final version. She had taken to writing letters she had no intention of sending. She wrote these on her nicest paper – small smooth squares the likes of which she had never been able to afford until she came to Ireland, in colours that would have delighted her son: lemon rind, dusk, peppermint green, fire. On the rare afternoons that she could get out, she went, usually, straight to the post office to stamp the consistent letters home, and then to Eason's, where she would ramble through isles of cards and reams of paper goods, walking amongst schoolgirls who were looking for a set of special markers or a birthday card, and who tried every pen available on the small scraps of paper left there on purpose. Sandrine had discovered recently a new stock of paper that was bumpy and uneven, that had rose petals strewn between layers of pulp; these seemed too pretty to write on, so she only bought an envelope with an early autumn scattering of fallen pink petals. Because it was a large envelope, about the same size as the usual saffron-coloured ones with metal hands that folded outwards to form a seal, Sandrine had taken to placing her unsent letters in it, enclosing the latest one in the pile before returning it, carefully creased, to the rose petals.

Most of the letters were to George, in principle, but they had quickly become, in the few weeks she had been writing them, letters to a different George, one that she imagined for herself in this new world of Ireland. Instead of telling him of her doings, she told him of nothing, just wrote words that she might have learned to reconsider (yearning, she wrote one afternoon over and over again, *yearning*, on pale cinnamon paper in black ink) or painted word pictures of things she had noticed about Ireland (more and more of us here, she told the page, every week, more and more of us here, our pictures even in the papers). Mostly, however, she wrote of the child, of how she was growing and moving and how her own body was distending and distorting in accordance with the child's needs.

This afternoon she looked carefully through her sheets of paper, deciding which to write on. She had felt a solid kick. What paper would suit this occasion? After almost beginning on a bright blue sheet with small white fish lapping around the edges in a neat line, she poised her pen over a textured page of white linen-like paper and began. *George,* she wrote, *she is moving. She is really and truly moving. I felt her toes today against my skin. It was a fine kick, you would have been delighted. She will be a fine child, George. I wish you could feel her.*

Clare awoke then with a yelp of remembrance. Tom, she cried,

Tom. And Sandrine put down her pen, folded the sheet of creamy paper in half, and put it away.

There seemed less time to herself now that Tom had died, and even beforehand her time off was unpredictable. Beyond her walks to the church and the local shops, her expeditions to collect her attendance certificates and to pay her school fees, what she saw now was through the glass of the windows – the sea and the sky, the slow parade of cars, the irregular green that separated the house from the water, people who walked as their dogs roamed frantically after scent.

She did watch Ireland on the television. It was brightly coloured – women politicians wore red suits, GAA players had splotches of pink that a child might have drawn on their pale cheeks, estuaries had green-booted fishermen, gleaming silver cranes perched over the expanding landscapes of cities and towns and villages whose names she could not pronounce, neat lines of blue metallic and black cars edging up against rows of countless houses attached to each other from the shoulder down, their chimneys, mostly unused, sticking up like necks into the sky. Mostly Ireland on the television was indoors, like she was, in pubs glowing with orange light and brown syrupy drinks, in official-looking buildings armed by black gates, in narrow-aisled shops full of bustle and bags.

Despite the warm light spilling through drink and the full shops, Ireland seemed angry. It was on strike: schools had rat infestations and no toilets; hospitals had no beds, nurses no money; trains were delayed by weekend improvement work; bus drivers threatened action over rumours of privatisation of their fleet. Farmers protested over the diminishment of subsidies, ministers defied the law. 'Tribunal' was another new word that Sandrine absorbed. From the airport, people were deported, people like her, weeping, stone-faced. Lawyers spoke, reporters stood by. Tension mounted about *foreigners, non-nationals, immigrants*. Her face grew hot when she saw reports claiming that women in their thousands were descending from Poland, Nigeria, and Bulgaria to give birth to their children so that they could be Irish citizens. *Birth tourism* provoked intense anxiety.

All of the exuberant colour and flagrant anxiety of the news was followed by the weather reports. But Sandrine heard forecasts indifferently. They were always the same. She woke each morning and slid the curtain back from the window, knowing from the light as it crept around the edges that it was cloudy, muggy, raining, gusting, everything at once, but not warm, not hot, not seething. That kind of heat was gone, vanished from her life.

Within weeks of Tom's funeral, though, the winter was stretched thin by spring, and things were changing. There was no longer any cry from Clare in the night. A week after Tom died, she decided – Sandrine believed she had decided – to say nothing. Life had humbled her into speechlessness. She sat and stared at the grey glisten of the television screen when it was off – the way it looked wet, almost – or looked in anguish into Sandrine's face as they sat together at the table. She did not cry. She did nothing.

And she wouldn't eat. Her bones seemed to grow. By the end of a week, ten days, two weeks, Clare vacated herself, allowing the bones to take over. Sandrine watched, and continued to talk. She knew it was no use. The *pain au chocolat* and doughnuts were of no interest any longer. The word 'Vietnam' failed to create a flicker in Clare's eye. It was over. And while Clare quietened herself towards death with a hard resolve, the thaw began, the air brightening and bringing the scent of summer in April.

⸗

When Sandrine is exposed to the heat of the sun again, it is like wandering in to another time. She stands still while it soaks into her, closing her eyes. The heat she had forgotten pours over her and she is, eyes closed, at home, standing in the dusty warm doorstep in weekend bare feet with the sound of her son's playing filtering through the maize that is growing and the radio behind her over the sink. It is the English-only station, for she is leaving soon and wants her ear to adjust to hearing only one tongue. The news is bad, as always, and she learns over and over again words like 'enquiry', 'commission'. She opens her eyes and the Irish street returns to her.

Cars prowl slowly as they do on the television, head to toe, windows rolled down as far as possible. The children on the paths are reddened, dusky rose, knees and noses awkwardly pink. Old ladies have tightly tied scarves under their softly rippled chins, workmen hold their ties in sweaty hands, their jackets already abandoned in offices and cars. Sandrine spies a white pregnant woman crossing the road, watches her pad slowly, back bewildered by its unnatural arch, a hand drawn over her forehead to catch the pearls of sweat before they trickle down the straining cords of her neck and plunge between heavy breasts. Sandrine moves her hand over her own belly, now protesting at the limits of her clothes, which have already been altered to accommodate. The baby is somersaulting in the heat, in the warm bath of her womb. She is not at home, but it is hot, and there is a child playing, and it is this Sandrine focuses on as the tears come.

Crossing the same road as the pregnant woman, who, to her relief, actually smiles at her in sympathy, she passes two African men in long pants and sweaters. They glance at her while they continue talking. She is startled. They do not feel the heat as she does. Has she forgotten so much? So much that the Irish late spring day has not only overwarmed but upset her? It is the child, she reminds herself, the child in her furnace, making her more susceptible than others to the sun's power. But the thought lingers as she walks past a greenhouse strawberry vendor whose fingers are pinkened and whose sign reads Irish Strawberries, First of the Year. *I am forgetting my home. It is no longer my home.*

She thinks of Clare. Clare would have recognised the heat, Sandrine knew. She would have sat outside in the garden on a hard chair and drifted back to Vietnam if she had been there. Sandrine frowns to herself. Now Clare had trapped herself inside, her life narrowed to the immediacy of two rooms. As a result, Sandrine found herself free to come and go more often as Elizabeth haunted the house more regularly.

Sandrine prowls the area near the house only, ambling along the seafront, staring at a residence like one in which she had slept her first few nights in Ireland, but no asylum seekers lived there any longer. She saw a few white pages had been hung, announcing the owners' desire to take the building down and turn it into a row of townhouses whose views would spill out over the sea and command phenomenal prices. Watching the news, Sandrine had learned something of the Irish property market. In the meantime, the low building's windows were caked with salt and the grime of traffic. Its painted front had weathered until the colour was indescribable, an anxious mixture of grey and white and butter.

Most afternoons now, Elizabeth arrived to sit with her mother for an hour or more, having left work early – she too sensed that an ending was on its way. When Elizabeth arrived, even if it was misting, Sandrine left Tom and Clare's house and walked straight ahead towards the sea, sat on a bench and stared towards Wales. Elizabeth needed now to be alone with Clare, Sandrine felt. And she herself felt a need to get out. The house felt empty, suddenly, and she had given up her sea-gazing from the window and had come out into the weather to face it directly. She had come to love the live noise of it, unmediated by windows, the variance of the days. She wouldn't have to stay by the sea for long, only a few moments, even, if it was raining, to feel her loneliness and fear collapse into the murmur and thrash of water that was before her. Afterwards she would walk, sometimes to Dun Laoghaire and out on an arm of the pier that hopelessly stretched towards the horizon, pointing at something. Sometimes she'd walk in the other direction to the tower, where she watched the swimmers' heads bobbing on the surface, their conversation skimming the waves.

This is all she does. Afterwards she returns to the house, cleans it as if Clare were still interested, peering in at her bed to make sure it is still made up. She watches Clare, stooping over herself, becoming something else in a chair under the window with the light of the sea shimmering on her face. Clare never speaks now. Sandrine watches Clare, reads, writes to her husband things that she will never send, and, as the light stretches into evening, reads his letters, over and over again.

ᴄ ᴄ ᴄ

Elizabeth has not read the letters. They are in a cardboard box that sags with damp. She is standing alone in the hallway of her parents' home. She does not want to read them. Her eyes take in glimpses of her parents' writing on yellowed envelopes. She has not considered this. She has been eminently practical about doctors and nurses and appointments, nursing homes, prognoses, death, dementia. She has been practical about dementia. But the feeling of it – this she has not spoken about. Beyond answering the usual platitudes from friends – I can't believe it, how awful, how are *you*? – she has said nothing. Elizabeth has always felt private, a legacy of her childhood, but this is a new type of retreat into the self, away from friends with whom she had discussed other serious things. It was like becoming a child again, and returning to her parents, but she looks older, the history of smiles and frowns etched on her skin in fine lines like the borders of countries: here sadness, there wonder, there dejection. Are any of the lines from the letters, from the death of her father, from the dementia?

She opens the door. The wind and the spring sea howl into the hallway. Elizabeth is in the evening cold that always follows on early sun, her elbows beginning to ache from the weight of the box. She brings the letters home and puts them into a closet, removing them from her parents' house where her mother sometimes roams from one door to another with a hat in her hands, searching for Tom. She says nothing. Clare will not put down the hat that Sandrine had pulled gently over her head before they went to mass three weeks ago.

Clare had not been to mass in years. In Vietnam? she'd exclaimed and looked at anyone in surprise when asked about how the services differed from Ireland. I have no idea, Clare would smile, knowing she was courting danger if the enquirer was Irish, particularly if it was Tom's brother Alan and his wife. But Sandrine took her to mass because she had not been to the funeral. Sandrine wanted her to have done something to mark the fact of her husband's death, even if unknowingly. What was the point in telling her? Elizabeth had argued with herself, crying then, in the nursing home still, her father's body in a room behind her. She knows that he is gone – why push her to the brink of herself just so that you have the high moral ground of having told her the truth? And so Sandrine, Clare on her arm, had walked at a child's pace from the house along the seafront and around the corner to the vacant church, where they sat in the back, Clare staring at the altar and the priest with her fingers swimming around the hat's edging.

When they were back home and Sandrine had taken it off, Clare had retrieved the hat and held it in her lap, not looking up. Sandrine excused herself to the loo moments later. She couldn't sit any longer in that silence that was the death passing between them and an announcement of the death to come. Elizabeth, watching her mother in the days afterwards, felt too that Clare knew that Tom was dead. The hat, the new blueness of it, seemed to say something to her mother, she thought, why else would she sit with it so preoccupied? Why else would she have ceased asking for Tom? Unless, of course, she had forgotten him.

Elizabeth remembered almost nothing of the funeral afterwards, who was there, what they had said. Only random details stayed with her: a little girl's flouncing skirt, her giggles that Elizabeth wanted to drink. She wanted to take her hand and leave the funeral, walk towards the seafront to Teddy's and eat ice-cream, loads of it. Get away from the space of the body and the box and the sight of faces streaked like a Pollock with tears. It was unbearable, all of the emotion that everyone seemed to feel, the way that she herself could feel only the desire to escape.

Several friends urged Elizabeth into cleaning out Tom's wardrobe right away. Clear it all out, they'd said, let someone else use the clothes. No point in hanging on to it. Elizabeth protested it was too soon, but she knew they were right, that she would have to do this sooner or later. Among the pressed shirts and awkward balls of dark socks was the box of letters.

This box Elizabeth puts on the floor in a wardrobe in the spare bedroom in her own home now, and closes the door, thinking that at least they will have some privacy. The dialogue implicit in all of those addressed envelopes, in the maturation of handwritings and language, can continue. The room, with only its bed and a dressing table and the empty wardrobe, feels like a hotel room, now has its first object of any meaning: this cardboard box full of words. Elizabeth pulls the door of the room shut and pauses, almost listening, then leaves the past there, where there is nothing else.

ᴄ ᴄ ᴄ

In a corner of the old-fashioned Chippendale children's desk in her room in Tom and Clare's home, Sandrine kept a handful of letters bound together by a red rubber band losing its stretch. These were not the ones that arrived most weeks at the house and contained the precious drawings by her son, the updates by her husband. Those were littered around the room, on the bed, on the desktop, even on the floor so that she could see her son, see his young life everywhere. These were not her own unsent letters kept in the gorgeous thick paper with the leaves protruding, nor the ones that were in progress on various surfaces around the room. This small packet that she always wished thicker, these were old letters her husband had written her. There were only seven.

They had seen each other daily, so there had been little call for letters before the move to Ireland. He had been at school with her, before she had gone away to further her studies at a boarding school after various relatives pooled meagre resources. Sandrine found after her education was completed that she wanted to go home, and so she returned and became one of two teachers in her old school. The courtship was brief. He remembered her, of course; they had played together as children. He was working on the farm, and had taken over from his father by the time she came back.

He was enthusiastic about her education, wanting to learn from her. He thought that she could put into place what he believed would be a revolutionary new education system – he was young, patriotic, and anything could be done, anything could happen – and Sandrine, already aware of the limitations of what she could do as a teacher here, had admired his energy, his smooth-as-velvet jaw-line. He would meet her at the school when the pupils had gone home, and their laughter would slip under the plywood door. Their love passed unspoken for only a matter of months. He was so in love, he declared, he could not wait. He had wanted her to write him letters, but she could not give them to him, too embarrassed by the strength of feeling in them. In her parents' home, when everyone was asleep, she sat up to prepare lessons (she told her father) but instead wrote George extravagant love letters that she reread to herself quietly before burning them outside with a match struck against the heel of her shoe.

Matches accumulated in the tin garbage pail until her mother confronted her, demanding to know if she was smoking and wasting precious money like an American woman. Sandrine had burst out laughing and showed her mother the scattered ashes. I am burning paper, Mama, she laughed, practice lessons. Why waste the paper in this way? her mother replied. Keep it for me, Sandrine, your sisters can draw on the backs of the pages and practice their letters. And so Sandrine produced odd pieces of paper for her mother, but continued to burn her letters to George. It made her feel terribly shy to think of handing these to him as they passed in the mornings on their way to work – to do as the children did – and then to have to see his eyes afterwards meeting hers across the front porch of the schoolhouse.

Once she had arrived in Ireland, she felt sure, thinking back, that he had done the same, written dozens, maybe hundreds, of unsent letters. Perhaps he had not even burned his. Perhaps he had carried his own in his pockets, hoping that she would arrive at the school with something for him. Perhaps, Sandrine thought, but perhaps he had not. Perhaps there had been no writing at all on his part until much, much later, when she had almost left for Ireland. Even the seven that she had with her were ones that he had written with a specific purpose in mind – they had decided to conscientiously practice their English.

When they booked her plane ticket at a fake marble desk in a travel agency in Harare, leaving their son at home with George's parents, Sandrine had begun to cry. George had comforted her under the barely averted gaze of the agent, who was bored with such scenes. Think of our son, what it will mean for him. And you must think of other things. I know, Sandrine, we will write each other letters, only in English.

After six years of marriage, through raids and the excursions of Mugabe's teenaged gangs, after the conception of their son, his birth and all of his firsts, from smiles to steps – things had begun to change. George's enthusiasm had waned. The farm would be able to employ him for only so much longer; the other farmers were all being driven out, and there was fear that theirs would be next. It seemed pointless to resist any longer. What were they to do if the thugs arrived? And there seemed to be little hope in the next generation. The pupils didn't wish to learn, he complained to Sandrine, they were uninterested in anything but the televisions that were now in so many homes, even those that lacked food. And those televisions described different lives than the one she could offer them with education, different from the example George offered in working the land.

He wanted to give up and get out. He was worn down by poverty, by the lack of possibility, by the scandals of the government. Sandrine had watched this happen, seeing his temper fraying around the other labourers that he suspected might not support the MDC, seeing the crease that became a ravine between his brows. He couldn't leave, his brother had been beaten within an inch of his life not many months before, and he was certain that the police would have their family name on records. He had no university education and would not be granted a visa so easily in any case. Despite Amahle's disappearance, she was a woman and more likely to be granted a visa. It would be up to her to get out, get a visa and a job and then a passport. Legality. A password into the west, away from this desire for the life of the television, away into the television itself.

His enthusiasm revived over maps and forms. He traced rivers with the pads of his fingertips, whispered to her of train journeys they might one day take, across Europe, into Russia, from west to east on the Orient Express. He wracked his brain for the English for odd things and leapt out of bed in the dark to look up a word in the dictionary. And this energy for maps and words sped after him into the fields, where other labourers now learned to recognise the small-dog shape of Ireland, knew the capital, knew that Ireland too had suffered under the British.

While George was infected with the excitement of the coming journey that he himself would not take, Sandrine tried to prepare herself for the actual journey, learning what it was like to look at everything around her out of fear that it might be the last time. George's exacting joy was matched by what she experienced as a lapsing sorrow. The roads would not be like this one, brown and dusty and soft underfoot during the dry season. Neither would the night sky contain such a sense of vast stillness. She would not hear the language that was her own except in her own mind, which was too quiet, or see the jacarandas bloom into blue and purple against the light. Her mugoti, the spoon handle worn smooth by her touch, would lie idle as others prepared sadza for George and Tobias and the family.

For two months, each week they wrote letters. She began the correspondence, tentatively, checking her work with a small, old dictionary with a cover made out of grey cardboard. When he replied, surer, resigned, desperate, she forgot to think of the letters as exercises, and began to write passionately. The separation was to come. It lay waiting in the sealed plastic bag holding her ticket that he had placed in the sturdy black Bible, which made her feel strangely as if she were making a pilgrimage. There was no avoiding it now, too much money had been spent on that ticket in the small bag, and, as a result, the letters were loud and raucous with love. After a month, the word relationship could not be contained on the page and spilled into their other life of the house and the child and the work.

This, Sandrine knew, was her soon-to-be child, this bundle of letters, this English language, the awkward verbiage of it. The daughter had begun with those letters on one of the several evenings her elder brother had been put to bed early. She would probably never know this, Sandrine thought, never know the how and why of her existence, so easily explained by the letters.

She had written him eight; he had given her seven. It was his turn, and the day of her departure so near. Her last letter she had handed him over breakfast three days before, just before he left for work, and she had hoped that he would hand her, in turn, his reply at the airport, something to take with her on the plane. The other letters she had put in her bag for the cabin (the idea of them being kept away from her in the cavities of the plane was impossible).

But at the airport he gave her nothing. She had been angry and said nothing, of course, for there was her small son with the lack of understanding rimming his huge eyes and the queues and the general chaos of her own emotions. Her sisters and their husbands were there, her parents, and some of George's family too, all there to send her off, so she could say nothing. She was even more angry at his silence than she might have been because she had already composed a reply to his unwritten letter and had sealed it in an envelope. *I am*, it read, self-conscious in its use of an old-fashioned phrase, *with child*. But when his hands put nothing into hers but their own nervous pressure, she did not hand him this line, and when she had passed beyond his gaze and walked to the plane, blindly, she tore it to pieces and later shoved them into the wastebasket in the airplane toilet.

As the months drew on and the daughter came closer to her own being, Sandrine fretted over the letters, worrying them with her eyes as soon as she entered her bedroom. How was she to tell him now, in another letter? On the telephone? This seemed a better idea. Sandrine bought a card for the phone from the shop down the road, hurried around the corner one Saturday morning when the sea spray was arching its way across the green and towards the house. The Chinese girl at the cash register had told her about the cards, very cheap call home, she'd said, handing Sandrine the two stamps she bought when she had not had time to walk to the post office. But the Chinese girl wasn't there that morning. A teenage girl with glittering nails sat flipping through a magazine in between ringing up purchases, her nails clawing and teasing strands of her unnaturally flat hair. Sandrine pointed to the cards, handed over her ten euro and hurried back to the house, determined to call right now.

Since she'd left home they had spoken only three times. Once when she started the job, once on her son's birthday, and once on George's birthday. She punched in the numbers and waited, her coat still cold from the air, her eyes still tearing. No one answered.

. . .

It was funny the way you got to know the other visitors at the nursing home, Elizabeth thought. She was on hands and knees in the kitchen pulling cupboards apart, sorting through half-used bottles of window cleaner with the labels coming unstuck, hard-caked shoe polish in surprising colours – mahogany, hot purple, hedge green. There were the weird items that crept into suburban homes everywhere: barbeque lighting fluid (although she found no barbeque anywhere and couldn't remember her parents ever grilling in Ireland or anywhere since they'd lived in Connecticut), cheap, yellow plastic handled screwdrivers, jay cloths stained cloud grey. Elizabeth opened a small wooden box that might once have been full of tender-leaved cigars, now full of nails and hinges and hooks, most gone rusty, bent, the tingling scent of corroding metal. She put the lid back on.

There was a man who always arrived at the home in a suit with a plastic bag of pick-and-mix sweets to see his wife, a frail woman with white blouses. Jack and May. She seemed so much older than he did. Elizabeth felt desperate seeing them together.

It's the way it goes, with dementia, Alzheimer's, all those things, her ex-husband had shrugged and said when they met for coffee. He'd dutifully called to see how she was after Tom's funeral, knowing from her demeanour on the day that she was a wreck. Elizabeth envied him that casualness, the distance he'd acquired.

She didn't know what to do with the house now that Clare had been moved into the home. She didn't want to rent it out because she was worried for Sandrine. Elizabeth had yet to speak to her about it, but the baby must be coming soon. She had agreed to meet Ciaran for coffee in part because she didn't know who to talk to.

I can't, Ciaran, I can't talk to her about it, I don't know what to say. I'm afraid she'll think I'm threatening her or something. They stayed quiet for a moment. I guess I'll have to, Elizabeth said doubtfully. But I don't have kids, I have no idea what this must be like for her. She knuckled her eyes so that he wouldn't see the beginnings of tears growing.

I don't think that matters, Elizabeth, he said gently. He waited. How are you doing on that front?

I'm grieving, Elizabeth said as the tears, the first ones she had shed in anyone's presence since her father's funeral, for the children I won't ever have. Ciaran reached across the table to touch her hair, cleared his throat and pulled his chair around the corner of the table so that he could hold her.

ᴄ ᴄ ᴄ

Sandrine steps wearily from the building that houses complaining voices and queues. It is a rare, hot day, but the heat of the building had been unbearable. There is a breeze or the memory of one on the river and she keeps to its bank. The lunch hour movement of bodies and bags is beginning to ebb. She crosses the Ha'penny Bridge amidst a flurry of legs, lingering along the railings to let them continue, and the breeze is captured in her skirt. She reminds herself, standing there with the wind, of a picture she once saw of a boat on Lake Kariba, and she feels some of the pressure of complaint leave her shoulders. Her eyes are unfocused and she stands, thinking.

Sandrine! a voice calls. Sandrine is bewildered for a moment, knowing that she knows no one – but there is Elizabeth, as planned. Her face is pink and Sandrine wonders again how she ever lived in Vietnam. Sandrine smiles at her.

Elizabeth had taken a wandering walk before coming to meet Sandrine. To her mind, Dublin was always rain-glossed and full of nameless streets. She had looked up at the gate as she strolled through the arch. Elizabeth's arch, she thought, the arch of a dead monarch, my namesake. Today, in the heat after rain, she did not intend to shop on her lunch hour. An amble (Elizabeth never did eat lunch when it was warm, her body returning to her warm-climate habits automatically) and then a cup of coffee with Sandrine would be lunch enough, would get her away from the computer and the inanity of forms that was her job. Even for her, it was warm: a dense, American heat, slightly shimmering and too blue, the edge of thunder hovering on the horizon. Mounting the steps she spotted Sandrine, her skirt floating about her knees, staring at the water.

Sandrine! she called.

Sandrine turned, startled out of her reverie of Lake Kariba.

How did it go? Elizabeth asked.

Oh, Sandrine said, tightening her one-hand hold on the thick-painted railing. So much to think about, you know, Elizabeth. I don't know what to do.

Why? What did they say? They stood atop the arc of the bridge, a small island of rippling fabric.

I think it's okay, for me, Sandrine said carefully. But I don't know about. She finished, said no more. Elizabeth frowned.

Sandrine, have you told them? They have to know. Elizabeth looked at Sandrine, whose thin body was swollen with the distortion of pregnancy. They can't *not* know, she said.

Sandrine shook her head. They said nothing. I was at a window, you know, so they couldn't see, perhaps. I don't want to tell them, Elizabeth, because I'm scared they will send me back. And I can't go back.

They said nothing. Dublin flowed around them and the water beneath them, the river was darkly gleaming, opaque with brown light and spotted with a Lucozade bottle, a Fanta can, Tayto crisp packets, all drowning.

Let's go get something to eat, Elizabeth said suddenly. She was so used to talking to Sandrine, to seeing her, but only indoors, in her parents' house, really now Sandrine's, since her mother was in the home these last few weeks. Here, in the air, Sandrine looked far younger, her eyes wide, her stance less certain, left foot hiding behind right. Elizabeth remembered that Sandrine's son was only small, having just turned six, and realised that she did not know how old Sandrine was herself. Only twenty-eight, twenty-nine?

Yes, Sandrine smiled, almost shyly. A cup of tea would be nice before I go back to the house.

Elizabeth steered Sandrine through Dublin, and it was a relief. Sandrine no longer had to keep her eyes on the familiar places, like the gates of the college, or the stout green glass building whose sickly shimmer she knew would lead her to a train and back to where things were familiar. Her eyes could now wander randomly.

Elizabeth left Sandrine seated at a shiny table and returned with her coffee, a tea, and a plastic-wrapped oversized biscuit. Only when she had been about to turn in to the coffee house and looked around for Sandrine had Elizabeth realised that the heat and the walking might be too much for her. The biscuit was the result of this realisation, of Elizabeth's remorse for seeming so brusque, but Sandrine only picked at it, politely.

It had been a mistake, their arranging to meet. Elizabeth looked around the café as she raised the small white cup of bitter coffee to her lips. There was nothing to say. Sandrine didn't like her. She'd only come because she had to. She was Elizabeth's employee. Sandrine was staying in a house for free because Elizabeth allowed it.

Elizabeth shook herself, mentally. She replaced the cup on the saucer and heard herself saying, Sandrine, you know that I'll help you, with all of this. And she meant it. She wanted to help and was prepared by the emotion of this instant for lawsuits and press conferences and family reunions at airports under hothouse suns of lights.

There may be nothing to do, Sandrine said quietly, her eyes heavy.

And would it be so bad to go home? Elizabeth asked, fingering an empty sugar packet.

I never told my husband, Sandrine blurted out. I had a letter, to tell him, she was crying now, and at the airport, it was his turn and I didn't give him the letter, I tore it up. I tore it up. And I tried to call and tell him and I didn't. And now I'm so afraid because what will he say? He might not believe me, that I was pregnant when I left. And then, I don't know, he might never let me see my son again. Sandrine lowered her face and moaned.

Elizabeth reached across the table and rested her hand on Sandrine's bare forearm. We have to tell him, Sandrine. I can tell him, if he doesn't believe that you were pregnant when you came. And he'll be delighted. He'll have another beautiful child soon. It'll be fine. I'll call a solicitor, see what we can do.

I asked, today, Sandrine said, pulling her hands from her eyes. They said that either I remain a student and pay a lot of money to do a course, or I will not have a visa any more. They say I was given a student visa only, and that to change the status of my visa I have to return home first. Then they'll reconsider.

You're on a student visa? Elizabeth asked stupidly.

Sandrine's eyes were swollen with tears. Yes, yes I am. It was the only way.

But you're not going to school?

189

I switched schools when I got here because someone told me about this one. They sign your card, say you have been attending, and you pay them money for the classes.

But there are no classes, Elizabeth said slowly.

No, and they were closed down recently, Sandrine said. When I called there was no answer, no one answers any more, and that's why I went in today, because there's no record of my attendance. They are looking. And if the record comes, then I can sign up for another course, and stay. And if it doesn't, I think I will be in trouble. They told me they are investigating the school. And if I have a baby here, Sandrine paused, if I have a baby here, I don't think she is entitled to citizenship. I don't think so.

Of course she'd be entitled to citizenship! Elizabeth cried. How could she not be? That would be ridiculous. That can't be true.

I think so. I talked to a woman in the queue and she told me her friend had a baby, and they told her the baby could stay but not her. The father was Irish, and he took the baby, and they sent the mother home to Nigeria on the plane. Only two weeks ago. This woman I spoke to, I think she told the truth, because she said she had not seen her friend in two weeks now. This vote that is coming up, she told me it will mean the baby will not be Irish, and that's what the radio has said too.

They sat in silence. The café around them was beginning to throb with workers on their way home from work early, snatching up the gleaming glass bottles of fruit juices to ward off the unusual heat on the buses and the Dart. The door opened and closed heavily, the heat escaping the streets and sneaking its way inside.

But you're not from Nigeria, Elizabeth said. Because it's Zimbabwe, she said slowly, and because it was a British colony, and because Britain's part of the EU, you must be entitled to stay some way. It's different. There must be some way.

Maybe, Elizabeth, but I don't think so. Maybe it would be a good idea to ring a solicitor, though.

I'll ring someone today, Elizabeth said, watching as Sandrine flapped the laminated coffee menu at her forehead. You don't want to go home, Sandrine, Elizabeth said flatly.

Sandrine's eyes began to fill with tears again. It is so hard, Elizabeth, to see it on the news and know that I am here and George and Tobias are there. Riots over bread, she said, and broke off, lowered her head. Elizabeth bit her lips.

I'll call a solicitor. Are you feeling okay?

Just tired, Sandrine smiled faintly.

I wish you had told me, Elizabeth added softly. You could have gone to the classes. I would have helped you.

Sandrine nods, slowly. I know that.

But you didn't know then, Elizabeth said, sighing, I know. I'll call a solicitor when I get back to the office, but come on, I'll find you a taxi.

No no no, there's no need, Sandrine protested. I'll take the train.

As they rose from the table Sandrine turned to Elizabeth.

You don't want children, no, Elizabeth?

Elizabeth's body continued with its movements: the stride of the legs, the gesture of the arm to raise her bag up over her shoulder. Her fingers wound their way around the bag's smooth leather strap. I can't have children, she said quickly, trying to make the sentence seem only like another physical movement, her lips and tongue moving the letters and words out, away from her.

I'm sorry, Elizabeth. I shouldn't have asked such a personal question.

It's fine, really, Elizabeth found herself protesting, even though it didn't feel fine, not in the body that had housed that private sentence that had not wanted to be spoken. She pulled the door open and waited for Sandrine to pass through.

Which way do you walk? Sandrine asked her, hesitating, trying to pull the conversation back from that brink.

Elizabeth pointed and then stopped. I've never said it out loud before, she said. I've known for a long time, really – I mean we, my ex-husband and I, we tried and we had tests, I've had so many tests, she half-smiled – but I kept thinking that somehow something would change and I'd be pregnant. Of course, I'm on my own now so –

Sandrine watched Elizabeth's face, which was set and serious and quiet. Maybe you will be one day, Elizabeth. I hope so. You would make a good mother.

Elizabeth smiled slightly but shook her head, then stepped into the street, flagged a taxi and hurried Sandrine into it, pushing a folded blue bill into her hand.

Sandrine reached up and rested her fingertips over Elizabeth's, tried to smile, said nothing, and left Elizabeth on the roadside with tears in her eyes and the aching emptiness of some extraordinary farewell. She looked around to locate herself, and began the walk back to work.

She passed schoolgirls, their skirts hemmed above the knee, socks shoved into their shoes to bare their skin to the sun. They laughed, bending their heads together, hair swinging, momentarily mingling before their necks arched to express the full scope of their giddiness, heads thrown back, eyes skyward. Their voices also arched, pitching themselves towards impossible heights, plummeting, screeching, falling into harmonies together, uttering the same phrase, the same names, laughing again: an orchestration of dissonance writing itself by the second. She had never recovered that giddiness herself, Elizabeth knew. She had sobered like a committed drunk in one attempt, on that plane out of New York so many years ago. Or in her own bedroom that night, when her mother had told her they'd be moving.

Her mother.

Elizabeth passed the French patisserie Clare had liked, paused, went in and bought, hastily, from the little that was left in the fingerprinted glass cases, miniature pastries that she would take to

Clare later on in the hope of getting her to eat something. The young girl behind the counter crooned *merci* at her as she gave her the change, the silver and bright gold cold in her palm. Elizabeth, out of habit, smiled and said thank you.

She no longer paced quickly. Her mind objected, forcing her into a slow, steady walk that allowed her to think without wishing to. Elizabeth felt tired out by the moments of sitting solemnly with Sandrine and somehow reaching into her, revealing something of herself. That was why the sentence had formed itself, wasn't it? Because something of herself had already opened out to Sandrine like a palm, the way that her hand had stretched itself for the coins, some reflex that inhabited her self. And such intimacy was exhausting.

It was exhausting to spend so much of her time worrying about another woman's pregnancy when what she had hoped to do this year was worry about a pregnancy of her own. Instead of buying pastries for her senseless mother, Elizabeth had hoped that by now she would have been buying such things for herself for no reason other than that she was pregnant and hungry and prone to all of those cravings of stereotypes of pregnancies she'd heard about. Pickles and ice-cream in the middle of the night. She'd hoped that Ciaran would buy such things for her, if not in the middle of the night as in 1950s films and American folklore, then on his way home from work, and she'd hoped too that her mother would be able to talk to her during the pregnancy of her own experiences, hoped that the impossibly physical reality of her changing body would force a change in their relationship and make it into something itself pregnant.

But instead Ciaran was gone, and Elizabeth was barren, a stark hopelessness to the word. She would not produce an heir, and while no civilization at all wrestled with this fact, her own existence did. Had Queen Elizabeth cared, towards the end of her life? Had she listened to the whispers that must have ran around the stone buildings of her castles and palaces like plague-ridden rats? Her own friends no longer mentioned it. Sandrine was the first person to ask her directly in years. She was now getting too old to be asked by conspiratorial colleagues whether she intended to have children, and friends had stopped asking.

And her own mother had asked, once, shortly after Elizabeth and Ciaran had married: do you want children? Clare's voice had been careful, aiming for dismissiveness, studied and even. I don't know, Elizabeth had shrugged, her veneer of indifference thin. And now that she was ready to answer that question, wanting desperately to pour out the problems of her answer to her mother, she could not. At the age of thirty-seven, Elizabeth found herself losing battles on two fronts: to become pregnant, and to be able to have any conversation at all with her mother. Because by now her mother was unwilling to speak in general, and seemingly unable to speak sense. She spoke only trails of words that seemed unrelated, even mispronounced, incomprehensible, some other language that no one knew. Elizabeth's blood tie to her mother gave her no further access to her mother's mind. It was not the strange reversal of parent and child at the time when a child learns to talk and its slurred, forming language is understand only by its mother and father. Elizabeth stared, trying to see what Clare was saying, but saw nothing, only the shape of madness.

You could think back forever, Elizabeth believed, and find clues to madness. Her mother had been trying to stitch in the worn patches in a complicated hall rug in shades of rust overwhelmed by sunlight. She had abandoned the painting of the downstairs hallway after one coat of slick vermilion matte on half of one wall. She'd begun redecorating the upstairs bathroom by eliminating the flimsy white shower curtain. Surely this had been a sign of madness, to have so many projects spinning out around one's self. Elizabeth thought this more and more until she believed it. Clare had been showing these signs for years.

Elizabeth entered the building and made her way up the bare stairs to her office. She was too warm to go directly back to work, her mind too swollen with thought. She arranged her desk and got rid of all of the paper scraps, the sticky, uncomfortable plastic pens, bent paper clips, ripped-open envelopes. Her files were smooth and labelled. But where had she put her keys? For fuck's sake! she murmured at the room, and then stopped, slunk into the chair and slid across the room to the window like the inglorious end to an ice dance. Losing her keys, talking to herself, imposing madness on her mother in retrospect. Jesus, every adult she knew had too many things to do, too many things that they wanted to accomplish, finish, even just start.

And she had nothing that she wanted to do except one particular thing, and that was the one thing she couldn't do. Ciaran had tried to get her to stop thinking about it. She could see in retrospect his efforts to distract her, the mental magic he had performed. But it felt like such a failure on her part that everything else – the losing first of Ciaran, then of her father, her mother, the casual ordinary stresses of working – these things, while not ceasing to have an effect, became a united problem that could be made redundant by the solution of the other problem, the problem of infertility. Some natural cycle had been disrupted, and by her own body, so that now, losing her parents, she could not be consoled by her own children, could not look to them as the continuation of a personal history. Everything seemed to be ending, nothing beginning.

Elizabeth grabbed a book off of her desk, one of her father's that she'd brought to read on the train. She flipped through it, trying to calm her mind. Arib ibn Saïd al-Katib al-Qurtubi, 918–980 AD, doctor to the caliphs. A remedy for inability to conceive suggested in *On the Generation of the Foetus*: ginger, pomegranate blossom, eggs, and pepper. She closed the book tightly in her palms.

VII

She had not yet been to a doctor. She had been pregnant before, and reasoned that she knew what to expect, but still, Sandrine thought that at some stage she should go to see someone. It had come near enough to the stage of pregnancy when she remembered taking the bus to the hospital with George, clean sheets in one of her bags, to give birth to Tobias, the terrifying exhilaration of being in labour upon her. George's family thought it crazy that she should go to the hospital at all – she herself had been born at home, too, but she wanted to make sure that everything was as safe as possible for this baby. But here, in Ireland, where there were hospitals enough nearby and signs for doctors' surgeries everywhere, she put it off, fearing that a doctor might report her and her daughter and then what would happen?

Sandrine was thinking this as she walked from the house to the shop around the corner. She had spent the rainy afternoon watching cricket on the television, because the *pok* of the balls relaxed the baby, and because at this stage there was nothing to do but wait for the child to arrive. Zimbabwe was winning. She would be back in five minutes, she told herself, the match would hardly be over by then. There were many overs to go yet and the walk would do her good. Outside the shop stood the Chinese girl, crying. Sandrine stopped.

What's wrong? She put her hand on the girl's shoulder, which was swollen and soft. She had grown big all over, Sandrine saw. The girl shook her head and turned away and as she turned Sandrine saw that her belly was gone. There was no child in it now.

Your baby? She went after the girl, who continued to cry and eventually shook Sandrine's hand away and walked wearily off, her sleek hair rippling like tinsel as she cried. Only an old woman crippled with arthritis out to walk her dog turned to see the girl as she cried her way down the road.

With her carton of milk, Sandrine stood at the counter and waited while the queue moved slowly past rows of newspapers slathered with grainy, pixelated photos of football stars, past bars of chocolate wrapped in coloured paper with their ends sticking out in naked silver foil, past displays of peppermint and spearmint gum. Instead of the girl, there was a Chinese man at the till. He must know her, he would know what had happened. When she arrived at the top she put the milk down and addressed him. His eyes were rim-red and he did not smile. What happened to Ling's baby? Sandrine asked.

Her question hung between them. His eyes flickered. Baby died, he said after considering her for a moment. Very bad. Baby come, and died, only two minutes. Boy. He die and my wife very sad.

Sandrine felt her own baby lurch while he spoke. Why? she gasped. Why? What was wrong?

Baby's brain, the man said, on outside. People were listening now, watching this exchange between a Chinese man and a black woman, listening to them talk about a dead baby.

I am sorry, Sandrine spoke softly. Very, very sorry. I will pray for you.

Yes, the man said again, very, very bad. My wife, she want go home, go back to mammy. No stay here. I no want go, he added. Very bad.

I'll pray for you, Sandrine repeated flatly as she lifted the milk, and he nodded at her.

Thank you, he said, and turned to an builder in overalls who was gripping a roll stuffed with pale slices of meat and straggling shreds of lettuce. That's terrible, man, she heard him say as he handed over the money for his lunch, that's fuckin' awful that is. Take care of yourself, right.

Sandrine went back to the house and stood at the wall that rimmed the small front garden. She turned away, crossing the road and walking across the grass to the sea wall. There she rested the milk on the wall and put her hands on the rough concrete full of sand and stared out at the curves of the water swelling towards her, the tide coming in. She had been foolish to avoid the doctor. Something could be terribly wrong, something as bad as what had happened to Ling, and now it was too late. If something was wrong it was too late. Sandrine clutched the milk and hurried back to the house, her fingers sifting through the keys to find the one she needed.

She had to call George and tell him. George! she cried out as he answered the phone. George! Can you hear me? The relief of hearing his voice spread over her. She felt her legs begin to tremble and give out. Sliding carefully into one of the wooden chairs that surrounded the kitchen table, Sandrine heard her voice. No everything is not okay George, I'm pregnant.

            ᴄ ᴄ ᴄ

Elizabeth hung the phone up and trawled through the rooms until she was back outside in the garden in the sun that was like warm metal against skin. Her book was still teepeed on the arm of the chair, and the clothes billowed and settled on the line. Everything was as it had been. She went to the line and gathered the hot fabrics in her fingers, testing them. Dry. She pinched plastic pegs open and draped the t-shirts and pillowcases over her left arm until the skin was heaped with their heat, then returned to the chair, which she straddled, tumbling the clothes on to the footrest between her legs.

One by one, she folded the shirts American style, the way her college roommates, who had experienced summers at The Gap, did. Thumbs over empty collar bones, fingers over the shoulders so that the shirt extended itself to her hips like a limp dancing partner, a flick of the fingers that whipped the sleeves and a few extra inches together behind the back, pressing the lines of the shirt against her body, the neckline tucked between chin and chest, catching the ends and drawing them up to her chin, mouth open. The square pile of shirts rose, then was covered in pillowcases that she mock ironed with her palms, thinking of her mother's maniacal attendance to the smooth sheets of the hotel and how much she had loved them. Elizabeth trundled the socks into balls that were themselves mockeries of globes, her own plain white cotton knickers cut in half by one single crease. Her hands cemented the pile of colour and its socky awkwardness, squashed it down and then shoved it to the end of the lounger so that she could put her feet up again, and think of Sandrine.

The baby was fine, she'd assured her, but then the story of the woman who'd worked in the Londis had come out, and Elizabeth found her palms damp. So she had called her own doctor who worked from a house nearby with a surgery sign that had been his father's, like a lot of his patients.

I'll take you, Elizabeth had told her, so don't worry. He's very nice. And sitting there in the heat of the sun, Elizabeth thought of the old-fashioned waiting room with its fanspread of *National*

Geographic magazines and the clean beige lino of the floor. She brushed the buzz of a bee from her face and knocked her book to the grass. That had been the first waiting room to which the words 'barren' and 'infertility' had accompanied her, but then they were only tiptoeing ghosts, possible presences.

The sun was yawning behind the trees now. She did not retrieve the book, which fluttered as if with its own life. The heat was still dense. Elizabeth closed her eyes against the sounds of the rush-hour traffic. Sandrine is having a baby, she said to herself. And her mind paused on the continual present tense of it all, the near year-long process of the child's growth in the dark quiet of Sandrine's body, and the near year-long worry of that growth. As if that wasn't enough, Sandrine's mind, while her body distorted itself into a sort of readiness, would also worry for almost a full year about the paper forms awaiting her when the child was finally its own body. Birth certificates, alien registrations, enquiries about when the mother had become pregnant, if she had become pregnant in Ireland merely to give the child Irish citizenship, and depositions, probably paperwork with lawyers and gardaí, testimonies by Sandrine, perhaps by her husband, perhaps by Elizabeth. And maybe blood tests, DNA samples. Elizabeth's eyes were suddenly open and the heat beat down on these ideas and made her sweat. This was what lay ahead: the immense, frustrating chaos of torts and bills and the insensible agreements between governments. The fear was what kept Sandrine from wanting to return, and what had kept her silent all of this time.

And here she sat, on a chair on a lawn trimmed by one of the neighbourhood teenagers, looking up at a house she and her ex-husband had owned and which was now hers, a house with rooms she might not sit in or visit for days at a time, and another room in which she only slept and abandoned thoughtlessly as soon as she had woken, and in one room (and again, she didn't know which) were her passports, an Irish one and an American one. She could go anywhere with those small booklets with their stamps and digits too large to contemplate, and it was these passports, Elizabeth realised as she drew her knees to her hot chest with its slight streams of sweat, that allowed her the house, the lawn chair.

The truth was she wanted to go nowhere. Elizabeth wanted to be still. She thought about how it made some kind of sense that she could not have a baby, as if her body felt itself that all the moving around had unsettled her too much to mind someone else. When her friends frequently took off for holidays, heading to Berlin for the weekend, the south of Spain for a week, planned long-haul trips to Australia, Elizabeth mostly balked, wanting, instead, to drive the coast south or north, head west the odd time and gaze across the sea at her past life.

ᴄ ᴄ ᴄ

Do you ever miss America, Clare? she asked. Elizabeth uncapped a tube of lotion and began rubbing it, gently, into her mother's hands. Clare watched her, watched the cream melt into her skin that was now so thin.

Clare said nothing. I don't, Elizabeth said, her voice drifting away as she turned to look out the window into the greens of the garden, now landscaped for late spring. Although, it's funny, she smiled to herself, sometimes I actually miss Vietnam. Can you believe that, Mom? she looked at Clare. And Clare smiled back, a small smile.

It was Elizabeth's idea, a barbeque birthday party for her mother, since the weather was fine and since there was a barbeque that Ciaran had built with red bricks salvaged from a skip outside the house next door. They would have a barbeque, she'd thought, admiring the jagged architecture of the old bricks, some scarred by weather, others chipped like teeth, some perfectly rectangular. The cake, store-bought because Elizabeth never had learned to cook much of anything, read 'Happy Birthday Clare' in startling gelled red icing on a snowy background, and there were marzipan roses scattered about the top and the base in unnatural colours: sky blue, neon yellow.

She had collected Sandrine first, and then they drove to the nursing home for Clare, who without protest had been put into a coat and led to the car. Back at the house, Elizabeth put an arm about her mother's stooping frame as they moved through the kitchen. Under her palm her mother's shoulder blade was sharp, rivets of bone against slack skin. Her collarbones created hollows, secret places of bodily change. Clare shuffled her feet, looking down at them in their blue leather shoes. Sandrine took her arm to guide her through the patio doors and into a chair, talking to her gently, telling her what she was doing: we're going outside now, Clare, so there's just a bit of a step, oopsadaisy, now it's flat again, and that's your chair there, the guest of honour's chair at the head of the table in that patch of sun. Isn't that nice?

Elizabeth had taken her hand away. She watched Sandrine's self-possession, her ability to say words that were the right ones, that made sense and brought a movement to Clare's eyes. She had only laid her hand on her mother, but offered no language, nothing of solace, because the ridges of bone and the sense that the skin would tear under her hand had silenced her. Sandrine, she thought, would not be terrified to bring a baby home from the hospital. She'd hold the head properly, make sure of support. Elizabeth would have had wordless wonder, that was all, and that was not good enough.

Fidelma was already there with her husband, and Clare's youngest siblings had made the trip as well, still spry, helping to pass around plates and serve salads. So Elizabeth, rousing herself, found blankets and hastily brought them to her mother's chair, where Sandrine had settled her into pillows. This was what was needed, she thought, just movement, just action. And kneeling down in front of Clare on the patio to tuck the cotton beach blanket around her legs, Elizabeth thought that she was rewarded with a twitch, a glimpse of teeth, the effort of a smile.

Elizabeth would refuse almond paste for years to come. In her mind, the garishly tinted roses on the cake were what killed her mother. Wasn't that all she ate that day? They couldn't convince Clare to eat chicken or to pick up a sausage, couldn't interest her in even a drink of fizzy lemon. Instead she'd sat at the table in the sun, the blanket wrapped around her shoulders occasionally sliding immodestly around her breasts, and the other tucked around her legs so that the bones made creases in the fabric, and her eyes had fastened on the cake. She said nothing, failed to smile, just stared at the cake, occasionally moving her head to the side to look at it. It was Sandrine who figured it out, that the cake was what had mesmerised her, and Elizabeth immediately moved it up in front of her. There you are, Mom, your birthday cake. Clare had smiled, her lips pinched upwards for a fraction of a second, and her fingers had extended towards the frosting, and had plucked the first rose.

When they rang from the home in the middle of the night, Elizabeth had been lying in the dark of her bedroom listening to the night noise of the suburbs, the screech of tyres, the flow of rain to ground, voices thick with drink bolting into the air in rapid arcs as footsteps paraded in strange times, the drag of a heel against concrete.

When she hung up she couldn't move for a moment. She just wanted to sit in the dark that was never really dark in the suburbs and be alone with this death. Tears slid down her cheeks as she sat up in bed, naked, the sheets shackling her ankles and knees. Her mother had died in her sleep. One of the night staff, the lovely Filipino man with the three children back at home, had been doing the hourly round and had found her. What was this grief? There was a silence to it that Elizabeth had not been prepared for, nor was she prepared for the image that lodged itself in her mind. The image was her mother, settled on the edge of her bed in the Connecticut house, her hands holding open the vee of a book, and her arched eyebrows the only indication that the words she read aloud conjured the fantastic world of the child into rhyme. Elizabeth could see her mother's lips moving, but couldn't hear the words. She could only see this silent picture of a past moment that wasn't really a particular episode, she knew, but a composite moment of many: all of those nights when Clare had followed her into the bedroom, read three, four, five books, then turned off the light, pressed her lips to Elizabeth's forehead and made her way to the light of the doorway.

Elizabeth, under that heat, lay, parentless, unable to close her eyes and unable to shift that image of her mother on the bed. Her mind began to hear the words, inventing them for the silent picture of her mother to say, over and over the way she'd wanted to hear books as a child. But now Elizabeth didn't want to hear the story. Her mother was dead.

It was better this way, she knew, and she knew everyone would say that – that Clare had simply died, instead of all of the gradual sinking that her father had done, rallying, slipping, rallying, slipping, going on like an absurdist play, going on after the point where the audience understood and wanted to go home. And still, even though her father seemed to be dying for months, when he had finally died, Elizabeth had felt bereft, weepy, uncertain of her grief because it was so strong. Now that her mother had died too, Elizabeth experienced something different. Lying there in the dark that was already being edged in by light (when was the solstice? soon, Elizabeth realised), she was frightened.

What did she do now that both of her parents were gone? It seemed to her that something should be done, as if there was a ritual that would be revealed to her, an experience one wasn't told would happen until the necessary moment. Wasn't that moment now? Elizabeth turned and saw the space in the bed vacated by Ciaran and thought, this is the ritual, nothing more than this – the lying frightened in blue half-light, the need to cling to another who was alive, to another whom one loved.

VIII

Elizabeth stared at Sandrine, who stared back at her. Both parents buried.

The day was thick with clouds that hung like blue grey gauze over everything as they walked away from the grave. Her father's gravestone was still a blank, smooth piece of heavy granite, because there hadn't been time enough to get someone to chisel his name and the date into it. It would all be chiselled together. Her father's grave, now both of her parents', had barely had time to grow a slight beard of grass, and now the sods had been peeled back, the wound opened. Elizabeth knew that she herself would not visit a graveyard, but in a few months' time the stone would bear their names and a set of dates that were wrenchingly close together: March, May.

It's hard to believe, friends and relatives said to her, more to say something than to say something true.

It is hard to believe, she agreed, realising that platitudes were perfect for such moments.

Clare had returned to her room while the sun was still up, pushed in the wheelchair down the smooth corridors by her daughter, who had helped her into her nightgown with one of the nurses. Elizabeth had kissed her on the cheek and said that she hoped that she would have a good sleep. In her hands Clare could still feel the shape of those roses. The sticky residue was gone, wiped away with a cloth someone had produced, but the shape remained. She lay there, quite still, the flower in her hands. It was the closest she had had to green bean candy in an age. Her thoughts were quite clear. It was her birthday, or had been, or would be soon – so the cake said – and she had had green bean candy. Tom had not been there, and she knew why. There was nothing to say about this; nothing that she could shape into words that made sense. It was as if all of the far corners of her mind were trying to come together, reaching so hard that it felt like a hurricane was behind her eyes. Outside her window, a light rain began to fall that would not last, but Clare closed her eyes and let herself go to Hanoi, to the porch, to where she would wait with her daughter for her husband to come home for dinner.

᠎ ᠎ ᠎

Elizabeth gazed at the new batch of letters. They were still there in a box, in the corner of the sitting room. She had tidied everything else. The laundry was no longer laundry but clothes in closets. Papers were now files, dishes had ceased somehow to be dishes because they were clean, become plates and cups and bowls again.

What was in them?

This was the question that had set her in a cleaning frenzy, not her mother's death. They unsettled her, all those envelopes with the trails of time traced into them, over and over again, the post-marks blurring or fading or stark and succinct: June 10th, 1972, PM, Dublin; March 17th, 1983, Marseille; November 16 1991, New York. Dates, times, places that she is excluded from. They are to her parents, these letters, to each other, most of them, but also notes and postcards from her, even letters from her.

Elizabeth felt quiet and removed, needing to dream in silence about the coloured envelopes, about the hands that had circled vowels and consonants and the tongues that had licked the gummy paste-white back of stamps with historical faces, abstract drawings, miniscule birds, buildings, boats on seas with horizons that could run only as wide as the stamp allowed. About the fingers that had released packets of words into post boxes on street corners and in train stations, during morning rush hours and in the small, still hours of deepest night. Her own, too.

She wanted to drift away from this impossible present of dead parents and empty houses and citizenship laws and babies. Drift away into the moments of the past when she was free to write letters and drop them away from her as one does the woody stem of a cherry while the juice bursts redly in the mouth. When she was not defined by a job, when sleep didn't overcome her like a dark drug at midnight, when she was unmarried and so desperate to meet her lover over even a phone's flimsy wire for even minutes. When a baby was a drunken possibility that one risked, on occa-sion, thrilling – and trembling too – at the idea of a pregnancy.

She is asleep, it begins, *my love.* Her mother's handwriting round and careless, inky, very young. *There was a long battle over bedtime, eventually settled when I promised the park and ice cream, and God knows what else for tomorrow. I'm counting on her memory failing her at breakfast, as I have a million and one things to do before you come home, not least of all the packing, which is impossible to do with her climbing me like a tree!*

How are you finding it? From your letter it seems that the office is fairly central. It's hard to make myself realise that you're looking out at Broadway while you write to me, and when you rang last week. Is it still busier than you had expected? Do mind that you rest and sleep well, and for God's sake don't continually eat boiled potatoes and spices for tea or go out to all the foreign restaurants recommended to you! When we arrive I am going to teach you to cook normal Irish food straight away. You don't have to try every single spice you're offered. And with potatoes! It might prove fatal. I don't think Elizabeth would appreciate scrambled eggs with cumin, coriander and Tabasco sauce or even Indian restaurants with strings of Christmas lights and metallic garlands, so perhaps if you have time you might nip in to the local supermarket for cereals and leave a box ready to go in the apartment in case she arrives with a screaming hunger.

I am sorry it has taken so long to write. It's three days since I received your letter, but Elizabeth has been a little imp and time is hard to come by (after midnight now). I'm amazed at how much energy such a small little person manages to store up in a nap, never mind a whole night's sleep! We miss you terribly, and look forward to your return next week, when we shall be a proper family again, and you can put the imp to bed. I will be too happy to do anything but enjoy seeing you with my own two eyes. And just think, dear, it will only be another two weeks and our new life together in Connecticut will begin properly.

Your loving Clare, Elizabeth's eyes read. She had missed him. She had known that kind of longing. Her father had kept this letter all his life, for nearly forty years. He'd carried it from Connecticut to Vietnam and eventually back to Ireland. It had meant enough to him to do that. Where was his letter that had brought this response? Was it as full of veiled longing? How old was her mother then? Thirties, with Elizabeth aged two, nearly three? And yet the emotion (Elizabeth's mind ran from facts and figures) was the same in some way, the plague of absence ravishing the heart.

‹ ‹ ‹

Elizabeth had been dazzled by the colour in the boxes – the wild mix of white, blue, gold, patterned envelopes – and by the promise of the envelopes themselves. She had sat there for a long while simply staring into that mix of colours and promises, her eyes churning through them. She recognised her own handwriting, from schoolgirl scrawl in pink ink to nearly horizontal adult, recognising in a distant way too the stamps that her own tongue had gummed and pressed on to corners, in the early days, and then, later, on to any section of the envelope at all, randomly. These, though, she brushed aside, her fingers first hovering and then diving through the sea of addresses. They dove through several years of her life (Vietnamese, Irish, American stamps) and rested only when they came to foreign handwriting.

She had intended to read only one or two, and ended up sitting there in the empty room before the boxes for the rest of the afternoon. She never made it into the office, and no one rang. Her sensibility returned enough that she began to put them in order, to study postmarks and penned dates and to group the envelopes by year. All of her father's were the same size: slightly rectangular, small. (Her own were of so many sizes and shapes that she ignored them completely, just bundled the rest neatly by date.) In one of the last envelopes, wedged in between two of her own letters from New York, she found a photograph of herself as a teenager, falling out of an envelope addressed in her mother's hand to Tom. There she was, standing by the window of the Hanoi living room, the heat a white glare through the sheer curtain. It was her image that Clare had sent through the Vietnamese and Irish postal systems to reach her husband, and on the back her mother had scrawled the date and a line: *a picture of your beautiful daughter*. Her eyes full of tears, Elizabeth gazed at herself and felt all of the loneliness of a distant lover, thinking how strange it was that her mother had seen her that way, had proudly sent a photo of her off to Tom, but had so rarely attempted to say such things to her.

Elizabeth went downstairs and made a cup of coffee, leaning against the edge of the white countertop until the kettle boiled, staring out at the day, empty, blue, almost violet. She thought neither of her parents being dead, nor of her work, but of the girl in the photo and her mother's floral handwriting and the absences they'd created in each other's lives. She took the coffee back to the letters and sat down again, cross-legged, the mug and its steam beside her. She didn't drink it, sitting instead in a dream of old words, old ideas, as, slowly, the coffee lost its heat. The room seemed constructed only out of words that surrounded her, all of the words laid out into sentences that were the narratives of lives. Her coffee was cold. She was beginning to feel an awareness of things beyond this mass of words. Elizabeth, slowly, forgoing any meticulousness that would focus her more sharply on the words again, gathered the letters into her hands and placed them back in the boxes, and, her mind beginning to clear, put them back into the closet of the otherwise empty bedroom.

IX

The solicitor had been quite clear. He was a friend, and was trying to be as helpful as possible. He'd even refused any consultation fee, waving it off. Sandrine sat all the way back in her chair, heavily, her ripe stomach a strange round presence in the room of hard lines, gleaming chrome frames and slatted white blinds. Having invested a great deal of hope in this meeting, she couldn't gather any enthusiasm after what he had said: it was useless. It was Elizabeth who inched towards the front of her seat, her fingers fidgeting in the air as she spoke.

There's nothing else we can do? The baby will be *born here*, for God's sake, and that means it will be Irish. To hell with this referendum, that can't be right, she said. Why does she have to go back to change the status of her visa? Can't we say that it would be too dangerous? I mean look what's happening there. And she can't travel now, obviously, anyway, or with a new baby. And the baby won't have the same opportunities back there.

They have deported women with small babies before, I'm afraid, he sighed. Only if the child had an Irish father would it be likely that it would be allowed to remain.

Elizabeth frowned, sat back. She felt heat in her face, wanting to say what she had been thinking for a while now, every time she gazed at Sandrine's belly. What if we said that the father was Irish? Sandrine looked startled.

No, Elizabeth, you'd get into DNA tests and all that, and it just wouldn't work. Look, really from a legal standpoint the best thing to do is for Sandrine to return home after she has the baby and to try to change her status then, based in part on the fact that her child was born in Ireland. That is the best chance. From here – it won't work. That the school she was supposed to have been attending has been shut down for illegally reporting attendance for money won't be in her favour. We can't find anything to corroborate that she has been attending classes, since the school didn't run any. The referendum vote might well come back with a Yes result and change the constitution so that if you're born here you're not entitled to citizenship automatically. It really is best to return to Zimbabwe and apply for a new permit to enter, not as a student, but as a worker.

How can they do this? Elizabeth cried, turning to see Sandrine's reaction – her face was working over itself, aiming for calm.

When they left, Sandrine felt the hot tears growing, but still tried to calm Elizabeth.

Thank you for trying, she said. I – she began – but Elizabeth cut her off.

I wish I'd known from the beginning, Elizabeth told her again, that you were supposed to be going to school, I mean. We could have found a school closer by and you could have really gone instead of paying all that money for nothing, and we would have paid for it. She said 'we' as though there was someone in addition to herself.

I wish the same, but I can't change it. I wish I had come and gone to school – Sandrine began to cry – and I wish that my husband had been able to come, and Tobias, and my parents. I wish they could all be here. I wish that it was different, that I wasn't foreign here. I wish that home was enough. I wish that this vote would go differently because we both know which way it looks to be going. I wish that the people didn't spit at me, and say – she took her breath in too sharply before the utterance – *nigger*.

Elizabeth covered her mouth with her hands. Oh Sandrine, she whispered through her fingers.

They reached the car and Elizabeth hugged Sandrine before opening the door for her; they stood, awkwardly together, the baby between them. After a few moments Sandrine nodded that she was okay. She climbed into the passenger seat, sighing. Elizabeth powered on the car and rolled down the windows, and as they sat in the heat of the car she looked at Sandrine and cleared her throat.

You know, I've spent most of my life feeling *away*, and not even sure where I felt away from. My parents' longing for – for *elsewhere*, it seemed so greedy. She paused. I don't know why I'm saying this.

Because we are friends, Sandrine said.

And also because – Elizabeth eyed Sandrine carefully – I wanted you to know that I know how different this is. And I ... I feel so – I feel like I want to tell you that I'm sorry.

Sandrine smiled. I know I should tell you, she replied, that it isn't your fault, but instead I am just going to say thank you. Maybe it'll be different, when I come back. If I can come back. Sandrine turned her face to the warm breeze coming through the open window.

They sat quietly until Elizabeth could not sit in the silence any longer. Sandrine, would you like the baby to stay here?

She would have a much easier life here, Sandrine said simply, in many ways.

Elizabeth paused, cautious. What if I were to mind her until you came back? She had said it. The sentence was there in the car.

Sandrine put a hand on Elizabeth's as it perched tightly on the steering wheel. I have thought that it's a funny thing, that I'm pregnant here in such a mess of circumstance, and you are longing to be a parent. I have wondered about it too. I wished that I could have a child just to give to you. Sandrine's eyes filled. But, and she watched Elizabeth's own eyes begin to shed tears, even though it will be such a mess, I could not leave her behind. You know.

Elizabeth nodded and nodded and Sandrine stroked her head and they cried together.

⸺ ⸺ ⸺

The hardest parts were over: the attic was cleared out, so were the kitchen cupboards, the closets, the drawers and much of the furniture. And they still had six weeks or so, Elizabeth reckoned, at least. Sandrine could remain in the house until the new family were ready to move in, which was a relief. The house would not sit hollow, and Sandrine would not have to move.

They had stretched their cups of tea to two, chatting about nothing, and then had moved slowly into separate rooms to sort out, pack up, and discard. It was all finished then: the house was empty except for basics and a scattering of rugs, and the baby things that friends had dragged out of their own attics for Sandrine to use – the Moses basket, the changing table. Elizabeth had bought nappies and there was now a neat pile of all-in-ones and minuscule bibs. Most signs of the lives of those who had once roamed the house was boxed up, thrown out, donated to charity, and the house itself began to be dominated by the promise of a child, the promise of life. The walnut floors, still gleaming, remained to reflect on what had passed.

That was a week ago now; they had finished up late in the afternoon, scrubbing their hands clean of dust and laughing for no real reason. Elizabeth and Sandrine had eaten take-away pizza in the deserted front room, where the light of the summer sea dazzled itself on the now-blank walls. Elizabeth had discussed baby names with Sandrine, listening with curiosity to her husband's choice, Anenti. And Elizabeth had gone home happy, feeling lighter. There was something strangely freeing in having just one home.

Then there is the text, one afternoon as she is in a meeting: Sandrine is on her way to the hospital in a taxi. Elizabeth begins to make her own way there. She passes through the throngs of business people in suits and notices that the referendum posters are still everywhere. She wonders if these same business people, these men and women that she pushes past on the paths – did they vote yes, vote to change the constitution and keep people like Sandrine out? It scares her, in a way, that this baby is about to arrive in a country that only this week has voted to disallow her citizenship. She will be born placeless on this day, an unwelcome baby.

* * *

There had been no time for anything. They only made allowances at all because of the baby being so tiny and new. Three months. After the child had been vaccinated, that was all, then Sandrine would have to go. The deportation officials were actually very nice, Sandrine reminded Elizabeth afterwards, once the shock had worn off, but they had made it clear that there was no point in trying to dodge them. Eventually she would need to bring the baby to a doctor or to school and then it would all come out. Elizabeth had wanted to ring the solicitor again, but Sandrine refused. Something had changed with the birth of the baby, and she was resigned to going home. Perhaps the officials had been too good at putting their case forward, too good at convincing her of the difficulties of going underground in a country after flouting her student visa status by never attending classes and working full-time. Perhaps she recollected with greater clarity, looking at the baby, the strain of walking down the street and having eyes resting on you as a *non-national*. But, Elizabeth thought, perhaps too there was something else, something hormonal, even, or physical, that had happened. Perhaps Sandrine just wanted to go home to be with her husband, to see her getting-bigger boy, to see her parents again, bring her daughter home, even if it was dangerous and difficult.

The farm on which George worked was still hanging on, though. There had been only a few minor incidents, and it was still able to employ him and the thirty or so others from the village. George was hopeful, Sandrine told Elizabeth, that things were calming down, that the land reform movement was more sensible now. There was a job between them, that was the main thing. No teacher had been hired to replace her, so she might be able to reclaim her job, if at a lower wage than before, until she applied to come back to Ireland.

Maybe Elsa will be able to claim citizenship, Elizabeth suggested. Maybe the laws will change.

It's a possibility, Sandrine replied, smiling slightly. Then we might all return some day. And George and Tobias will meet you. Elizabeth gazed down at the sleeping baby in her arms. She had spoken to George for the first time this week, calling him to tell him of Elsa's arrival, glad that he, like her, was in tears at the news. Will you hold her for me while I take a shower, Elizabeth? Sandrine asked.

Elizabeth knew that Elsa, named for her, was the most beautiful child she had ever seen. She knew this was because she had seen her in that first moment, as if she and Sandrine together were the parents of this child with the deep, liquid brown eyes and perfect brown skin and pink gums that had emerged from Sandrine's screams and sprawled knees. Elizabeth found that she could gaze at this baby for hours, stare at her asleep or awake, marvelling at her being. That she knew that Elsa was going away within weeks of the birth made it all the more important to gaze and marvel. Elsa would disappear, and even if she tried to visit, even if on a regular basis, the child would be a stranger to her. Promise you'll write to me, she pleaded with Sandrine.

So there had been that three months of being almost a mother, of changing nappies and feeling somehow as if work had disappeared. There had been three months of shopping frenetically for everything she could think of that Sandrine should bring home with her, clothes and toys and books and vitamins, which were terribly expensive at home, Sandrine had mentioned once, months before.

Elsa mesmerised Sandrine, too, of course, and this, accompanied by how tired she was from feeding and caring for the baby, made her more sanguine about having to leave. In some moments, sitting in the now near-empty study while her child fed and slept on her lap, Sandrine would gaze around at the vacant shelves of the bookcases and remember the loneliness she'd felt earlier in the year. That had abated, and now she would return to her family, to George, with the sense that it would be okay, because it simply had to be. This Irish experience would somehow be subsumed into her family life, a gap in time that she went away to bear Elsa. How strange a space it had been – she had spent her pregnancy across the world, and would now return, empty herself, her arms full. The longing to see Tobias was so intense that it brought on her milk whenever she thought of him, and this alone made her feel that going home was the best thing.

As they had packed her things into boxes and shipped them ahead, Sandrine gathered all of the unsent letters she had written, considering them. There were no fires burning in the house during this hot summer, or she might have been tempted to destroy them. She wouldn't bring them home. They didn't belong with her, and she couldn't bring herself to give them to George, not now.

They belonged to this gestation, this spell of time that had been as much a meditation on her life, a pause in the midst of it all, as an attempt to make a life elsewhere. That prospect had failed; she had failed – and yet now, knowing she was going, she felt no shame. She was coming home with a beautiful, beautiful baby who had been born in Ireland. The letters could not come too. They were too full of those fears of memory failing, a record of disintegration. But rather than throwing them out, Sandrine felt something wordless that made her bundle them into a plastic shopping bag that she left in a corner of the wardrobe in what had been her room. In their stead, she put strange things into the space that had opened in the box – a pepper mill that Elizabeth had put in one of the many boxes of items to be discarded, along with the smallest three of a set of ascending bronze Buddhas that she wanted Tobias to hold in his hands. Instead of the articulation of the letters, Sandrine wanted to bring these silent objects back home as private placeholders of memory.

Once the new family was ready to move in to the Sandycove house, Sandrine moved in with Elizabeth, and the spare bedroom finally heard the wails of a child. Then there came a series of lasts: last dinner with Sandrine and Elsa, last stroll to the park with the buggy, last night with Elsa in the house, last nappy to change. Elizabeth had amassed hundreds of photos of the baby and Sandrine, but mostly just Elsa on her own. In only a few hours those images would be all that were left.

The thought of this was too much, and at the last minute Elizabeth felt unable to go to the airport to follow it all through and say goodbye. She rang Ciaran and asked if he would go with Sandrine to the airport that evening, that she couldn't face it. Ciaran, startled, said yes quietly, don't cry Lizzie, it will be okay. I'll go, don't worry, he said. So Elizabeth had said goodbye to Sandrine and Elsa in the house, both women crying, the baby asleep in a sling on Sandrine's breasts. I'll write, Sandrine said. You must write too.

In the coming years, there would be letters, scribbled notes that Sandrine dashed off when Elsa napped and Tobias was at school and George was not yet home and the family out and about doing their business. There would be printed missives Elizabeth typed in her office on darkening autumn afternoons and evenings before she emerged into the Dublin traffic.

There would be the more leisurely, thoughtful letters that resulted when either woman managed an hour to herself at a table by a window as night descended. In these letters would be the small details of lives lived out at distance: Sandrine's remembrances of the rain in Ireland, of the wooden-floored house in Sandycove strewn with rugs of crimson and ochre and cinnamon, of Elizabeth herself with her shiny blond hair that was so flat and smooth like her mother's, Elizabeth's questions about Zimbabwe, about how they were managing, about her remembrance of Sandrine and her belly growing bigger with the baby, about the vision of Elsa that first moment. A drawing by Tobias of his mother, his father, his sister and himself might be neatly folded into the crease of Sandrine's letters; into Elizabeth's might be tucked twenty euro for the boy's birthday.

As the years progressed the letters would increasingly mention Sandrine's new baby, the little brother who had replaced Elsa as the smallest member of the household. The letters also turned to the new agreement between Ireland and Vietnam to speed the adoption of Vietnamese babies by Irish people. Sandrine would write full of eager questions, Elizabeth would reply with the ferocity of hope and with a growing desire to return to Hanoi, to see it again, to reconstruct it in her memory, that place where she had lived for so long with her parents.

Elizabeth began to want to see the new buildings, the new streets, and to visit the Metropole. And then, as the winter folded into spring into summer, there would be nervous notes about Elizabeth's upcoming trip to Vietnam, where she would meet the little girl who would come home with her and grow up as her Irish daughter, Anh. The first letter after they returned would be full of photos and exclamation marks. Sandrine's letters would come back full of joy at the event, reassuring Elizabeth too that the farm was still holding out, that the townships being destroyed were in the cities, away from them. And as the years went by the letters would ripen with stories of bold toddlers, lost jobs, fear, the way that Ireland had fallen – as if off one of its own sheer cliffs – into a state of bewildering bankruptcy, marked by dole queues reminiscent of an earlier era. Elizabeth would often feel that it was just as well Sandrine had left and had not returned. So many were out of work now, including her ex-husband, who finally went off to Canada with his new family, a wife and two small boys, an immigrant himself. Sandrine herself would sometimes stare at the three Buddhas and think of all that had been lost in that year of her life, that confidence in the solidity of memory and mind, but she didn't write this to Elizabeth. It would go unsaid between them.

But as the women said farewell in the hallway of a nondescript suburban house in the late afternoon July sun, all of that was in the future, unavailable to them as knowledge, as feeling, unavailable as anything but imaginings and hopes. As Ciaran pulled out of the driveway, Elizabeth stood, emptied, to wave, and then turned into the house, headed straight for the garden, where she lay on a deck chair under the sun without moving, examining the sky.

It was a beautiful, still afternoon, the sky open and wide as eyes. Later on, she thought, if anyone was watching Sandrine's plane from the ground, they would be able to follow it until only their own human vision failed them and the speck that was the plane's movement across the sky would disappear into particles, ions, nothingness, and all that would be left of the flight would be a white streak that was like flight itself – a vacant arrow into space that would trail off until, finally, it ceased to be.

Acknowledgments

Of the books that I read while researching this book, I would like to acknowledge a few that caught hold of my imagination: Jack Turner's *Spice: A History of a Temptation* and Giles Milton's *Nathaniel's Nutmeg* contained vivid, memorable writing and astonishing facts. Andreas Augustin's history of the Hanoi Metropole was a book that for a certain period hardly left my desk; Andreas was also kind enough to answer questions by email, for which I am grateful. Of the books I read on Zimbabwe, *Zimbabwe's New Diaspora*, edited by JoAnn McGregor and Ranka Primorac, and Daniel Compagnon's *A Predictable Tragedy: Robert Mugabe and the Collapse of Zimbabwe* were particularly enlightening. The International Pepper Community's website (*ipcnet.org*) was also invaluable. My father-in-law, Tony Lenehan, was a font of information about pepper in particular, and the spice trade in Ireland more generally. The Immigrant Council of Ireland (*immigrantcouncil.ie*) makes available far more information than was available to my character in this book, as does The Irish Network Against Racism (*enarireland.org*). Background on the 'Citizenship Referendum' held in June 2004 in Ireland is available from the referendum commission: *http://www.refcom.ie/en/past-referendums/irish-citizenship/*. Any inaccuracies, historical or otherwise, are, of course, my own. Finally, profound thanks and love to Donal for all of our 'international dinner nights', which no doubt led me to imagine a spice trading character, and for tolerating me talking about people-who-do-not-exist.